Die in my Dreams

Christine Green

MACMILLAN

First published 1995 by Macmillan

an imprint of Macmillan General Books
Cavaye Place London SW10 9PG
and Basingstoke

Associated companies throughout the world

ISBN 0 333 64073 X

9 8 7 6 5 4 3 2 1

A CIP catalogue record for this book is available from
the British Library

Phototypeset by Intype, London

Printed by Mackays of Chatham PLC, Chatham, Kent

To Yvonne, the unforgiving. Remembering the night we imagined we'd won £250,000 each and we still didn't manage to buy the new outfit.

Chapter One

The prison officer on the gate muttered, "Bye Forbes. Don't come back.'

Carole Ann Forbes didn't answer, didn't look at the prison officer, just strode out of the gate, head in the air, not wanting to show that, deep inside her, anxiety was spreading as fast as blood on blotting paper.

She stood at the bus stop, waiting. The prison itself was behind her. Middleton Grange, open prison, well named because it was in the middle of nowhere, but about as 'open' as an oyster shell. She smiled to herself as she watched the empty road. There had been pearls in the shell. Women she'd always remember but would never see again. No one would be likely to be 'just passing' her new 'home'.

Her prison visitor, Nina Gardener, had arranged for her to board with an elderly woman who took in ex-prisoners in a town in the Midlands called Fowchester. Nina lived in a village nearby and had said she would try to find her a job, but, of course, in a recession she couldn't promise.

Wheat fields surrounded the prison and a slight breeze ruffled their surface. Carole Ann stared at the moving wheat for a while. The wheat heads were still green, still growing. She lifted her head to the sun for a moment, wondering if anyone in the prison watched her as she stood there. From her cell – she called it a cell, the screws called it a room – she could just see the bus stop.

She'd seen others leaving. Now it was her turn. She didn't feel happy. There was no elation, just relief mixed with a gnawing anxiety.

The sun was shining. She was completely alone, no traffic passed, no pedestrians passed either, unless they were visiting the prison.

At the bus stop she stood for some time, still holding the suitcase

1

that now contained everything she owned. After a while she set it on the ground. She smiled to herself. She'd already made two decisions; one had been to ignore the prison officer at the gate and the other, to put down the suitcase. She half expected someone to shout, 'Pick up that suitcase, Forbes.' She half *wanted* someone to say that.

For ten years she had made no decisions other than what to spend with the meagre 'wages' she'd earned working in various prisons, or whom to accept as friend or lover. Now she would have decisions to make every day. And no one to give a damn.

She stared at her watch. It was 8 a.m., on an early May morning and the bit of world she could see seemed bright and very green.

Back inside, the noisy prison breakfast would be over and the inmates would be making their beds and tidying their cells. Trish would still be crying. Crying because she'd lost a friend and crying because she was still on the inside.

Carole Ann fumbled inside her handbag and found her tobacco and cigarette papers. She rolled a thin cigarette, carefully lit it with a match and inhaled deeply. She'd been a non-smoker when she went to prison but somehow smoking was a comfort, something you could share with other inmates, a bond. There wasn't much else you could share, except dismal past experiences.

She'd only had two drags on the cigarette when she saw the bus. She could see as it came to a halt that there were only two other passengers. The driver opened the door and said, 'You can put that out. No smoking on board.'

She threw down the cigarette immediately, picked up her suitcase and stepped aboard. So much for 'freedom', she thought.

'The station, please,' she said as she took her purse from her handbag.

'Rail or coach?' he asked as he looked her up and down.

Carole Ann murmured, 'Coach please,' and smiled. He didn't smile back. He knew, of course, she'd just been released. There was nowhere else to come from.

He was, she supposed, in his early thirties, like her. Sullen-mouthed and with black greasy hair. When he told her the price of a two-mile journey she thought he'd made a mistake but she tried not to show surprise. As she counted out the money he still stared at her and she knew he was trying to guess her crime. As she put the money onto the little shelf in front of him she whispered, 'It was murder.'

He didn't blink in surprise. His sullen mouth didn't alter one jot but in his eyes she saw . . . respect.

At the coach station she ordered a pot of tea in a café. She'd got used to prison tea, had hardly noticed it was different from tea on the outside. This tea was fresh and hot and strong. It was a completely different drink from prison tea. She stared around her. There were several men in the café. Some in suits, some in jeans, one in black leathers. She couldn't help it. She lusted after them. Especially the one in black leathers.

As she drank her second cup of tea she supposed she should check on the coach times, but it didn't matter when she arrived. What was she going to do when she *did* arrive in Fowchester? She only had a few pounds in her pocket. There was no one to contact. Except for Nina. She imagined she would unpack her suitcase, have a bath, perhaps look round the shops, and then what? Go back to some grotty boarding house and lie on the bed staring at the ceiling. There would be no Trish, no laughs, no shared fags, no baiting the screws. Just an aching loneliness. Oh Christ, she thought, I want to go back.

In the ladies she stared at herself in the mirror. In prison the mirrors had been small and cracked. This mirror was large and new. She could see most of herself in it. She was slim and pale – A greyish paleness but her face was unlined, her complexion clear. Her blue eyes needed some mascara to make them look larger. She'd buy some today and some blusher. She did have a lipstick Trish had given her as a going-away present. It was red. Carefully she applied it, pressed her lips together and stared at the result. Her lips were as red as blood. She smiled at herself in the mirror, flicked her comb through her long fair hair and murmured to herself, 'Here I come, Fowchester. Ready and willing and free.'

Somehow, though, the words needed an audience. Needed a Trish or a Sharon to say, 'Go for it, girl.' She had no one to show how brave she was trying to be. She felt totally exposed, like those nightmare dreams when you're walking about naked. She'd been full of bravado on the coach, within sight of the prison. Now, she had no familiar landmarks, just the sounds of her friends' final goodbyes echoing in her ears. And the rising sense of panic in her chest.

Miss Enid Braithwaite rested her weary legs on her mock-leather pouffe and after a few moments inspected them carefully. Her ankles and knees looked swollen and her varicose veins were raised and beginning to throb. She knew it was her own fault, she'd done too much housework this morning. She'd dusted the room, aired the bed, vacuumed the floor, prepared an extra meal, and now she waited for the girl to turn up.

Enid had thought of having a little nap, but she didn't want to be woken up from it so she decided to play patience for a while and then perhaps listen to records. She lowered her legs, stood up stiffly and slowly, and moved her occasional table in front of her. She sat down again equally slowly and set out her playing cards. She'd been playing for a few minutes when she noticed she had indigestion and the sun that shone in from her back window was almost blinding her.

I shouldn't have bent over the cards so soon after my dinner, she thought. Enid believed in having a good hot 'dinner' in the middle of the day, it was more 'proper'. In the same way, she believed in changing her clothes in the afternoon. Women didn't do that nowadays, she knew, they wore scruffy jeans and bought packet meals.

She rested back in her armchair and closed her eyes and thought about the last girl she'd had, who stayed for three months and was nothing but trouble. She'd told the Prison After Care Service and the Probation Service that she wouldn't have any more women, but she'd been persuaded now to take a 'quiet' one.

Men, thought Enid, were a lot less trouble: three meals a day and that was it. No trouble at all. Just like Mr Reynolds. He'd done time for armed robbery and GBH and he'd been as good as gold. He still was. This new one, Carole Ann Forbes, was going in the room next to his. Any problems at all, Enid had already decided, and she'd be the first to go.

The clock on the mantelpiece showed three-thirty. Time for tea. Enid gave her knees a quick massage and then began the process of standing up. It took her longer and longer each time.

In the kitchen she measured out two teaspoons of tea into her small teapot and poured on boiling water. How people could use tea bags she didn't know. The tea just didn't taste the same.

Enid stood to drink the tea; she wanted to sit but couldn't face the prospect of getting up again. Then she walked into the front room, pulled aside her net curtains, the whiteness of which she was very proud, and stared out onto the mid-afternoon quiet of Cherry Lane. Where was that girl?

Dave Reynolds, too, waited for the arrival of the new lodger. He lay on his bed watching black and white television but the old film hadn't penetrated his consciousness. Like rain or sun it was just . . . there. He hoped this new woman wouldn't talk too much. He didn't talk much and he didn't know what to say to women. Not surprising that, he thought, because he had spent most of his adult life in prison.

During his last stretch in prison he'd come to the conclusion that he was a criminal for two reasons – one, he was bone idle; two, he liked other criminals.

Only 'career' criminals, though, not perverts or child molesters but blokes who were ambitious and tried for the big time – the bank jobs, big-time fraudsters, safe breakers and the like. Men he could admire. Some of them 'hard' men, but not all. A few of them were real nutters and would think nothing of gunning down anyone who got in their way. He'd tried to be a hard man but he wasn't, never would be now. He was forty-five and still a petty criminal, but what made him stand out from the crowd was that he was ambitious, and in Dave Reynolds' mind that made a difference.

As the afternoon wore on he become aware of how warm he felt. He stood up to take off his vest and watched the lane through the net curtains. A few women walked by but when he saw *her*, he knew. He recognized the pallor, the wariness in the walk, the slight suspicion in the way her head turned occasionally as though a screw still observed her every move. He watched as she lingered at the front gate. She was a looker, he had to admit, but he hadn't seen her bum yet. He willed her to turn round, but she didn't. He heard Miss Braithwaite shuffling to the door and then the front door opening.

He went back to his bed, took out the girlie magazine from under his pillow, lay on the bed, smiled to himself, opened up the magazine and carefully registered other bums for future reference.

Carole Ann Forbes had spent the afternoon walking slowly round Fowchester. There were no big department stores, just little boutiques and charity shops. She'd never been in a charity shop before

5

and was amazed at what you could buy. She bought two paperback books, two cotton tops which looked relatively new, and debated for ages about a blue cotton dress. She had so little money that any purchase seemed a painful decision. Once she'd actually parted with most of her money, leaving just ten pounds, she felt relieved. As long as I have enough for stamps and tobacco I'll manage, she thought, and managing, she supposed, was what she'd have to do on the 'outside'.

She paused outside a tea shop and stared at people drinking from real china cups and eating scones and cream. Her mug of tea in the coach station had cost sixty pence – real china and real tea, she guessed, would cost much more. She walked on and eventually asked an elderly lady leaving the post office where she would find Cherry Lane.

The lane was at the back of Fowchester's main street. There were no cherry trees in sight, just small terraced houses with neat front gardens and white net curtains. Number 15 was the least neat, the paint peeling on the window frames, but the nets were white and an assortment of pansies grew in two wooden tubs set on a concrete garden.

She lifted the brass knocker and knocked loudly three times. This is it, she thought as the footsteps slowly approached the front door. Your new gaol, your new gaoler.

Chapter Two

'There's been another one, boss.'

Detective Sergeant Fran Wilson walked into their shared office and waited for Chief Inspector Connor O'Neill's response. He was staring out of the window on to Fowchester's main road. She waited.

'Be saying that again, Fran.'

'There's been another burglary A couple just back from holiday have reported it. Usual style: smashed window, small things taken – jewellery, cash, a radio, tapes, table cigarette lighter. Nothing of any great value.'

O'Neill turned and stared at his young DS. 'Jasus, I'm fed up with this bastard.'

'You're always fed up,' muttered Fran.

'What was that?'

'I'm fed up too,' said Fran with a weak smile.

That was true, she thought, as she sat down and placed another sheet of paper in her typewriter. She'd been working in Fowchester for over a year now and still she felt she didn't belong. Her past had preceded her and occasionally when she came into a room the atmosphere and the conversation changed. Sometimes it was a subtle change, sometimes verging on the downright obvious. She couldn't have felt worse had she been a known spy for the KGB.

Yet all she'd done was tell the truth, reporting a fellow officer for beating hell out of a suspect. The fact that she had suffered too seemed to have escaped her colleagues' attention. The fellow officer had been her lover and, she'd thought at the time, the love of her life. Now she was stuck in Fowchester, dullsville of the Midlands, with a boss who fancied her and who was fanciable in return. The fact that he was good-looking with a boyish smile and an accent as smooth as Irish coffee made her very wary. One heartbreak in a decade was quite enough to cope with and she prided herself on the ability to learn from past mistakes.

'I'll be having to make a decision on this, Fran,' said O'Neill thoughtfully. 'The Super's after me. This makes six burglaries in three weeks. Presumably by the same person. We've interviewed everyone who's as much as snitched an apple from a stall and we've still got nowhere.'

'What about surveillance?'

O'Neill shook his head. 'There's uniformed men doing extra patrols but they're either blind and deaf or our man has got a vantage point on that estate. I'm supposing the latest one is in the same area?'

Fran nodded. 'Should we talk to Neighbourhood Watch again?'

O'Neill laughed drily. 'They want to be starting a vigilante group and if we don't put a stop to it that's just what they'll do.'

Fran stared at the blank sheet of paper and from there to the sunshine outside and the strolling inhabitants wearing sunglasses, shorts and smiles, and felt envious of their freedom. She was still five reports behind, she hated typing, and today was Wednesday and so far this week she hadn't been outside the station.

She began painstakingly to type with two fingers. Aware that O'Neill was staring at her, she continued doggedly until she'd finished the first page. She snatched the paper from the machine and placed it on the desk.

She'd noticed that O'Neill seemed more distracted than usual, and was aware too that he wasn't really staring at her but that his greenish eyes, at that moment, were fixed but unseeing.

'Can I help, boss?' she asked.

'What are you meaning, Fran?' he asked.

'I'm meaning, boss, with respect, you're getting on my nerves.'

He rested his head on his chin and stared at her again. 'I'm thinking we haven't been out for a drink together in weeks.'

Fran shook her head wearily. 'You drink enough for the two of us anyway.'

'Now is that any way to be speaking to your boss, DS Wilson?' he said, sounding mildly irritated. 'I'll not be having any cheek. Just write your reports and for God's sake do better than the last lot.'

He stood up, walked to the door, stood there for a second or two as if waiting for her to respond, then walked out. Fran knew exactly where he was going – to the pub.

8

She carried on typing her reports. Two hours went by. There was no sign of O'Neill.

At four o'clock Detective Inspector Pete Preston knocked on her door.

'Super wants to see you – now. Where's the Chief?'

'He's out on the burglary case.'

Pete shrugged. 'Well, I should get along to Ringstead's office this minute – a happy man he is not.'

Ringstead's happiness, Fran knew, depended on neatly filled-out charge sheets, the cells being full, reports in on time and a CID that had the best crime clean-up rate in the Midlands. Fowchester police station, just emerging, it seemed to Fran, from some weird time warp, hadn't yet caught up with the 1990s. Consequently he was always miserable.

She knocked on his door and waited. And waited. He did it on purpose, of course, making people wait. Giving them time, no doubt, to think over their inadequacies. Self-evaluation it was called, his one sadistic attempt to be 'modern'. He'd been on a course – Management and Self-Evaluation: The Way Forward – the result of which was yet another long form to fill in every three months, elaborating on personal strengths and weaknesses. Fran had been used to that in Birmingham. And it had taught her an important lesson. Lie through your teeth. Admit no inadequacies. Profess confidence and project confidence. Because if you didn't you got sent on some ghastly course.

'Come in,' he yelled. By shouting, Fran was sure, he inferred that this was the second command and that the first had been missed. Consequently the poor unfortunate outside already felt at a disadvantage.

Superintendent Ringstead was round and pompous with sharp dark eyes and a tendency to state the obvious.

'Ah! Detective Sergeant Wilson, there you are. Sit down, sit down.'

Fran sat, upright, uneasy, eyeing him with the vague distaste she'd feel for a cat retrieved from a sewer.

'Well, Francesca,' he said, lapsing into the avuncular style he used for all women officers, as though they were schoolgirls in for the headmaster's pep talk. Fran gritted her teeth at the sound of her full name.

'How do you feel it's going?' he asked. She paused. By 'it', she supposed he meant Fowchester police in general.

'Fine, thank you, sir.'

'Good. Good. And O'Neill not working you too hard?'

'No, sir.'

'Not drinking too much, is he? I know he does like a tipple, but then all of us men drink more than is good for us.' He laughed at what he thought was a little witticism. She didn't answer. Ringstead's brief laugh gave way to his watching her steadily.

'You have nothing to say on the subject?'

'No, sir.'

'I see.' He rubbed his hand around his chins slowly.

'So you feel that you are working well with O'Neill?'

She nodded. 'I've learned a great deal from him.'

One of Ringstead's eyebrows rose questioningly.

'Hmm.' He sat back in his chair and Fran knew by the awkward pause and the eyebrow that he had something more to say on the subject. 'I'm going to get rather personal now, I'm afraid. It's come to my attention that you are – how shall I put it – getting rather attached to him. While I realize . . . relationships do build, I'd prefer it not to happen on my patch.'

Fran hadn't been prepared for this. She felt so angry she couldn't speak, so instead of speaking she stood up, intending to gather something sharp-tongued and pithy to say as she did so.

'Sit down, Sergeant Wilson,' said Ringstead coldly. 'You must understand, I value a senior officer of O'Neill's calibre. He's got a tragic past and I don't want to see him going through any more trauma. You girls are just as likely to move off to pastures new while men like O'Neill stay the course.'

Fran sat down, her back stiff, her hands clenched. She felt insults and death threats jostling for space in her brain. But along with the insults a warning voice saying, this is your job, maybe your last chance, lose your temper and you blow it. She took a deep breath.

'In that case, sir,' she said coldly and deliberately, 'I'd like to formally request you assign me to someone else.'

Fran could see he was a bit rattled by her reaction. She stared at him as she waited for his answer. 'I can see you're upset,' he muttered, 'but there's no need. I really only meant it as a little unofficial warning.'

'Even so . . . I would like a change.'

Ringstead stood up and walked over to the window. Fran

watched his back, still seething. He turned. 'It's not possible to reassign you, Sergeant Wilson.'

'Why not, sir?'

He paused to stare at her for a moment. 'Because, my dear, no one else would have you.'

It took a second or two for that piece of information to sink in. Fran could feel her eyes begin to water. She hadn't expected this. It was like a blow.

'I see, sir. Well, in that case I shall have to treat DCI O'Neill with the proverbial bargepole. Or maybe I should go into purdah?'

'There's no need to be sarcastic, Sergeant. You must understand, some of the staff here are a bit outdated in their attitudes.'

If she hadn't been so upset she would have laughed.

'Yes, sir. Thank you, sir,' she answered, her voice still thick with sarcasm.

As she walked to the door, he said, 'Oh, and by the way, try to chivvy O'Neill on these burglaries. Neither of you seems to be getting very far.'

Back in her office Fran stared at the reports still to be typed. She wasn't actually seeing the words, she was too annoyed for that. She muttered 'bastard' a few times, referring to both Ringstead and O'Neill, and by the time O'Neill did appear she felt marginally better – or at least more calm and full of resolve to show Ringstead she would stick it out and one day make DI just to prove she wasn't like the other 'girls'.

O'Neill ignored her at first, walking, deep in thought, to his desk and then sitting down and swivelling on his office chair to study the map behind him. He didn't turn round to speak to her, just said in a low voice, 'You'll be wanting to tell me about it, Fran.' This was his opening gambit with most people. And it worked! To say 'No, I don't' sounded incredibly childish. So most people muttered, 'Yes, of course I do, Chief Inspector.' Fran guessed that he'd been told on the way in that she'd been called to Ringstead's office and that she hadn't been dancing a jig when she came out.

'I'd rather not talk about it, boss, if you don't mind.'

He turned round and smiled. He had an attractive smile but Fran wasn't in the mood to be swayed.

'I'll tell you what,' he said. 'We'll go out for a breath of air. And then you can be telling me.'

11

'I'm not going to the pub, Connor.'

'I didn't ask you. We'll walk round the Ferndale estate. That's where I've been. I haven't been to the pub.'

Fran picked up her shoulder bag from the hook on the door and followed him out. Going past the offices and meeting people in the corridor was like running the gauntlet. A single officer gave no bother, acknowledging O'Neill but ignoring her. A twosome or a threesome always had a comment, usually mumbled, but she heard nevertheless – 'Mind your back!' or, worse, 'Grass!'. The animosity of some of them had increased. O'Neill was fairly easy-going and liked a drink, and others in the CID felt resentful a woman had got the job. Especially a woman who had broken their code.

They walked to the Ferndale estate in bright sunshine, O'Neill silent, striding ahead, Fran still feeling raw and defensive. She liked O'Neill but she wasn't prepared to get involved, didn't want either of them to get hurt. It was just so humiliating to be accused of 'getting rather attached to him'. It made her sound like an abandoned mongrel dog.

The Ferndale estate had been built on waste ground behind the main Fowchester road. During the last few weeks it had been burgled so often that the residents were beginning to feel slighted if they hadn't been burgled. It was almost an insult to the desirability of their possessions.

'What do you think?' asked O'Neill.

'About what?'

'These houses.'

'I don't like them much,' said Fran, glancing around vaguely. 'They're a bit crowded together. I don't think they're worth the money.'

'O'Neill smiled. 'What about the facilities?'

'You mean schools, shops, that sort of thing?'

He nodded.

'From that point of view, boss, it's quite convenient. The schools are near, you can walk to the shops, there's a park for the kids—'

'Precisely, Fran.'

Fran frowned. 'I don't understand.'

'Come on, I'll show you.'

The park was on the edge of the estate, bordered by trees and a narrow river, and with swings, slides and a roundabout. It was the local dog walk and hanging-about place for local teenagers in the

12

evening. O'Neill stopped near the swings to watch two boys of about ten, one swinging backwards and forwards, not on the official swings but on a homemade wood and rope contraption hanging from the hefty branch of a tree, the other boy just watching.

'They've been here for hours,' said O'Neill.

'School holidays?' suggested Fran.

O'Neill shook his head. 'Another week before they break up for half term.'

'I suppose they're just playing truant.'

'I think,' said O'Neill. 'They're sussing out their next job.'

Fran paused. From this distance she could hear them laughing.

'But they're so small,' she heard herself say in shocked surprise.

'Sure they're small, Fran, small enough to get through wee windows and no one takes much notice of them retrieving their ball. I watched them earlier on. Now they're on the swing and seeing who goes in and out of the houses. I know it's only guesswork but I think we've cracked it. One's the lookout. The other gets in. If you look you'll see they've got a sports bag by the tree.'

Fran saw the red and white sports bag resting by the tree trunk. Was O'Neill right? she wondered. Could these two really be responsible for Fowchester's worst series of burglaries in living memory?

'Be holding my hand,' said O'Neill suddenly. 'We don't want the little sods to run off. They're bound to outrun us. Just act casual.'

Fran held his hand. If Ringstead could see them now he'd be puce in the face. That thought somehow gave her a great deal of satisfaction.

'Talk to me, Fran,' said O'Neill as they walked nearer to the boys. 'Tell me about Ringstead.'

She smiled. What the hell, she thought, he probably knew anyway.

'Ringstead thinks I'm after you. Thinks I have sexual designs on you.'

'And you haven't? To be sure, Fran, I'm brokenhearted.'

'You can drop the corny Irish accent, boss. I've made things very plain.'

'Sure you have, Fran. Sure you have.'

The boy waiting for his turn on the rope swing saw them coming and watched them warily. He had fair hair, blue eyes, and chocolate round his mouth.

'Is that safe?' asked O'Neill.

'Course it is, mister. You got the time?'

'Five-thirty. Is your mum expecting you?'

He shrugged, eyeing O'Neill even more warily. 'What if she is? What's it to you?'

O'Neill hadn't replied when the boy on the swing landed on the ground. He had a round face with a crew cut.

'You an old perv?' he asked belligerently. ''Cause if you are, you can leave my friend alone.'

O'Neill shook his head in a seriously denying manner. Both boys now watched him with equal wariness. O'Neill smiled at them. 'We're only here for the day. Do you know anywhere we could go . . . sort of private?'

The round-faced boy was the taller. Fran guessed he could have been eleven. He smirked, thrusting a thumb to his left. 'You could go along the river, mister – everyone goes there.' He giggled. 'And make sure your girlfriend's careful. She might get nettles up her bum.' Then, turning to his friend, who was grinning inanely, he said, 'Come on, Danny, let's go.'

O'Neill put a hand on Danny's shoulder. 'Just a minute, boys. I'll be wanting to have a word with you – police!'

Fran expected a bit of a fuss but both boys looked nonchalant.

'So?' said the older boy.

'So. I want your names and addresses.'

Danny laughed slightly nervously and the other boy gave him a warning look. Then he said, 'Mister, we ain't done nothing. And if we 'ad you couldn't charge us.'

O'Neill kept his grip on Danny, but when the other boy kicked out at Fran's shin and Fran, taken by surprise, gasped, Danny slipped out of his loosened grasp as fast as a marble down a greased drainpipe. The boys had almost legged it to the edge of the park by the time O'Neill and Fran started running.

Once outside the park, the boys had disappeared and the two police officers stood side by side, breathing fast and scanning the empty narrow roads of the housing estate as if their eyes had played them a cruel trick.

'Come on,' said O'Neill. 'They'll be back some time. We'll catch them then . . . and another thing—'

14

'What?'

'It's opening time.'

Fran smiled in a resigned way. If you lived in a small town the pub was the only place to go. It was one better than being at home and talking to a mouse which might or might not be behind the skirting board.

Chapter Three

The thumps on the front door came just before midnight on Friday.

It was four weeks since the burglary duo Danny Webber and Spencer (known as Spen) Tate had been found and cautioned, and Fran half suspected they or their friends were causing the noise, a reprisal for being caught, a sort of 'knock up Ginger' with a hint of menace.

Fran had gone to bed early and then lain awake listening to homeward-bound traffic, doors opening and closing, and giggling coming from next door. Students had rented the house after her elderly neighbour died suddenly, and it seemed Friday night was fun night.

The thumping continued. At first she had hoped it was next door's door that was being thumped – with it being a terrace it was sometimes hard to decide which door was being knocked at.

Sighing, she slipped on her towelling robe and, in bare feet, padded downstairs. She paused in the hallway. All was quiet. She turned to go back up the stairs. Then the thump came again. This time there was no doubt that it was her front door. She glanced behind the curtains but couldn't see a thing.

Opening the door just a fraction, she peered out, then she looked down. The body on her doorstep moved, the bloody face illuminated only a fraction by the streetlight.

'Connor – oh my God! What's happened? Stay there. I'll call an ambulance.'

Before she had a chance to move, his hand had grabbed her ankle.

'Jasus, woman, just help me in.'

'But—' She hesitated.

'Just be getting me in,' he murmured between swollen lips.

The blood seemed to have tracked down his face, onto his shirt, over the lapels of his jacket and come to rest in a dark sticky mess on his chest. Her eyes rested on that patch and the thought flashed into her mind – he's been shot! O'Neill watched her with his left eye; his right eye seemed to be swelling as she watched him.

'I'm all right, Fran. I haven't been shot. Do as I say and get me off this bloody step.'

As she bent down to try to haul him into the house, the smell of rampant alcohol hit her nostrils.

'Boss or no boss, you are a—' Anger made her struggle for words.

'Stupid bastard?' he suggested.

'Come on, you'll have to help yourself,' she said, pulling him ineffectually by the shoulder. He was too heavy for her to drag indoors bodily, although she knew she would have managed it had he been even half sober.

O'Neill began to get slowly to his feet. He lurched against the doorjamb. He was so drunk he couldn't stand properly. Fran stood watching him, wishing she could feel something other than anger and disgust. He staggered into the hall, knocking against her round table and a vase of white and pink carnations as he did so. She grabbed him quickly by the arm and led him to the sofa. As he fell back clumsily over the sofa's edge, with his long legs dangling, Fran felt resentment and anger bubbling inside her like porridge on the boil. He was so bloody selfish! So irresponsible.

'What happened?' she said coldly.

He waved a hand at her dismissively, 'Don't you be getting high and mighty with me, Sergeant. I've had a spot of bother, that's all. Just look after me . . . I'm needing the touch of a tender woman.'

'Well, boss, you've come to the wrong place. I'm off duty—'

He stared at her, the blood still wet on his face but beginning to clot. 'You're looking as pretty as—' He broke off, obviously trying to maintain his train of thought. 'You're in the CID now, Fran,' he said, his voice slurred, 'and you're never off duty. Now you be getting into the kitchen and make me some hot strong coffee with a dash of something.'

'Arsenic or cyanide?'

'You're a cruel woman, Fran Wilson. If you had any compassion you'd be looking after me like Mother Teresa. I could be dying.'

'But you're not,' answered Fran tersely.

Connor's hand clasped her wrist. 'Put a steak on my eye and I'll tell you all about it.'

17

'If you were sober, boss, you'd remember I'm a vegetarian. All I can offer you is a packet of frozen peas.'

He smiled crookedly because of his swollen lip. 'That would be grand.'

In the kitchen Fran filled the washing-up bowl with hot water, took out a packet of frozen peas, searched in the kitchen drawer for a plaster, without success, but found an unused dishcloth still in its plastic wrapper. That would do, she decided.

'You're not geared up for first aid, are you?' he commented, on seeing the dishcloth.

Fran said nothing. She began to wash the blood from his face. It took some time because she had to be careful to avoid the wound. Once the blood was off she examined his face. His right eye was swollen, his lower lip was swollen. She examined his head – there was no wound. She sat back on her heels and stared at him.

'Connor, this isn't your blood,' she said.

'Sure it is,' he answered. 'You must have missed the wound.'

She thrust the frozen peas on his eye and stared at him. 'Where did this happen, boss?'

'I'm glad you're remembering I am your boss, Fran. I'm not enjoying this.'

'You could have fooled me,' muttered Fran.

'What was that?' he asked sharply.

'Nothing.'

He stared at her, one hand holding the peas against his eye. Eventually he said, 'I got into a fight.'

'I can see that,' said Fran. 'You seem to have come off best. What happened?'

He smiled sheepishly. 'Now there's a question. My memory's a bit hazy.'

'Try.'

'You're a hard woman, Fran. I thought I'd get coffee and sympathy here. It seems I was wrong.'

'Why did you come here, Connor?'

He looked away from her. 'There was nowhere else to go. A lorry driver found me in the gutter outside a club in Birmingham. I gave him your address. I told him you were my wife.'

Fran was no longer surprised at what O'Neill said. His wife had committed suicide three years ago and she had a vague feeling that he *did* wish she was now his wife.

18

He shrugged. 'I go to clubs sometimes. Hoping to meet some-one, I suppose. A fair colleen. It was an Irish club.'

'Tell me about it.'

'I would if I could, Fran,' he said, wincing slightly as he spoke. 'I remember coming out of the club and seeing a fight. The rest of it's just a blur of flying fists and feet.'

'You were kicked?'

'A mild kicking, Fran.'

'Where exactly were you kicked?' she asked, concerned now that he'd ruptured his spleen or something equally dire. He pressed a hand to the side of his chest.

Fran sighed. 'Let me look, boss. You could have fractured ribs.

'I'm all right. Don't start fussing. It was my own stupid fault.'

Fran shrugged. She knew O'Neill well enough to know that the expression on his face meant he wasn't going to discuss it any further. 'I'll get you a drink,' she said.

In the kitchen she ran the tap for some time and then filled a tumbler.

'Drink this,' she said. 'Water is the best thing for a hangover.'

His lips hinted at a smile. 'I haven't got a hangover – yet—'

'If you drink plenty of water you won't get one at all.'

'Christ, you're a know-it-all,' he said good-naturedly.

As he drank the water, still with the frozen peas pressed to his eye, she asked, 'Why drink so much, Connor? I know you're not happy but alcohol won't help.'

'What do you know, Fran? You don't get the flak I do from Ringstead. I'm tempted to lay one on him.'

Fran perched on the edge of an armchair. 'I know he's a pain but you make him worse. You need professional help, Connor.'

O'Neill sighed. 'I'm not needing lectures, Fran. Tonight's little fracas wasn't that serious—'

'How do you know? Maybe the other person's in a worse state than you. That wasn't your blood, after all.'

'Go to bed,' he said.

'Suit yourself, boss,' said Fran. 'I'll throw you down a duvet and some pillows.'

Later, in bed, Fran lay in the dark staring at the ceiling. Was O'Neill the nice guy she thought or did he have tendencies like Rob, her one-time lover, who was teetotal but beat up a suspect with no more compunction than he'd feel on swatting a fly? Perhaps she wasn't a good judge of character at all. Maybe she was in the wrong job or the wrong place – or both.

The thought occurred to her, too, that maybe O'Neill had instigated the fight. Perhaps his blackout was a homicidal rage. Maybe the other person was badly injured. Would she ever find out what had happened? Had anyone seen the fight? Telling herself she was being melodramatic and that there was probably a simple explanation, she tried to sleep.

Falling asleep was easier than she'd expected, but she still slept badly and then woke at 6 a.m. with a start. There were noises coming from her bathroom. Then she remembered O'Neill. He was vomiting.

He came down later, looking tired and ashen. 'I feel like death,' he said. His right eye, although swollen, hadn't turned black and apart from the pallor he looked relatively normal, if she could ignore the blood stains on his jacket.'

'You can't go out like that. If you want I'll walk over to your place and get you some clothes.'

'Thanks a million, Fran,' he said as he handed her his house keys.

The walk will do me good, thought Fran, and she wanted to be away from him for a while. His house was on a newish estate near the racing circuit. She supposed it would take her about ten minutes to get there. Then when she got back she could tell him she'd got plans for the day and suggest he went home for a proper sleep.

The day was already warm, and being outside made her feel more cheerful. She passed a few early morning dog-walkers and a jogger, red and puffing, who looked about to expire at any moment. When she arrived in Byron Close she was surprised to see a For Sale sign outside O'Neill's end house and she couldn't help feeling slightly hurt that he hadn't told her he planned to move.

Inside, the house was a mess. Unopened mail lay on the hall floor, newspapers, empty mugs and glasses were strewn across the sitting-room floor. Two full bottles of Irish whiskey plus a half-empty one were lined up on the floor beneath a standard lamp. In the kitchen the washing up was piled in a bowl, although there was only one pan in evidence and that was a frying pan. Just as well he didn't go in for big meals, thought Fran as she firmly closed the door.

In the bedroom a photograph of his dead wife stared, smiling, towards the bed. She was blonde and pretty with soft gentle eyes. The bed was unmade, socks and underwear lay scattered on the floor. This was, she decided, the house of either a very depressed man or just a lazy, whiskey-swilling slob.

She collected a black polo-necked sweater and black jeans from his wardrobe, some clean underwear from a sparse selection in a drawer, and then returned to the kitchen for a carrier bag. On the kitchen table she noticed his mobile phone. Should she take it or leave it? She left it.

Once back at home, she handed him the carrier bag and made no comment on the state of the house or the fact it was up for sale.

'Do you mind if I have a shower?' he asked.

Fran smiled. 'You'll be lucky. The shower only produces a tea-spoon of water at a time. The bath works, though.'

Fran made tea and toast while he was in the bathroom and she'd finished by the time he reappeared. She had to admit he looked really none the worse now. His lower lip was still slightly swollen, likewise his eye, but in general no one would really have noticed.

'You're looking better, Connor,' she said.

'Is there any breakfast going, Fran? I'd be grateful for a bite to eat.'

She smiled, 'There's variations on toast.'

'I could take you out for breakfast.'

'I've had mine, thanks.'

'I'll go then.'

'Yes. I'm off out to see a friend.'

'Male?'

'Yes,' she lied.

'I'll be going then.'

'Fine.'

He walked slowly out of the kitchen. Fran followed him. At the front door she touched his arm. 'Please Connor, get some professional help for your drinking. You do have a problem.'

'You'd be thinking that, would you, Fran?' he said. 'I'll decide if I have a problem. If you've got any complaints, take them to Ringstead.'

She paused. 'I might just do that, boss. You can mess up your life and career but why should I be dragged down with you?'

He stared at her for a moment. Then he said softly, 'You're an ambitious little bitch.'

21

As the door closed she muttered, 'You bastard!'

Her day was ruined. She felt tears of anger pricking her eyes. She went into the kitchen and began washing up furiously. She'd had her night's sleep ruined, she'd worried about him, she'd tried to help and what did she get? – he called her a bitch! Well, O'Neill, she thought, maybe I am ambitious, but next time you come calling I won't be in.

O'Neill walked slowly towards the house. It wasn't home now. Not since Jenny had died. He just couldn't maintain an interest in mere bricks and mortar. Jenny had been the heart of the house and with her gone there wasn't much point in staying there. He'd put the house on the market a year ago and two miserable viewers had had a desultory look round. Now was *the* time to sell, or so the long-haired estate agent had told him.

He was sorry Fran had seen the house in such a mess, it wasn't usually that bad. He hadn't exaggerated when he spoke of Ringstead being on his back. Ringstead lived somewhere in a more law-abiding era where the majority of the population would grass their nearest and dearest on a moral issue. Now most people, if a crime didn't affect them, ignored the more trivial crimes such as housebreaking, robbing building societies or fencing goods that fell off the back of a lorry. Crimes against property, it seemed to O'Neill, were almost admired by a good many otherwise law-abiding people. Unless it was their car or their house, in which case even hanging was too good for the perpetrators.

As for his relationship with Fran, that seemed to have worsened. She had more confidence now in herself, and less in him. She was so pretty, had a great figure, and what really riled him was that he needed her far more than she needed him. She disturbed the flatness of his equilibrium. He'd actually been drinking more since she arrived. He couldn't blame her for that, but alcohol gave him optimism for the future that he didn't feel when sober. Most of all he needed a woman. And at the moment, alcohol was his only woman.

He let himself into the house and wandered straight into the sitting room. He picked up a used tumbler, bent down for the whiskey bottle, hesitated for only a few moments, poured himself a deliberately small one and gulped it down quickly.

'You bitch,' he murmured. This time he was referring to the whiskey.

The whiskey had barely hit his stomach when the phone rang.

'O'Neill,' he said wearily.

'It's Pete, boss. Word's just come in there's a body down by the river about two hundred yards from the park. A dog sniffed it out.'

'Did the dog make the report?'

Pete Preston murmured, 'Very funny,' then in his normal loud London accent said, 'The dog's owner, a bloke called Barry Jakes, says the body's in the nettles. Looks as if he was fishing before he keeled over. I've contacted Scene of Crimes and they should be on their way, plus I've arranged to have both entrances cordoned off.'

'So it could be a natural death?' said O'Neill.

'Don't think so. Blood on his chest.'

'I'm on my way,' said O'Neill, about to put down the telephone.

'Where were you, boss? We've been trying to get you for an hour.'

'I was jogging – forgot to take the mobile.'

O'Neill smiled to himself, if Pete believed that he'd believe anything.

He rang Fran and heard the frostiness in her voice. He wanted to apologize but couldn't quite say the words. Instead he said, 'You'll have to ring your friend, Fran, and tell him you can't make it. There's a body by the river – you've got ten minutes. I'll see you in the park.'

'Thanks boss,' said Fran, still frosty.

O'Neill tried to suppress his feeling of triumph that some unknown man was about to get the elbow, and he felt a tinge of guilt that another's death had caused that feeling.

As he left the house he was aware he was walking fast, feeling better, feeling more alive, experiencing the excitement that came with the start of a murder enquiry. He supposed it was the same feeling a hunter felt at the first sight of his quarry. It was an emotion that whiskey could never provide.

Chapter Four

By the time Fran and O'Neill arrived, the number of people in the park seemed to indicate that a rumour had already circulated that there was something available for free. Fran supposed a gruesome sight was a freebie, but they'd be unlucky today. The uniformed police had cordoned off the path to the river on both sides and were standing guard, trying to look impassive in shirt sleeves and bright sunshine.

Just as they were about to slip under the yellow ribbon a middle-aged man with a mouth set in misery approached with his dog and said to Fran, 'I want to walk down there.'

'Not today, sir, I'm afraid. It's been closed off.'

'You're going through,' he said, with a hint of envy.

'We're police,' said O'Neill crisply.

'Bugger,' said the man as he began to drag his disappointed mongrel away from his favourite sniffing ground.

'That's typical,' said O'Neill. 'He's trying to pretend he's a dog-walker – really he's a ghoul, he had a ghoulish expression on his face.'

They walked further along the river, past banks of high nettles, tall grasses and a variety of white and yellow weeds that swayed only slightly with each whisper of breeze. Soon they could see the main area of activity, where a yellow tarpaulin tent was being erected.

'Leave that,' said O'Neill to the constables. 'Where's the body?'

A sergeant pointed to the large red and white striped umbrella that lay on its side in a clearing near to the river's edge.

'He's behind there, sir. A Mr Jakes found him' – he pointed to a bored-looking man who stood some distance away with an Alsatian slumped near his feet – 'Or rather his dog did. Kept sniffing around until his owner took a look behind the brolly. He says he put it back in the exact position.'

'Be getting a statement from him, Sergeant, and if you're satisfied you can let him go home.'

Fran handed O'Neill a pair of surgeon's gloves and he moved the umbrella aside to look at the corpse. He stared at the dead man's face, and brown eyes seemed to stare back at him. The corpse looked surprised, as if death had come so quickly he'd had no time to blink. The face itself was an ashen colour tinged with blue, as if his whole face was preparing to become one large bruise. Fran, too, stared at the dead man, noticing that even in death he was good-looking and still young. Blood had trickled from his open and fixed mouth into a cracked line like a dry river bed that reached down to the open neck of a navy sports shirt. He wore blue jeans and black trainers.

As they stood staring at the dead man a butterfly with porcelain-blue markings fluttered over the forehead, moved to the open mouth, hesitated for a moment and then flew away.

'Draw the scene,' said O'Neill, without taking his eyes from the corpse. It took a second for Fran to realize what he meant.

'The photographers will be here soon, boss,'

'Don't argue, Fran. You can draw, can't you?'

'No.'

'Just be doing your best then.'

Fran took her notebook and pen from her pocket, crouched down and began painstakingly to draw the scene. The river was, she supposed, about six yards wide; on the opposite bank were the same high nettles but no path, just fields, with a few sheep grazing contentedly around a clump of shady trees in one of the fields. This side of the river the body lay to Fran's right with the umbrella now cast aside and the various equipment an angler needs surrounding it: a portable canvas seat, a basket, a net, a torch, a vacuum flask, a tartan blanket and a black leather jacket, but, strangely, no fishing rod.

'This notebook's not really big enough, boss,' she said to O'Neill, who was busy emptying the dead man's pockets.

'You can enlarge it later, Fran,' he said as he laid out a wallet, a packet of condoms and a biro from the dead man's jeans pockets. Fran stopped drawing to glance at the business card O'Neill handed her: Alan Lattaway. Financial Adviser. The Tahill

25

Insurance and Investment Group. 3 Swanley Close. Fenway. Fowchester. The wallet also contained two ten-pound notes.

Fran continued to draw. Also to her right, in the distance, was the Wanderer pub. She guessed it was over two hundred yards but she found guessing distances quite difficult. She could see the pub sign but not read it; the pub itself seemed to be built on raised ground with a sloping garden that led down to the river's edge. Hastily, she drew the pub and its side extension. On her left the river continued and the path eventually opened out on to the park area and the grass and swings and slides. Fowchester residents often wrote letters of complaint about the rampaging nettles but at least these prevented children getting too close to the water's edge. Although the river did continue for miles, most of it was wild and overgrown, walkers no longer braved brambles and nettles with no reward at the end other than fields marked 'Private'.

Finishing her plan of the area, Fran closed her notebook and noticed O'Neill was gazing across the river, deep in thought. As she came to stand beside him he said, 'I'm taking your advice, Fran. I'll be getting some professional help.'

She smiled broadly and touched his arm. 'That's great, boss. I'm so pleased.'

O'Neill felt a wave of pleasure. It was almost as if he'd cracked his drinking problem just by saying he'd seek help. He knew it wasn't going to be that easy. But he wanted to try for Fran. To prove he was man enough and therefore go up in her estimation. And now there was a body and a murder enquiry and he had a chance to show her that although he was in a second-division force, he was a first-division detective.

When, moments later, the police surgeon Graham Gretton rushed along towards them in an obviously 'this has ruined my Saturday' state, he did manage to pause long enough to smile briefly at Fran and combine this with his usual nervous tic.

Again Fran was caught unawares, thinking he was winking at her when no such thing was intended. O'Neill and Fran both moved back on to the footpath to allow Dr Gretton to have his first look at the body.

After a cursory glance at position and general condition he called out for someone to help. Fran was the first to make a move and she began to help by undressing the corpse so that the rectal body temperature could be taken. O'Neill looked away at this point. Sudden death was always without dignity. Soon the photographs would be taken by the Scene of Crimes team and then would come the final assault of the post-mortem.

'Chief Inspector – come and look at this.'

Somewhat reluctantly, O'Neill moved nearer to the body. Gretton had the navy shirt raised and the bloody chest exposed.

'Death caused by two stab wounds to the chest. No marks on the hands from fending off the blows. He didn't put up a fight. Could have been killed by first wound. I'm only guessing but he's been dead some hours. Probably killed last night some time after midnight and before 4 a.m. Stomach contents might be a help there. And that's it really.'

'Weapon?' asked O'Neill.

'Your trouble, O'Neill, is you want jam on it. The knife is probably in the river.'

'Any idea what type of knife?'

Gretton smiled. 'Sharp and pointed is my guess. I can't tell the depth of the wound. If he'd had a beer gut he might have survived. Nothing like a thick layer of fat to give you a bit of protection.'

'Thanks, doc. I'll be remembering that,' said O'Neill.

When the doctor had left, with a wave and a brisk involuntary wink, O'Neill stood for a few moments staring at the body. He crossed himself and prayed silently for the soul of the dead man to live in everlasting peace. As he stood over the body of Alan Lattaway he thought wryly, once a Catholic, always a Catholic. The ritual and the comforting words were ever with you. Even a lapsed Catholic hedged his bets, just in case—

'Boss?' Fran interrupted his thoughts. He turned to her, glad to look away from the body and the staring surprised eyes.

'Why did you want me to draw the scene?'

O'Neill smiled. 'It fixes it in your mind. Photographs can't give you the same perspective. Outdoor murders yield up fewer clues in my experience. The elements can confuse and destroy.'

Fran hesitated. 'Yes . . . but the weather's been good lately, no high winds or rain.'

'True. And no footprints either. But if we'd found this man – Alan Lattaway – in his own home; we'd have found out more about *him* in an instant. When we tell the relatives, in an hour or so, we'll be more aware of what we're doing and saying and how the relatives are reacting than thinking about what sort of man our victim was. And what enemies he had.'

'It could have been a random killing.'

27

O'Neill shook his head thoughtfully. 'I don't think so. He didn't put up a fight. He was taken off guard – probably by someone he knew and trusted. Fear is a great incentive. If he'd met some thug he'd have had a chance to get his adrenalin levels up.'

'Perhaps the fishing was just an excuse,' murmured Fran.

O'Neill nodded. 'So we'll be assuming for the moment he arranged to see someone here and, on that basis, we'll also be assuming he was a married man and he was meeting someone here because he didn't want his wife to find out.'

'So you think this assignation at night was a sexual encounter?'

'Sure I think that.'

'But—'

'But what, Fran?'

'A man who lives in a detached house would probably have a car. Why come down here pretending to fish, with nettles as big as trees, when they could have met on some lonely road and gone off in the car? Also, it wasn't a frenzied attack. A crime of passion somehow would have been more . . . uncontrolled.'

O'Neill thought about that one but couldn't come up with an answer. 'I don't know,' he said eventually. 'Maybe he has a small car and they were both too large for . . . whatever. And maybe the passion had waned.'

Fran smiled and shrugged. 'It's all academic so far, isn't it, boss? We're only guessing.'

'Don't knock your first thoughts at a murder scene, Fran. Sometimes that intuitive flash is what you stay with.'

Fran laughed. 'I thought intuition was something to be slightly ashamed of, like . . . dandruff.'

O'Neill smiled. Fran was young, still a bit naïve but getting less so. He wondered sometimes if she realized yet the true depth of chauvinism in the police force. It wasn't so overt these days, it was true, and officers did attempt to be politically correct, but there was always that undercurrent.

'It is. Just don't be using the word "intuition" to Ringstead,' he said with a smile. 'Male officers call it a hunch. Female officers call it intuition. The "hunch" theory sounds more macho, so gets more credence.'

'Oh,' murmured Fran. Not having thought of the politics of sexism, she resolved to weigh her words more carefully in the future, especially where the top brass were concerned.

O'Neill crouched down in the space between the nettles. 'We've a few minutes, Fran,' he said. 'Let's see what we can find.'

Fran donned her rubber gloves again and was glad she was wearing sturdy cord trousers to protect her legs from the nettles. The sun was pleasantly warm now but she knew that by midday it would be so hot she'd wish she could wear shorts. Dead bodies, she thought, belonged with damp weather and miserable grey skies, not bright sunshine and heat waves. Murder seemed more obscene in the sun.

On closer inspection of the ground surrounding the body, they found more items than expected – a matchbox, an apple core, a half-eaten rubber ball, an empty lager can and a dead rat. They lined up their finds, waiting for Scene of Crimes to bag and label them.

O'Neill and Fran left shortly after the team had arrived. The onlookers in the park still milled around, waiting in vain for their grisly view.

Fenway was a modern addition to Fowchester. A cul-de-sac of so-called 'executive' houses. All detached, all expensive but rather small, each one with its own garage. They were as neat and soulless as a stack of cans in a supermarket, and for once Fran felt glad to live in a house with a bit of history, a mouse and a smell of damp.

They hesitated at Number 3, Swanley Close. Fran knew O'Neill was nervous, knew that this was a part of the job no one got used to. The body was now the deceased occupant, an empty shell, stiff and without pain. The living they were about to assault with cruel words were as yet unaware of the pain to come. With a few words, their lives were about to be changed for ever.

'I'll do the talking,' said O'Neill.

As he knocked at the door he would have given either arm for a shot of Irish. That would have steeled him, loosened his dry tongue, eased his words. Instead he sighed, straightened his back and tried to harden his heart.

The door was opened by a woman in her thirties. She wore a straight cerise skirt and a cream blouse. The smell of cooking rose from behind. A smell O'Neill couldn't recognize. Her short fair hair was slightly mussed, as if she'd been running her hands through it. She was fiddling with one pearl earring in her left ear.

29

Her right ear was bare. 'Whatever it is,' she said, 'I can't afford it or I've already got it.'

O'Neill guessed she'd just come home from working in an office. She looked slightly harassed but she was obviously well used to getting rid of door-to-door salesmen.

'Police,' he said. 'I'm Chief Inspector O'Neill, this is Detective Sergeant Wilson.' He showed her his warrant card and she nodded at it.

'Mrs Lattaway?'

'Yes, I'm Jill. It's serious, then?' she asked. He could see now the naked fear in her eyes and he felt his guts tighten as he simply said, 'Yes.'

'You'd better come in. I've only just come home from work. I'm all behind.' She walked ahead and then turned sharply, as if realization had just dawned. 'Oh my God! It's not Stephen, is it? I've just left him at the sports centre. Has there been an accident? Has there?'

'Not to Stephen. Stephen is your son?'

'Yes, yes. What's happened. It's not my mother, is it?'

'Just be sitting down,' said O'Neill. 'And I'll be explaining.'

She perched on the edge of the sofa, tense and pale. Fran sat down beside her.

'Could you tell us where your husband is at the moment?'

She frowned. 'Alan? He could be fishing or gone away somewhere. Sometimes he goes away early for the weekend.'

'But you're not sure?'

'No, I'm not sure.'

O'Neill could hear the defensive tone in her voice, and it troubled him. That, and the fact she didn't seem to have noticed her husband was missing.

'What's happened?' she asked. 'What's he done?'

'I'm sorry to have to inform you,' began O'Neill slowly, 'that the body of a man carrying a business card in the name of Alan Lattaway was found by the river an hour or so ago.'

'Oh God,' she whispered. Then she repeated, 'Oh God,' and shuddered.

O'Neill waited for tears or a more voluble outburst, but when neither came he said, 'Could you describe your husband to us?'

'Alan – yes. He's about five foot eleven, medium build, brown hair, dark brown eyes . . . does that sound like him?'

O'Neill nodded.

30

'What was it? Heart attack?'

'It wasn't that at all. It seems he was murdered.'

Her chin trembled and she clutched at the cushion on the sofa. 'Poor old Alan. He didn't deserve—' She tailed off as if realizing all the implications.

Fran glanced at O'Neill questioningly, as if to say what the hell's going on?

'We would like you to be coming with us shortly to make the formal identification,' said O'Neill.

'Yes of course. I have to collect my son. He's fourteen. He'll be very upset. They got on quite well under the circumstances.'

'What circumstances are those, Mrs Lattaway?'

'Call me Jill. I'm not really Lattaway any more but it made it easier all round to keep the name.'

'Could you be explaining?'

'We're divorced. Four years ago. It's been a terrible situation but he couldn't cope on his own. Alan tried living in a bedsit and he lost two stone in weight. It upset Stephen and my in-laws. I felt sorry for him. So in the end I said he could rent a room here. It meant he could see Stephen. He had his own room, I did his washing but I didn't cook for him.'

'And why did you get divorced?' asked O'Neill bluntly.

For a second she stared at him as if to say that's none of your business. But then she managed a slight smile. 'I met someone else.'

'I see,' said O'Neill.

Fran watched O'Neill, noticing that his 'I see' didn't sound as if he comprehended at all. She had to speak up and ask some questions herself now.

'Did your husband have any girlfriends?' Fran asked as she flashed O'Neill an 'it's my turn now' look.

Jill Lattaway smiled warily. 'Of course, he's a good-looking man—' She broke off. 'Was good-looking. Not that he spoke about them. But I always knew, just by the way he dressed, where he was likely to be going.'

'And when was the last time you saw him?'

She frowned. 'Yesterday – I think—'

'You're not sure?'

'Yes . . . it must have been yesterday morning. I went out on Friday evening about . . . eight.'

'What about Stephen?'

'What about him?'

'Where was Stephen?'

'He was here. He's old enough to be left alone for a few hours. He is fourteen.'

Fran smiled and nodded.

'So what time did you get back?'

'About midnight. Stephen was asleep. I went straight to bed.'

'And no sign of Alan?'

'When you're in this sort of situation, Detective Sergeant, you try to ignore an ex-husband as much as possible. I don't know if he was in or out. And I didn't care.'

'Call me Fran. Were you with your boyfriend?'

'Yes. What of it?'

'No reason, just that your ex-husband's death makes life just a little bit easier, doesn't it?'

'I don't know what you're getting at.'

'Don't you, Jill?'

A few seconds elapsed before Jill realized. 'Oh my God! You think Ian had something to do with Alan's death, don't you? That's ridiculous. He wouldn't, he couldn't.'

'I haven't met him. But I'm sure you must have made plans for the future. Unless of course it's just a . . . fling.'

'It is not a fling, as you put it. I love him.'

Jill flushed an angry pink, well aware that she had dropped Ian firmly into the frame.

'Come on, Jill,' said Fran softly. 'I can imagine you two sitting in your car murmuring sweet nothings. Planning your wedding or a little holiday or even just a weekend away. Cherishing the moments when you could be alone instead of just snatching the odd few hours in a car or . . . along the riverside.'

'We don't go along the river,' said Jill sharply. 'And we don't have to sit in cars. Ian does have a place of his own.'

'OK. Where did you go last night?'

Jill shrugged. 'We went for an Indian meal in Castleton. Then we went back to his place.'

'Castleton?'

'Yes. It's a large village north of here.'

'Why not eat in Fowchester?'

'We like to go where no one knows us.'

'So Ian is married?'

'I didn't say that.'

'No . . . but is he?'

'Separated. He's separated. Satisfied?'

'We'd like his full name and address.'

Sullenly, Jill intoned, 'Ian Bishop. The Gatehouse. Hadon Lodge. Fowchester.'

O'Neill stood up. 'Would you come with us now to verify that the body we've found is that of your ex-husband?'

Jill's eyes flicked anxiously from Fran to O'Neill and back, as if she was trying to think of some excuse. 'I want to pick my son up on the way.'

'Sure,' said O'Neill.

At the sports centre O'Neill drummed his fingers on the steering wheel of his Mercedes. They waited in silence. Five minutes later Jill appeared with a tall muscular boy wearing blue jeans and a grey sweatshirt. As the boy neared the car O'Neill could see how alike father and son had been. Those same dark brown eyes. He was crying, just letting the tears drift down his cheeks as if he hardly noticed.

As he got into the car he said to his mother, 'You slag! This is all your fault. I bet you're happy now.'

Chapter Five

Nina Gardener glanced at her wristwatch. She normally timed meals more by instinct than by her watch, but this dinner party she wanted to be perfect. It was a welcome to the firm for her husband's new partner. There were three now, it was a growing firm. Gardener and Langmore were *the* solicitors in Fowchester. Langmore, whose name was still embossed on the brass plate, had been dead for years but Charles's father, Edward Gardener, was still alive – just – and living in a nursing home near the coast.

Nina could hear Charles singing in the shower. Something Mozartian, she guessed, although he had such a dreadful voice she could never be sure. She was still a little worried about the menu. Would it be substantial enough? There was asparagus soup to start, then rack of lamb, new potatoes, courgettes with ginger and garlic, baby carrots and, to follow, caramelized oranges. There would, of course, be cheese and biscuits. She smiled to herself. She always had food left over. When they'd first married and Charles had been in the final year of his law degree they had been rather poor and she'd invited four friends for supper and there hadn't been enough food. She could remember the mortification even now. Charles had been understanding then but he'd become gradually less so and now, in middle age, could be pompous and impatient. She felt sure that not having plenty of well-cooked food now would be a cardinal sin in his eyes, something akin to her being caught shop-lifting.

'How's it going, darling?' Charles asked. 'It all smells jolly good.'

He stood by the open kitchen door with his greying hair, what was left of it, still slightly damp. He'd dressed casually in grey trousers and a navy blazer with shirt and tie. Charles was the type of man who'd wear a tie in the desert. But in the navy blazer he looked like a man who'd mislaid his private yacht.

'All under control,' said Nina. 'I would love a drink, though.'

'The usual?'

'Please, darling.'

As he went to get the drink Nina thought how unfailingly polite they always were. Their lives went by in a parody of trivial but polite questions and answers. 'Yes darling', 'Thank you darling' 'More wine darling? It's jolly good', 'What about the Maldives this year darling?' 'Sounds wonderful darling, I can't wait'.

Only occasionally did Nina wonder if Charles was quite human. He was decent, fair-minded, logical, reasonably intelligent, had fathered two boys, both at boarding school, and drank moderately, with only minimal change in his personality. He made love to her once a month on average, taking ten minutes for foreplay, which he seemed to regard as an obligation rather than a pleasure, and three minutes, on average, for vigorous sexual intercourse. During the action time he undoubtedly expected her to reach orgasm and he thanked her, sincerely, after each monthly encounter.

Those are just his good points, thought Nina sarcastically.

On the minus side he was often arrogant, pompous, opinionated and completely without a sense of humour. In truth, he was as passionless as a cooked prawn.

Charles returned moments later with a gin and tonic. She sipped it and tried to smile. He was already short-changing on the gin. When his back was turned she'd top it up.

'Oh, by the way, Nina, some female rang yesterday while you were out. Forbes I think the name was.'

'Oh yes, thank you, darling.'

'Who exactly is she? Not one of your social misfit types, I hope.'

Nina opened the Aga to check on the meat. 'She's looking for a job,' she said casually. 'I thought we might be able to use her.'

'What for, darling?' he asked, frowning slightly.

'Mrs Marriot is thinking of retiring, you know, and I do need some help in the house.'

'Of course you do, darling. As long as you think this Forbes woman will be hard-working and reliable, why not?'

Nina had forgotten about Carole Ann, she had to admit. She'd ring her in the morning.

'Anything I can do to help, darling?' asked Charles.

She smiled. 'All under control, captain.'

'I'll . . . er, wander off, then.'

'Put your feet up, Charles, darling. You've got half an hour before they come.'

'I'm sure you'll like Lawrence Morgan,' he said, pausing by the door. 'He's a very knowledgeable chap on the law.'

'I'm sure we'll get on brilliantly.' He smiled as he turned to go.

Cross off the reasonably intelligent, Nina thought, he couldn't even tell when she was being sarcastic.

Nina had her own supply of gin in the kitchen cupboard, behind the bleach and disinfectant bottles. She bent down when she heard the sitting-room door shut and topped up her tonic with gin. Charles thought she got through these evenings on a splash of gin and two glasses of wine. He didn't let his hair down, so why should she? Her husband of twenty years didn't know how to relax anyway. Sometimes when Nina was interested enough to spend time observing him she almost saw the ramrod keeping his back straight. He reminded her of a bit-part actor playing a very stiff role and overdoing it.

The guests arrived punctually. Nina would not have expected otherwise. Their friends, new and old, were not the artistic, raffish types. They were lawyers and barristers. Trained to be correct and punctual and . . . law abiding. Charles had invited just the partners and their wives for this meal. The partners' wives were meek souls doing good works – meals on wheels, organizing charity events, making jam, giving dinner parties.

The first to arrive were James and Harriet Sharbrook, both in their forties. Harriet had, in the dim and distant past, qualified at the bar but four children had long since dulled her professional ambitions. And although they found the school fees a dreadful burden she had once confessed, after three large gins, that the grandparents did help out. Nina studied her first guest as though how Harriet looked really mattered. She noticed her shoulder-length dark hair appeared unbrushed and that the clothes she wore tonight were her usual style – a white embroidered blouse buttoned to the neck and the black velvet skirt she'd had for years. Harriet was reasonably slim only through a regime of self denial and aerobic exercise, and she could have been striking but she'd long since stopped bothering.

James kissed Nina on both cheeks. 'You're looking wonderful,' he said. James was fair with a markedly receding hairline. This sparsely covered skull, Nina was convinced, lay over a brain that had never held an original thought. In her jaundiced view of the legal profession, lawyers didn't think much; they remembered, collated, sifted and came to conclusions. There wasn't much room for innovation or the odd spark of radical thought. Maintaining the status quo was the most important, even vital, attribute of their lives.

Nina smiled and hugged Harriet. 'Lovely to see you both again. You're the first, do come through and I'll persuade Charles to be generous with the drinks. You haven't brought the car, have you?'

'Came by taxi, Nina,' explained James. 'One can't take risks these days.'

Nina nodded in agreement. They were not a risk-taking couple. In fact, if she had to describe James and Harriet to a stranger in a single phrase she would have said: they wear matching white towelling robes – with identical motifs. They were a 'together' couple, so 'together' Nina could only think of them as a pair. They even had a combined voice. 'I do love your home,' said Harriet. 'We both do.'

Nina thanked her. She said the same thing every time she came.

The house, dating back to God knows when, had low beams, huge fireplaces and the in 'character' appearance that was not achieved without considerable effort.

Charles fussed with their drinks as if the mixing was of great technical difficulty. Halfway through he was interrupted by the door bell. Nina took a quick swig of neat gin from the bottle in the kitchen and went to join her husband at the front door.

The new partner, whom she hadn't met before, was, Nina had to admit, a dish. Tall, slim, with blue eyes and neat dark hair, he stood beside a petite blonde in a black dress who had a weak, nervous smile and bare skinny arms.

Charles introduced Lawrence Morgan so proudly that for a moment she wondered if Charles had developed delusions of grandeur. As if he had not just recruited him, but created him. Meryl, his wife, continued to smile somewhat nervously, confessing, 'I haven't been out for ages. We have a new baby, you see – our second, a boy, Giles.'

'Congratulations,' said Nina with a fixed smile. 'Charles didn't tell me.'

'Didn't I, darling? I'm sorry. I was so delighted to bag such an excellent divorce lawyer it must have slipped my mind.'

The last couple to arrive were Lionel and Georgina Douglas. They were in their fifties. Nina found them quite amusing because they never failed to have a row. Usually about some fondly held memory of utter triviality. These memories were shaped and stored in their long-term memories but the couple didn't seem able to conceive that each had collected separate and unique trivia. So they argued constantly and with such passion that Nina was quite jealous. Charles never argued with passion. Just deadly dull logic. He was usually right, which incensed Nina, and she compensated by drinking too much of her private supply of gin. How Charles didn't guess she couldn't get drunk on his measures she couldn't fathom.

Lionel kissed Nina enthusiastically on both cheeks and said, 'Charles, you're a lucky fellow. Nina grows more ravishing every day.' And more ravished, thought Nina with a wry smile. Lionel was good-looking in a worn and craggy way, his hair was still thick and black, his dark eyes twinkled, but not with ideas of dallying with the senior partner's wife. His eyes grew bright with the fanaticism of the DIY man. He was a man with a mission – converting as many barns as possible in his lifetime.

Georgina stood a few inches taller than him and was of general Amazonian build, which for some reason led her to try and disguise the fact by being a great fan of puffed sleeves and ultra-feminine dresses. She, too, was interested in barn conversions, but only in choosing the soft furnishings and bath taps. She rang Nina on many occasions to describe in graphic detail the brochures and catalogues she'd just minutely scoured. Apart from her rows with Lionel Nina found her incredibly boring.

Charles, wary of his drink stock dwindling too fast, began ushering the guests to the dining room. Nina stirred the soup and tasted it. Just before pouring it into the tureen she drank a double gin quickly. That steadied her. By God, she didn't care now if the evening was a flop or not.

Halfway through the main course Nina began to sense things were getting quite lively. Lionel and Georgina were bickering nicely about the weather on their holiday in Tuscany five years before.

'It was the Saturday it rained most of the day, Georgie,' said Lionel, slamming down his fork.

'It was not! I remember perfectly well it was the Sunday. I saw people going to Mass and the church bells were ringing.'

'You imagine things, woman. It was Saturday.'

38

'Don't woman me, Lionel. It was Sunday.'

Beside Georgina sat Lawrence, the new man, watching and listening with avid interest.

'Shall I ring home, Lawrence?' murmured Meryl from across the table. 'Just to make sure Giles is all right.'

'Do stop whingeing, darling,' said Lawrence tersely. At that, Meryl seemed to shrink in her chair and Nina signalled to Charles with a meaningful glance that he should top up her glass. If ever a woman needed another drink it was Meryl Morgan.

Shortly after this James had a minor altercation with Harriet about eating disorders and Charles glared at Nina's too quickly emptied wine glass, refilled it reluctantly and mouthed 'that's the last'.

As the evening progressed Charles became noticeably perturbed that his attempts to talk about the practice were stonewalled either by his own wife or by Lionel, who no doubt found plastering and woodwork a damn sight more exciting than the conveyancing and probate work he'd done for the past twenty-five years. Nina watched with gin-detached amusement as Charles floundered in their general lack of interest in talking shop until during a slight lull he said, 'Have you heard about the local murder? Let's hope we get the business on that one.'

Lawrence sipped at his wine. 'Did anyone know the victim?'

Everyone shook their heads except Nina. She was too busy feeling under the tablecloth for Lawrence's left knee. Giving it a gentle squeeze she gauged his reaction. It was a test she usually performed, with plenty of gin coursing through her veins, on men she'd just met. It was an infallible guide to their general bedworthiness. His reaction was the reaction *par excellence*. He returned her hand to her furthest leg and let his warm hand find her inner thigh. She was so impressed she spilled her wine, the red stain spreading wide over her white lace tablecloth.

Charles raised a warning eyebrow at her but went off to the kitchen for cloths and soda water. Before Charles came back Nina began unsteadily to serve the caramelized oranges and said to no one in particular, 'Don't tell Charles, darlings, but I knew the dead man.'

Chapter Six

Enid Braithwaite had already laid the table for the evening meal. The plastic tablecloth, she noticed, was getting a bit worn but the artificial daffodils looked as good as new. Luckily her lodgers weren't fussy about food. They got what she cooked and if they didn't like it they went without – just like in prison. I've no truck with faddishness, she thought; only the other day she'd seen a big purple thing being cooked on TV. An ober . . . something or other. You slice it, salt it, and then wash it and pat it dry. Then you could stuff it or fry it or use it to make that foreign dish with mincemeat and a cheese sauce. What a performance! She saw to it that her lodgers had plain-cooked wholesome food. There was nothing wrong with cabbage and carrots and tinned peas, nothing at all. That was the trouble with this country, she thought, everything was getting too foreign. Even ex-prisoners sometimes had the cheek to ask for exotic meals like curry or spaghetti something or other. She couldn't even say some of the words. She kept strictly to the same two-week menu and had the food delivered from the small super-market in the High Street. Today was Saturday, so it was hot boiled bacon with a parsley sauce, mashed potatoes, fried onions and carrots. And for afters it was rice pudding. It was all simmering away nicely.

In the week she served breakfast from seven-thirty till eight, and not a minute later. And the evening meal was at six. For those not working she made a sandwich and some soup at midday because she didn't want people cooking in their rooms. No, she wasn't having any of that.

Her front room was for the use of her lodgers but she never allowed them into her back room. That was private. That was where she listened to her collection of Cliff Richard records.

'Now, he is a good singer,' she muttered to herself, 'and a Christ-ian.' He wasn't into drugs and filth like some of these modern singers. She smiled to herself as she thought about him. He was a bit on the thin side. He could do with a few of her bacon dumplings. That would fill him out.

In the kitchen she checked the time by her kitchen clock and then she wiped a newly bleached dishcloth over the condensation on her cooker. She believed in clearing up as she went along. In one more minute she would serve the meal and then wash the pots. Miss Forbes and Mr Reynolds could wash their own plates. She'd been a little wary of Miss Forbes at first, not because she was a murderess but because she was so pretty. No male followers, that was Enid's creed. When she was young Enid had had two very nasty experiences, once coming back from church. She should have fought back harder and she admired women like Miss Forbes who did.

Carole Ann lay on the bed and stared at her bedside clock. Ten minutes to 6 p.m., Saturday – July 1994. More than two months of so-called freedom. Two months of sheer misery. She'd been to the job centre and signed on but no one there held out much hope of a job for an ex-con or anyone else. She'd rung Nina Gardener several times but she never seemed to be in, and then last night her husband had answered the phone and he sounded as friendly as a Rottweiler, and then there was the old bag of a landlady. She could have coped with the food but the Cliff Richard records were wearing her down. Occasionally in the evening she left the house quietly when the records came on and was usually back by midnight when the old girl bolted the front door.

Carole Ann, she preferred to be known as that because both names on their own were so ordinary, sat in the back yard sometimes on fine warm days but mostly she stayed in her room. She'd joined the library and read several books a week, wrote to her penfriend, sometimes walked round the town aimlessly, even, now and then, finding a man to talk to on a park bench. She had seen one or two beggars in the town but she couldn't bring herself to beg, although money was very tight. The DSS money covered the cost of a stamp, a few ounces of tobacco, a newspaper and a bottle of cider, and that was it. When her Giro was due she was always broke. She desperately needed new clothes and shoes but there was no way she could afford them. Sometimes in her idle moments, and there were plenty of them, she thought of ways to make money. Ways she had studied in prison. Prison had definitely opened her eyes to the opportunities of crime. She'd learned something new in each of the prisons she'd been in. But what stayed with her was the concept of 'them' and 'us'. She was with the 'us's'. As one fellow con put it, 'The "us" stands for "useless sods".' Once she'd accepted what she was, that she didn't belong with the 'thems', she could plan an alternative strategy. And that, of course, included crime. And if Nina Gardener didn't contact her soon she really would have to do something.

At six the landlady shouted, 'Supper's ready.' Carole Ann smiled grimly to herself. One day she'd fix the old girl's record player. In the meantime it was Saturday, which meant boiled bacon and thin glutinous parsley sauce with overcooked carrots, not forgetting the fried onions. She'd smelled the onions all the afternoon. The smell had drifted up the stairs, reminding her of prison and causing little ripples of homesickness. What did taking risks matter if the only result was that you went back to a place you preferred?

Carole Ann smoothed and tidied the pink candlewick bedspread and walked downstairs. She practised smiling for old Braithwaite as she got to the last three stairs. So that by the time her landlady presented her with the food she would look fairly angelic.

After she'd eaten she'd go out. Maybe hitch a lift. Pay Mrs Gardener a personal call.

'There you are, dear,' said her landlady, Miss Enid Braithwaite, as she walked slowly into the front room carrying the plate of food. She was an odd shape, with a great shelf-like bosom atop narrow hips and thin spindly legs. She always wore one of those all-encompassing aprons over a Crimplene dress, but the most memorable thing about her was her black hair, dyed to perfection with not a grey hair in sight. In contrast, her face was pallid, her features lost, though her tiny grey eyes reminded Carole of . . . mould. Enid, she thought, could have been related to one of the Munsters.

'No Mr Reynolds, I see,' said Enid as she placed the boiled-to-death meat and sloppy sauce in front of her. 'He's been late two Saturdays in a row. Goodness knows where he gets to.'

Carole Ann knew Enid would put the meal at his place on the table anyway. And there it would sit. If he wasn't back by six-thirty it would be removed and thrown away. Miss Braithwaite definitely had a ruthless streak.

She started to eat but after a few mouthfuls began to feel nauseated. The sight of Dave Reynolds' meal coagulating on the plate turned her stomach. He was a strange guy, in his forties, thickset, a bit rough-looking but with a quiet voice. They'd only had two conversations, both when Miss B. was out of earshot. He'd talked about his last two jobs. Not the wage-packet-at-the-end-of-the-week jobs but the snatch-it-with-a-shotgun jobs. H'd been quite animated on the subject and Carole Ann had listened carefully. She'd wondered then if he was a psychopath; he didn't display any signs of conscience but now she knew more about criminals she knew that wasn't unusual. Most criminals had discriminating consciences and avowed horror of certain crimes, but armed robbery remained firmly in the upper echelons of crime. It wasn't his lack of conscience that made her doubt his sanity; it was his facial expressions and his habit of turning his head, as if he were listening to voices. It would only last a few seconds but when it did happen it unnerved her.

'Is that all you're going to eat?' asked Enid as she collected her half-full plate. 'No wonder you're skinny. By the time you get a job you won't have any strength left. You'll have some of my rice pudding, won't you?'

Carole Ann nodded. She didn't really have much choice as it had already been placed in front of her.

At that moment Dave Reynolds appeared. He wore black jeans and a green T-shirt. 'Sorry I'm late,' he muttered, not looking at either woman. He sat down and began to eat straight away. He was obviously well used to cold prison food. Carole Ann found it impossible to watch him eat and she stared down at her rice pudding and reluctantly swallowed three spoonfuls. Enid, standing by their table observing them, made Carole Ann think of prison meal times where screws stood on guard. At least in prison, though, she'd never had to eat with someone quite as remote as Dave Reynolds.

'I'm going to my room when I've cleared up,' said Enid warningly. 'So I don't want to be disturbed. You can help yourselves to tea and biscuits. I'll leave a tray in the kitchen. And I'll be bolting up at midnight as usual.'

Dave didn't look up from his plate until he'd finished, then he took his plate into the kitchen, came back, started on his rice pudding and after the first mouthful asked bluntly, 'What were you in for?'

Carole Ann smiled at him. 'I thought you'd never ask. Murder.'

43

His brown eyes showed a flicker of interest. Murder of an adult had high status in prison. A 'lifer' would always have a share of respect from inmates and staff.

'Who d'you kill?' he asked.

'My lover.'

'Was he giving you a hard time?'

Carole Ann shook her head. 'No, he was a great guy.'

'Why d'you kill him, then?'

'I don't know,' said Carole Ann.

He turned his head slightly, as though listening, and then said, 'You must know.'

'I don't.'

He carried on eating. Carole Ann stood up. 'See you later.'

He gave her a half smile. 'You going out?'

'Why?'

'Just wondered, I thought you might want me to let you in.'

She shrugged. At that moment Cliff Richard's voice began to reverberate around the house. Carole Ann smiled at Enid's choice – 'Devil Woman'.

Chapter Seven

The formal identification upset O'Neill.

Stephen had insisted on seeing his father's body. Both Fran and O'Neill had tried to persuade him not to, but he'd insisted. They'd stood, mother and son, side by side, stiffly, as if to attention, beside the white-shrouded body. Jill Lattaway seemed the more composed of the two until the sheet was lifted from his face, then her face paled and her knees sagged and O'Neill had to support her.

'It is him,' she murmured. 'But it's not him, if you know what I mean.'

O'Neill did.

Stephen, with tears coursing silently down his cheeks, touched his father's purple face. 'I'm so sorry, Dad,' he said in a high-pitched shaky voice. 'I'll miss you—' He broke off and stared at his mother with such hatred that Fran took his arm and said softly, 'Don't, Stephen, take a deep breath. This has come as a terrible shock to both of you.' He stared at her but didn't seem to see her. O'Neill noticed he was clenching his fists so tightly his knuckles were white.

O'Neill drove them home. No one spoke. Except once, when O'Neill said, 'Would you like us to contact any relatives or friends to stay with you?'

'I'll tell his parents. They'll come over,' said Jill. Stephen stared out of the car window. Occasionally he wiped his face with the back of his hand.

At the house O'Neill parked the car and said, 'You'll be wanting to be alone. But I'll have to come again in the morning. And I'll be needing to talk to your friend Ian.'

'Ian didn't have anything to do with this,' she said sharply.

Stephen, who'd sat with bowed head, suddenly jerked upright and said, 'He's not coming in my house. I'll kill him. I will. He's not

45

coming in my house.' The boy's voice rose hysterically.

'Be quiet,' ordered O'Neill.

Stephen choked back a sob but said no more.

'He won't come to the house, Stephen, I promise you,' said his mother. Tentatively she put an arm around him and although he stiffened he didn't shrug her off.

Mother and son walked into the house together slowly, heads down, arms around each other.

O'Neill drove slowly away. He hadn't gone far before he said, 'Christ, Fran, I need a drink.'

'Please don't drink now, boss,' said Fran. 'It'll make you feel worse.'

'I couldn't be feeling worse. This bloody job crucifies me.'

There was silence for a while. Fran stared out of the car window at the shoppers in their summer clothes. Eventually she said, 'Are we going to Hadon straight away?'

'Might as well.'

'If you stop off on the way, boss, I'll make you some good coffee and a sandwich.'

He smiled bleakly. 'You're devious, Fran. You're only trying to stop me going to the pub.'

'Someone has to,' she murmured. 'And could you park round the back of the house in case someone sees us?'

Irritated, he said, 'I don't give a tinker's cuss,' but to please her he drove round the corner and parked in the small courtyard at the back.

Once in Fran's tiny terraced house, he sat morosely at the kitchen table. He couldn't get the boy's grief out of his mind. His own father had died on the first day of his retirement. A heart attack. Sudden and fatal – he couldn't even think about it now, seventeen years on, without wanting to cry. Although he couldn't articulate the feelings, he knew the loss of a father would continue to be a yawning chasm which no one else could breach.

He glanced over towards Fran, who was busy making him a cheese sandwich. She hadn't smiled in ages. God, he wanted her to hold him. She walked over with a plate of sandwiches and placed them in front of him. He could smell her. The image of the boy stroking his dead father's face came back. He put a hand over his eyes. He knew the tears were welling up.

'Connor?' She placed a hand on his shoulder.

'I'm all right,' he said.

'Was it the boy?'

'Jesus, Fran, don't ask.'

She put her arm round him and hugged him. He tried to choke back the tears but her body was soft and he felt so bloody weak. He swallowed hard. He couldn't give in. He didn't move. He wanted to, but he didn't. After a few moments he said, 'Where's that coffee you promised me?'

She removed her arm slowly and patted his back. He took a deep breath and looked up at her. Her eyes too were overbright. But she smiled. 'It's great coffee, boss. It'll do you more good than whiskey.'

He felt his guts wrench. And he knew it wasn't the thought of whiskey that caused it.

They drank the coffee in silence, and a little later on the way to Hadon O'Neill said, 'I want you to know, Fran, I've been remembering about my night in Birmingham. Well, some of it. And I'm sure I did nothing to be ashamed of.'

'Will you still go for some help with your drinking?'

'Sure I will. I wasn't trying to make excuses. When it's all sorted in my mind I'll tell you about it.'

'I trust you, Connor.'

'I hope you do, Fran. Someone needs to trust me.'

The Hadon estate was about five miles out of Fowchester. There were private signs marking the single-track dirt road that led to the lodge and pastures full of sheep.

'Lord Hadon owns this pile of land,' explained O'Neill. 'Past the gatehouse there's a proper road and about a mile or two along is the manor house, with its lake, stables and the estate workers' cottages.'

'You sound as if you don't approve,' said Fran.

O'Neill shrugged. 'I'm not sure I do. Acres and acres of God's earth, what right has anyone to own it?'

'It is beautiful,' said Fran, looking out on to the fields of sheep that seemed to go on and on, each field separated by a wooden gate and in the corners of the fields large oak trees with the late evening sunlight filtering through their leaves. It seemed a million miles from murder.

The lodge was oddly shaped, almost octagonal, made of stone with a thatched roof. The windows were leaded and the oak front

47

door boasted a handsome brass knocker in the shape of an eagle.

O'Neill banged hard on the door. It was opened immediately.

'Ian Bishop?'

He nodded. He was a man in his late thirties, tanned, broad-shouldered, with short dark hair, brown eyes, and saved from being too handsome by a broadish nose. He wore cream slacks and a navy short-sleeved shirt. He smelled strongly of aftershave. For some reason O'Neill thought he might have been ex-army.

'Police,' said O'Neill.

'Come in.' Then he added, surprisingly, 'I've been expecting you.'

The gatehouse was tiny inside. The front door opened straight into the living room, and O'Neill's overwhelming impression was of a dim, masculine shelter rather than a home. There was a battered leather sofa, a drop-leaf table and two chairs, a shotgun propped up just inside the door and a black and white portable TV in the corner.

'I'm Detective Chief Inspector O'Neill and this is Detective Sergeant Wilson.'

'I'm honoured. Usually I get a PC.'

'You'll be explaining that, sir.'

Ian Bishop frowned. 'You've come about the sheep rustling, haven't you? I lost three sheep last night. Five last month.'

'No, sir. I've come about a more serious matter.'

'Sheep stealing is serious. I'd shoot the buggers if I caught them at it.'

'We've come about murder, Mr Bishop.'

Ian Bishop fell silent.

'Today,' said O'Neill quietly, 'the body of Alan Lattaway was found by the river in Fowchester.'

'Oh my God!' Bishop's face paled slightly beneath his tan.

'You'd better sit down,' said Fran.

Bishop sat down heavily on a straight-backed chair.

'How well did you know him?' asked O'Neill.

'I didn't know him. I never met him.'

'But you were having an affair with his wife?'

'His ex-wife.'

'Very well, ex-wife.'

'I'm telling you, Chief Inspector, I didn't know him.'

'Where did you meet Jill?'

48

'How is she? Is she all right?'

'Could you be answering my questions, sir?'

Bishop rubbed his hands over his face. 'This is a bit of a shock. You don't expect murder in a place like this, do you?'

'Nor sheep stealing, but it happens. Now then, sir, back to my question. Where did you meet Jill Lattaway?'

'Originally, do you mean?'

'Any way you like, sir.'

'She works in the bank. That's where I first met her. I pick her up after work, sometimes we come back here, sometimes we go out for a drink or a meal. There's not much to do in Fowchester, is there?'

'No, sir, agreed, you'd not be finding it the entertainment Mecca of the Midlands.'

O'Neill signalled to Fran with a raised eyebrow to take over.

'How long had you been seeing Jill?' she asked.

He shrugged. 'About two years.'

'So you met after her divorce?'

'Yes. I didn't break up her marriage.'

'And where is the relationship going?'

'What's that supposed to mean?'

'I mean, sir, is she just a good lay?'

Fran's question hit home. His mouth tightened. She could see the flash of temper stiffen his body. 'For Christ's sake, I love her.'

'I see, sir. But you hadn't yet decided to make an honest woman of her.'

'It's not that simple.'

'Well, it is now, sir. The ex-husband has been . . . eliminated from the equation.'

'I didn't know Alan Lattaway. I didn't kill him.'

'Where were you last night, sir?'

'I was out with Jill, as well you know. You must have asked her.'

'What time did you leave her?'

'Round about midnight. I came back here.'

'Was there any reason she didn't come back here with you?'

'She was tired. She'd been working all day.'

'What about her son?'

'What about him?'

'Have you met him?'

'Yes. I have met him.'

'And?'

'If you must know, he hates my guts. I've tried, but we just don't get on.'

'Is he the reason you haven't got married?'

'One of them.'

Bishop looked from Fran to O'Neill. Then he said slowly and deliberately. 'I had nothing to do with Alan's death and nor did Jill.'

'Why do you say that, Mr Bishop?' asked Fran with a smile. 'We hadn't supposed that Jill murdered her husband. What makes you think we did?'

Fran could tell he wasn't prepared for the question and he stuttered his answer. 'Look you're c-c-confusing me. This . . . this is a nightmare. I'm not answering any more bloody stupid questions.'

Fran smiled again. 'That's your privilege, sir, at this moment. We'll be back of course.'

As they walked to the door, O'Neill said. 'I've been thinking, Mr Bishop, that there's one question you haven't asked us.'

'What's that?'

'You haven't asked us how he died.'

'So?'

'So. I'm just wondering in an idle sort of way why you didn't ask.'

Bishop glowered at O'Neill. 'Does it matter how? He's dead.'

'And you'll not be sorry about that.'

'I wouldn't say that I'm heartbroken.'

'That much is obvious, sir. Don't be worrying about the sheep, sir, we'll be sending a PC along about the rustlers. And don't be shooting anyone in the meantime.'

Ian Bishop glared at them both. His pent-up anger was obvious and as they opened the door they heard him kicking it closed in fury.

O'Neill's mouth formed a little victory smile as he walked away.

'You're looking pleased with yourself,' said Fran.

'Did you notice? He still didn't ask, even then, how he died.'

'I did notice. I think we rattled his cage.'

O'Neill laughed drily. 'You rattled it so hard he was left only just clinging to his perch. You've improved Fran – I think you had the edge on me there.'

Fran didn't answer. She was just glad her boss had cheered up.

In the car O'Neill said, 'There's not much more we can do today.

Tomorrow, with any luck, we might have a preliminary pathologist's report. Forensic will be taking for ever. It's time of death we need to know. But we'll be starting again in the morning, Fran. Be at the station by eight.'

He dropped Fran off, smiled, said, 'I'll be seeing you in the morning,' and drove away.

Fran opened her front door and felt a sense of disappointment. She wanted to discuss things, to talk. Now she was alone and he'd rushed off much more promptly than usual as if . . . as if . . . as if he wanted a drink! 'Stupid sod,' she muttered under her breath.

She wandered round the small house restlessly. It was too early for bed and her mind was too agitated to read or even watch television. She stared at the insipid rag-rolled walls, which she'd intended to change and hadn't, and knew she couldn't spend the whole of a summer's evening indoors.

For a while she listened for her mouse, pausing at the cupboard under the sink. She guessed that was where he had his entry and his exit point. All was silent. Even the mouse has deserted me, she thought. She put down a few crumbs as a test, slipped on a jacket and left the house.

O'Neill spent some time tidying up. He'd had no viewers yet, which was probably just as well, no one in their right mind would buy this tip. He'd been ambivalent about the house before, but now that there was a vague possibility it might sell he felt nervous about moving. He knew it was part of letting go of the guilt of Jenny's suicide but recently those feelings had become less acute, although he still found it hard to let go of that pain, he still wanted to feel it. It meant he was alive.

He planned, once he sold the house, to buy a small flat. Live the bachelor life. He found it hard to bring women here, as if his wife were still in the house, watching. As though he was committing some final treacherous act by making love in the house they had once shared happily, he thought.

In the lounge he stared at the whiskey bottle. He was driving, he wasn't fool enough to have even a small one before driving. His small ones led to larger ones. He was determined to stop drinking, or at least to cut down. Part of the reason was Fran. He was aware, especially now, with this murder enquiry, that if he cocked up it could reflect on Fran's future too. And to be sure she wasn't flavour of the month among some of the Fowchester police. He didn't want to make things worse for her.

He showered and dressed in his best blue-grey suit, splashed on aftershave, checked his appearance twice and left the house. To get to the motorway to Birmingham he had to go past Fran's house. He was going once more to the Black Cat club. Maybe she'd come with him. He wanted to find out what happened that night and with her there to help him he could at least show that he was trying.

The curtains remained closed at Fran's place. He peered through the window. She was out or she was hiding from him. Unreasonably, he felt angry with himself and her. Where the hell was she? She hadn't said she was going out. As far as he knew she still had no friends locally. Not because she wasn't attractive and good company, simply because those in ordinary jobs didn't want friends in the police; thinking as they did that the police were constantly on the lookout to grass their friends for minor breaches of the law like having an out-of-date tax disc or buying a watch from a man in a pub.

He banged the front door once more and yelled 'Fran' loudly through the letter box, but to no avail.

As he drove away he decided to take more cognizance of his DS's social arrangements in the future. And she could like it or lump it.

Chapter Eight

The landlord of the Wanderer pub, Roger Taylor, made his Sunday lunch time's reconnoitre, his 'recce', at 10.30 a.m. He toured the kitchen, checking the meat was in the oven, the vegetables being prepared, the desserts defrosting. He cast an eye over his live-in staff, his wife being one of them and Julie the new cook/barmaid being the other. They were scraping carrots side by side. Neither of them liked him very much, so they didn't look up as he passed through. He walked into the bar, checked the pumps were working and the optics, then he ran his fingers along the bar's counter – he didn't like any sticky patches. He altered the position of two beer mats, swept his keen eye over the main floor of the pub, noted the ashtrays were in place, six tables were laid ready for lunches and that the alcoves had been swept and cleaned. He decided he could have his drink in peace.

He selected a bottle of Glenmorangie, poured himself a generous double and sat down to drink in the empty pub. He did this every Sunday. He needed a drink before the busiest lunch time of the week. Even busier since the murder. It's an ill wind, he thought. He knew the man who'd got himself stabbed; he came in at least once a week but they'd never had a proper conversation.

'I'm going upstairs to get changed,' called his wife, Connie, from the door of the kitchen.

'Don't be long,' he called back without looking up from his glass.

'Get knotted!' he heard her say. Things hadn't been too good between them, especially since Julie had arrived. He'd wanted a barman to live in, but Connie had got stroppy as hell, saying she wasn't going to be cooking chips all week and doing roasts on Sunday. 'I'm not a bloody skivvy' were her exact words. So he'd given in, in the end. He didn't like letting her have her own way. He felt she was trying to ease him out of the pub towards her idea

53

of 'retirement'. Well, he was only fifty-five and he wasn't planning to retire yet. Being a publican had its drawbacks but he was his own boss and just lately business had picked up. They concentrated more on food now and he had to admit Julie was a damn good cook. Sullen she may be, but she could make old-fashioned puddings and her steak and kidney pie was getting quite a reputation. He'd just have to keep a close eye on them, otherwise he could see the two of them ganging up on him.

With ten minutes left till opening time he shouted up the stairs, 'Connie – move yourself!' He took a final look round the alcoves and again congratulated himself on the old-fashioned cosiness of his pub. There were wall lamps in each of the alcoves and old books on shelves and plain wooden tables and floors. Decorative plates lined the walls and fresh flowers always graced the tables. Outside, there was a small pub garden which looked out on to the river, and on fine days the punters would be packed in like sardines both inside and outside. Off the main pub lounge there was a small games room with a darts board, a shove-halfpenny board and a pool table.

'Do you have to yell at me?' asked Connie as she appeared behind the bar.

'You're so bloody slow,' he said.

She'd got some make-up on now and a flimsy cream blouse and skirt. The blouse was a bit too see-through for his taste. He could see her bra.

'What are you staring at, Roger?'

'Nothing.' There wasn't time for her to change now. He'd let it drop this time. Connie was ten years younger than him and he'd seen the way men looked at her. Even men in their twenties. And she encouraged them. He kept an eye on her of course, or as much as he could. He'd only had trouble once. And he'd got that sorted pretty quick.

The sweat ran down Julie's forehead. With the oven going full blast it was suffocatingly hot in the kitchen. Today the choice was turkey or beef. Why people should want roasts in the summer she didn't know, but they did. She opened the oven door and poked the turkey in the fattest part of its body, just above the leg. The juices still ran pink.

She ran the tap and poured herself a glass of water. Perhaps it had been a mistake coming here, but it was reasonably well paid and she wasn't going to do it for the rest of her life. Most things were bearable in the short term, she'd decided. Roger Taylor didn't help make the job more pleasant. Obnoxious and domineering, he'd tried to make her life a misery. But at least she wasn't married to him – thank God – and Connie compensated. Connie was great, she had a sense of humour and behind his back they had a good laugh – usually about him.

Julie turned on the potatoes to parboil and stood just watching the water come to the boil. She was twenty-eight years old and she'd landed up in some grotty town on her own. Not for long, though, she told herself. She was attractive – well, if she made an effort. She didn't feel very attractive at this moment with a white chef's cap on her head, her face flushed and with sweat seeping from every pore. But later, when she was showered and fresh and in a summer dress, she'd feel attractive again.

'Are you ready, Julie? I'm opening in two minutes!'

Julie caught a glimpse of her boss out of the corner of her eye. His paunch preceded his face as he crept round corners. He had gimlet blue eyes, fair to greying hair with a big bald patch like a monk's tonsure. He reserved any smiles and charm that he could dredge up for customers.

'As I'll ever be,' she replied after a short interval, knowing full well how irritating he found this. To disgruntle Roger was the only fun she ever got. One day he might retaliate. She smiled to herself, wondering if Connie would spring to her aid. Together they would make quite a team.

A few moments later she heard the bolts being drawn back. The lunch-time trade at the Wanderer had begun.

In the Lattaway house no Sunday lunch was being prepared. Stephen had hardly left his room for two days. Jill took him up some tea and toast for breakfast, leaving it outside the door. An hour later it was still there. She knocked softly on the door.

'Please, Stephen, you've got to eat. Your Dad wouldn't have wanted you to behave like this. If you won't eat, let me come and talk to you.'

The answering voice sounded aggressive. 'I've got nothing to say to you.'

'Come on, Stephen, there's a good boy. The police will be round later on. They'll expect you to be sensible.'

This time the answer was a stream of filth. Jill covered her ears and could feel tears building up. She didn't know he knew such words. Suddenly the 'good boy' seemed to have grown into a lout. A lout who accused her of being responsible for his father's death.

'Just piss off and leave me alone – you murdering bitch!'

Jill ran down the stairs and stood pressed against the wall in the kitchen. She was trembling, she couldn't stop. She had to speak to Ian. She couldn't manage this on her own. With shaking hands, she dialled his number.

'Oh, Ian, thank goodness you're in,' she said, feeling immediately calmed by the sound of his voice.

'What's up?' he said.

'It's Stephen. He's still in his room and he's . . . he's calling me terrible names. I can't cope, really I can't.'

'You're going to have to, sweetheart. What can I do? I can't come to the house, I'd be like a red rag. You know what he thinks of me.'

'Can I come over, Ian – please—'

'Now come on, love, that's not a good idea, is it? The police will be backwards and forwards like bloody yo-yos. We'll both of us have to stay put for a while.'

'You do still love me, don't you?' she asked tearfully.

'Come on, Jill, pull yourself together. All this will get sorted. Stephen will come round in the end.'

'Say it!'

'Of course I still love you. But we do have to be . . . careful now.'

'Why? What do you mean, Ian?'

'We don't want the police to think we had anything to do with Alan's death, do we?'

'No . . . It's been such a shock. I need you . . . you won't—'

'Stop it, Jill. You're getting hysterical. I promise you in a couple of weeks all this will seem like a bad dream. There'll just be you and me—'

'And Stephen.'

'And Stephen.'

As Jill put down the phone she felt uneasy. It was as if Alan had been a buffer in their relationship and now he was dead they were grating on each other. It shouldn't have been like that. This wasn't how it was supposed to be.

O'Neill had arrived back in Fowchester on Sunday morning at

2 a.m., after visiting the Black Cat club to find a woman and his memory. If Fran had gone with him he wouldn't have felt the need to find a woman. He'd gone there several times before because the members were over twenty-one and it attracted a fair number of good-looking women. He was only thirty-five, but completely sober he found it almost impossible to chat women up. He could interview women easily because they were in no position to ignore his questions, but in a social context among strangers he was reduced to being blunt and merely offering to buy them a drink. Which they often turned down. For Christ's sake, he'd once kissed the Blarney stone. Irish men were renowned for their chat-up lines, so why was he failing? Fran didn't respond, either. She was warm on the outside but inside, he was convinced, she had a heart like a steel trap.

The club was dimly lit by small red tasselled lamps, the drinks were mortgageable, the males cruising the scene were mostly balding and had the slightly addled look of once-married men. The women came mostly in pairs and O'Neill noticed the white marks on some of their ring fingers. Married but just out for a night's fun and happy enough to stay with the girlfriend they came with. O'Neill didn't approve of married women in night clubs, he knew that was probably old-fashioned but he couldn't help it. 'Going Dutch' was another practice he didn't understand. If you couldn't be affording to take a woman out then you wouldn't be asking her.

He drank tomato juice and loathed every mouthful. He stood watching from the corner of the smaller of the two bars. After a while he got into conversation with the middle-aged barman – an Irish man from Dublin called Dennis O'Donnell.

'I'm wondering, Dennis, where I'm going wrong with the women?'

Dennis shrugged, 'It's a mystery, all right. When I was a boy the girls then were all over us like a rash now . . . well now they'd rather dance with each other. It's us men that are to blame – we've encouraged them to have careers and then, when they do, they can't be having more than one-night stands.'

He spoke in the breathless manner of a set of bellows in overdrive. Once O'Neill had got him started, a whole pack of troubles came out. His wife had left him for a man with more of a future and fewer debts and now he was alone in England. His mother had died in Ireland and now the family were squabbling over the inheritance, a derelict farm in the South.

'Are you a bitter man?' asked O'Neill.

'Bitter! I'm as bitter as lemons in vinegar,' answered Dennis with a hint of a smile, not at O'Neill but at a pretty girl who came at that moment to the bar to buy a drink.

'I was here last Saturday,' said O'Neill. 'I heard there was a fight. Did you hear about it?'

'I heard about a fight,' said Dennis as he watched the girl's rear move away. 'Are you the husband?'

O'Neill shook his head.

'Well, it seems a husband, fed up with sitting at home alone, came to the club and caught his wife leaving with another fella. As you can imagine the sparks began to fly. He's just grabbed her by the hair and the other fella's run off in the meantime. He's giving her a slap or three when this knight in shining armour comes along and tries to come between a man and his wife. Well, Jasus – some men haven't the sense they were born with. So one almighty row starts and the knight gets one in the kisser. He's on the floor, drunk as well, of course, and he staggers up and she does it again . . .'

'Does what?'

'Well she'd knocked down the knight, but he manages to stagger to his feet again and then she ups and bangs their heads together. There was blood flowing in rivers, I'm telling yer. I've never heard nothing like it.'

'So no one was hurt?'

'I'm not saying no one was hurt. I did hear the knight in shining armour was seen crawling away from the scene. The husband was covered in blood but that came from a nose bleed. And of course the woman was as right as rain. She went off arm in arm with her husband like nothing had happened.'

After a decent interval O'Neill slunk away from the bar and drove home. He didn't think Dennis had guessed, but he felt as stupid as an Irish mule. On the drive home he resolved to keep off the drink and away from the Black Cat. He hadn't found his memory, someone else had relayed it to him. And for a DCI to be drunk and brawling – he knew he should be ashamed of himself. And he was. But most of all he was relieved. He hadn't killed anyone.

Chapter Nine

On Saturday evening Fran walked towards the river. She was only slightly surprised the police had already left the area. It was a small force and everything was done as cheaply as possible. She thought that if the general public knew just how many cutbacks were being made they'd be very uneasy. Murder cases were nearly always wound down after six weeks, but as yet this one hadn't even started the winding-up process. It was O'Neill taking the night off that had really surprised her.

The evening was warm and mellow, the sort of evening that encouraged lovers out of doors. The sort of evening that encouraged everyone out of doors. The park and the river side had never been busier. Among the hand-in-hand couples and the families were a few souls who'd come to stare at the murder spot. Someone had placed a bunch of flowers near the spot where Alan's body was found. Someone else had trodden on them. They lay, summer roses and forget-me-nots, by the nettles, squashed, like his life.

Fran continued walking towards the pub. She was thirsty. She'd never been in the Wanderer before and now was as good a time as any. There were still a few families sitting in the garden, the children running about excitedly. The water's edge loomed uncomfortably close to the screaming kids and Fran felt that sitting there with a soft drink wasn't going to be a treat. Anyway, she wanted to see inside.

It was so packed she had to wade through the crowd of young men holding pint pots and saying 'Hello darlin'' as she passed. She fought her way to the bar and stood next to three men waiting impatiently to be served. 'Come on, Julie – we're dying of thirst,' said one of them.

'Die then,' came the caustic but cheerful reply from Julie.

'You don't mean that, Julie, you know you fancy me rotten.'

'You are rotten. What do you want, another lager?'

'Make it two lagers and a strong cider.'

'Pints?' queried Julie.

All three men seemed to laugh in unison. 'Now would we drink halves, Julie?'

She poured the drinks, took the money, continued to smile and, finally, with a 'What's yours love?', took Fran's order of a bitter shandy.

'Is it always this busy on a Saturday night?' asked Fran.

Julie smiled. 'Well, it's extra busy with the hot weather, and I think the murder has brought a few customers in. The landlord's pleased.'

Fran guessed Julie was in her twenties, she was about five feet six, healthy-looking, not exactly pretty but she had attractive dark brown eyes and long lashes, a small mouth but a friendly smile. Her skin was pink with the stifling warmth in the pub and she wore a blue denim blouse that had grown damp under her strong-looking arms.

There were no seats available so Fran stood by a corner of the bar next to the men, who probably propped the bar up every night. She sipped her shandy and watched the landlord stagger in carrying a crate of soft drinks. She heard him say, 'Put these away, Julie, I'll carry on serving.'

The man beside Fran turned to her and smiled, 'You waiting for someone?'

Fran shook her head. He was about thirty, tall, with slightly receding fair hair and the healthy-looking skin of a man who worked outdoors. He looked harmless enough.

'I've been stood up,' he explained. 'She said eight o'clock. It's eight-thirty now. I don't think she's coming, do you?'

'Is she usually late?'

He shrugged. 'Not this late.'

Personally, Fran thought half an hour late wasn't too bad. She'd been kept waiting longer than that.

'You from round here? I haven't seen you in here before.'

'My first time. I walked along the towpath.'

He smiled, 'Everyone avoided it before, now they're coming in droves.'

'Why did they avoid it before?'

'There's no lighting. And there was a rape about five years ago and since then people avoid it after dark.'

'They never caught the rapist?'

He shook his head and stared into his beer. 'A few courting couples use it in the summer, and the anglers of course. They fish all year round but I'm not convinced they catch anything.'

'Did you know the dead man?'

He gave her a look which verged on suspicion. 'I wouldn't say I knew him. I'd seen him in here. He used to fish on the towpath.'

'I've never understood the joy of fishing,' said Fran.

'Nor me,' he said. 'But I suspect it's just an excuse for doing sod all.'

Fran laughed. 'Would you like a drink?' he said. 'I'm Colin Fellows, by the way.'

'I'm Fran Wilson. I'd love a shandy – a bitter shandy.'

They chatted for a while longer, Fran dreading him asking what she did. It was as much a conversation stopper as saying you were a tax inspector or had just left a Carmelite convent. Most people rallied though and then said something fatuous, like, you don't look like a policewoman. Which meant you didn't look butch and unfeminine. At least, that was the reaction from men. One day, thought Fran, I'll meet a strong man who won't feel fazed or threatened by my being in the police. By Monday, when they began interviewing in depth, all the regulars would know who she was anyway. Just as she thought she might tell Colin Fellows what she did for a living, a woman approached, took him by the arm and kissed his cheek.

'Sorry, Colin. The baby-sitter didn't arrive. I really am sorry.'

Colin didn't seem too forgiving. 'I'm used to it, Denise. What do you want to drink?'

Denise had long tumbling fair hair, wore denim shorts and a faded black T-shirt, gave Fran a 'piss off and die' look and said, 'Bacardi and coke, please, Col.'

Fran quickly swallowed her drink and fought her way out to the side door. The light was beginning to fade and just for a moment she wondered if she should risk the dark riverside walk. But only for a moment. Fear was something she'd had to conquer time and time again on the beat as a police constable in Birmingham. She wasn't going to allow herself to be scared in a one-horse town like Fowchester. After all, how many murderers or rapists could there be in a small population? One is too many, murmured a sensible voice inside her head.

She'd just got to the beginning of the park when she saw a group of teenage boys hanging round the swings. She knew then she'd made a mistake. There were five of them. They'd stopped their conversation as they heard her approach.

'Get a load of those knockers,' shouted one of them. 'Like a couple of melons, ain't they?'

They began to move towards her in a body. She felt fear twist deep inside her. Knew she had to make a decision. Everything seemed to be happening in slow motion. Fran, having had some experience of the psychology of crowds, knew that two, even three, might be deterred – five was a crowd and it was unlikely they wanted to ask her the time of day. They wanted to have fun with her, they wanted to make her afraid, they wanted her to show fear and then they could . . .

'Come on, love, show us your melons. We only want a feel.'

Fran began backing down the towpath. Could she outrun them? She certainly couldn't overpower five of them. Could she talk her way out? She turned to run back in the direction of the pub. They were close on her heels, jeering and shouting. Oh God, they are going to catch me! Then in front of her she saw the cavalry in the shape of a man with a dog, a large red setter.

'Quick!' she shouted, waving her arms wildly. 'Set the dog loose.'

She ran towards the man, arriving breathless in front of him. She looked back. There was no sign of the boys.

'Cowards – bloody cowards,' she said to the puzzled man. Now she was up close she could see the man was elderly and the dog was even older.

'You all right dear? Was it those yobs hanging round the swings? I saw them on my way down.'

She nodded.

'They're a flipping nuisance. There's always a few of them hanging around in the summer. You shouldn't be down here on your own, you know. Times have changed. Where do you live?'

'In the High Street.'

'You walk with me, then. I'll make sure you get home in one piece.'

The man, whose name was Harry, and the dog, who was called Rocket, accompanied her home.

'He's twelve years old. Always been docile. Wouldn't know how to bite anyone, but a growl is usually enough if they give me any bother.'

Fran thanked him and he watched her go through her front door.

'You take care,' he called out. 'Young girls like you shouldn't be out this time of night.'

Once in the house, she looked at her watch – it was nine-thirty. Nine-thirty on a summer's evening and she had been scared to death by a group of young boys. Eleven-year-olds were doing burglaries, grown men were being murdered – this wasn't what she'd expected in Fowchester. And she was angry. Angry that as a detective sergeant she couldn't feel safe to go out alone in the early evening. Angry that any woman should have to feel unsafe on the streets at any time. She'd get them somehow, she would. She'd didn't know on what charge – intimidation maybe, threatening behaviour, she'd think of something.

Having made herself a pot of coffee, she sat in the kitchen to drink it. Afterwards she felt a lot better. It was a pity, she thought, that O'Neill couldn't get the same feeling from caffeine. Did he drink to blot out his fear, she wondered? And where was he now?

That night she dreamed of being pursued and she saw Alan Lattaway being chased too, only this time she was the one who was knifed.

Fran met O'Neill the next morning on the way into Fowchester police station.

'Wait here, Fran,' he said at the entrance. 'I'll just see if there are any messages.'

He came back moments later, saying, 'Only one, no PM till this evening. It seems being murdered too close to the weekend creates problems. I think there's a danger the pathologist might be missing some golf.'

'What about the Personal Descriptive Forms?'

'Ringstead's organized that. Neighbours, friends, drinking companions, known clients – the lot. They'll take at least a week or so to do and then another week for us to sift through, unless of course we've found the killer by then.'

'You sound quite optimistic, boss.'

'Sure I am, Fran. I've not had a drink in twenty hours and I'm feeling you and I are going to rise like stars in the firmament of the Fowchester CID.'

Fran said nothing. She'd slept badly and she found O'Neill's cheerfulness misplaced. Last night's episode had soured her view of Fowchester, and somehow she felt reluctant to tell him what had happened. The policewoman in her felt guilty about that but she couldn't help feeling he might say it was her own fault. And she knew that was how all victims, especially women, felt.

'What about breakfast?' said O'Neill once they were in the car.

'I've had mine.'

'Fran, you can be a killjoy at times. I'm thinking it's too early to visit the Lattaways again, so we could have breakfast together. You could be managing coffee and toast?'

O'Neill drove two miles out of Fowchester to a Little Chef and ordered an Ulster fry.

'You're quiet today, Fran,' he said as they waited for their order in the deserted restaurant. 'No intuition yet on our murderer?'

'Only a hunch.'

He smiled. 'Quite right, Fran, a hunch. And what is it?'

'I can't believe Ian Bishop would be stupid enough to kill Alan.'

'Perhaps he didn't do it himself.'

'You mean, hire a hitman?'

'It does happen. But I'm not convinced the motive was strong enough, unless of course we find out he's insured to the hilt.'

Fran thought about that. 'He was selling insurance. He may have wanted to make provision for his son.'

The waitress arrived then with a massive plate of eggs, bacon, sausage, mushrooms, tomatoes and fried bread. O'Neill smiled broadly at the waitress and began to eat hungrily. Fran waited patiently and eventually said, 'What about the insurance angle, boss?'

'Murder for gain is common,' said O'Neill between mouthfuls, 'committed by people who don't read the papers, because if they did, they'd realize they were backing a loser.'

'Don't even mention the word loser, boss, we haven't started yet.'

O'Neill raised an eyebrow, 'I love your enthusiasm, Fran, and I'm not slacking, I've been trying to arrange for divers to search the river for the knife. The fishing rod was found a bit further down the river. But Ringstead's quibbling about the cost. He thinks dragging the river is going too far, he says we'll have to manage – and I quote – "within our budget".'

Fran sighed. Then she laughed.

'What are you laughing at, Fran? It's not funny.'

'I was just thinking, boss, perhaps Ringstead thinks we should put on our wellies and snorkels and do it ourselves.'

O'Neill smiled thoughtfully. 'A bit too deep,' he said slowly, as if a DIY diving job really was a possibility. 'The current is quite strong . . . and by the way, Fran, I called round for you last night. You were out.'

'Yes.'

'Yes, what?'

'Yes, boss.'

'Don't you be getting clever with me, Fran.'

'I am entitled to privacy.'

'Did I say otherwise?'

'No, but do I have to keep you posted on my social arrangements?'

'On a murder investigation, yes. I want to be knowing where you are and preferably who you're with.'

'Why?'

'Don't give me a hard time, Fran. You're my bagman and I want to know you're available. You know as well as I do there's no free time until we've cracked this one and, by God, as you pointed out, we haven't started yet.'

Fran sipped her coffee and tried not to show her irritation. 'Why exactly did you call round?'

'I wanted you to be coming to Birmingham with me. You remember – my missing memory.'

Fran smiled.' I remember. Did you find it?'

'Somebody else did.'

Fran waited for him to explain.

'I did nothing to be ashamed of Fran – except get drunk. All that blood on me was from a nose bleed that I didn't cause. No one got hurt.'

'Except for a busted nose.'

'I'm telling you, Fran, I was a bit misguided, that's all. I should have known better but we all make mistakes.'

Fran knew that was her opportunity to say something about the night before but she restrained herself. She knew he wouldn't let it pass and she felt . . . embarrassed.

Fran would have liked a few more details about that night but guessed he might elaborate in time. Somehow, drinker or not, she did still trust him.

'I thought we might make an early morning call to the Lattaways and then go on to the Wanderer pub—' said O'Neill. He was interrupted by the waitress collecting his empty plate. He flashed her a smile. 'I haven't eaten that well since I can't remember when and that was fantastic. Thanks a million.' She smiled back, gratified that one of her customers was so well pleased.

It was ten-thirty by the time they left the Little Chef to visit Jill Lattaway.

'Oh, it's you,' she said as she opened the door. Somehow Fran thought she seemed vaguely relieved to have company, even police company. Her hair was lank, there were dark lines under her eyes and she looked like any other grief-stricken widow, and yet technically she shouldn't have been heartbroken – after all, they were living separate lives.

O'Neill sat next to her on the sofa. Fran sat opposite on an armchair watching them both closely.

'You've had a bad night, I can tell,' said O'Neill gently.

Jill's lower lip trembled and she bit it in an attempt to control the flow of tears. 'It's Stephen,' she said. 'He's taking it very badly . . . he says it's all my fault. That I'm a whore, a slut, a slag, every insult you can think of . . . he's so . . . angry.' She began to sob and O'Neill put his arm round her and she continued to sob for a while into his shoulder. O'Neill handed her a packet of tissues and she wiped her eyes and tried to choke back her sobs. 'I'm sorry,' she murmured. 'I just can't cope at the moment. At least, I can't cope with Stephen. I just don't know what to say to him.'

'Would you like me to talk to him?'

'Would you, Inspector? It might help.'

'Sure, I'll do that. Just a few more questions then I'll have a word with Stephen.'

Jill sniffed, nodded and then sat alert and ready for his questions.

O'Neill smiled at her encouragingly. 'Now then, Jill, you'll be wanting to tell me all about Alan and Ian.'

'Oh yes, I would like to,' she said.

Fran watched with vague incredulity. He had Jill eating out of his hand. She was putty . . . already in shape. And did she talk. She hadn't got much past the honeymoon stage when the door opened and Stephen burst into the room.

'Don't believe a word she says . . . she's lying. They planned this

66

– they did! I overheard them; you didn't know that, did you?' He paused and walked towards his mother, who began to tremble. 'They murdered my dad, the pair of them. And I can prove it.'

Then he grinned with horrible satisfaction.

Chapter Ten

After Sunday lunch Carole Ann went up to her room and counted the money in her purse. She had five pounds. Five pounds was her worldly wealth. She had to do something. Staying with Miss Enid sanctimonious Braithwaite was worse than prison. In prison there had always been someone to talk to, someone to listen. Here there was Cliff Richard and an oddball ex-con. She'd go mad. The news of the murder had shaken her. Made her feel very exposed.

Why Nina hadn't contacted her she didn't know. She had promised to help her. People should keep their promises.

She walked downstairs and into the kitchen.

'Would you like a hand with the washing up, Miss Braithwaite?' she asked.

'That's kind of you, dear,' she said, handing her a tea towel. 'Aren't you going out this afternoon? You should go for a walk, it's a lovely day.'

'I did think of going out to Magham Green – I know someone out there.'

'That's a good idea, then.'

'How much do you think it will cost by minicab?'

Miss Braithwaite shrugged, which caused her bosom to gyrate upwards, and Carole Ann wanted to avert her eyes but couldn't.

'About five pounds single, I think, dear, but I'm not sure – you know I don't go out very often. You can use the phone and ask.'

Carole Ann went back upstairs and stared out of the window for a while. When you've only got a fiver it becomes pretty important to hang on to it. She needed more tobacco and she wanted enough for a drink. She couldn't go into the pub without enough to buy just one drink. She'd hitchhike. That was the answer.

She changed from jeans into a dress, a blue-sprigged Laura Ashley that she'd found in a charity shop, put on some make-up, brushed her hair and crept quietly down the stairs. Somehow she liked to come and go without anyone knowing. It was one advantage prison didn't have. She passed by Dave Reynolds' room. He was in; she could hear the dull drone of a local radio announcer.

Cliff Richard was already at it behind Enid's back-room door, belting out 'The Young Ones'. Carole Ann could imagine her sitting in a straight-backed armchair, arms folded under her breasts, lifting the weight from her stomach, eyelids beginning to droop.

She closed the front door quietly and began walking.

Dave Reynolds watched her go. She had a great bum and good legs. He knew she wasn't interested in him because he hadn't got any money. But one day, he thought, she'd be keen, especially when he'd done his next job. Crime was just like any other profession. It took time to perfect, it was all in the planning and the experience. And the tricks of the trade. He really needed a shooter but maybe he could do without one, he'd managed in the past. When he got to know her perhaps she'd be interested. She'd done time for murder, she'd probably learned a thing or two in prison. At the moment he could afford to bide his time.

The only drawback to his plans, he realized, was the fact that after the job the police would be round here like starving fleas on a dog. His alibi had to be cast iron. In the meantime, before the 'biggie' he'd have to do a bit of petty thieving – cars, perhaps, or a bit of shoplifting. The shops in Fowchester were a doddle, they couldn't afford security cameras – or maybe he could go further afield.

He'd get her a present, he decided, that's what he'd do. Maybe some earrings or a nice wristwatch. It was so long since he'd had a woman. He knew he'd be good to her. Get her anything she wanted. Maybe they'd even get married.

He lay back on his bed and smiled to himself. Then he felt with one hand under his mattress and brought out a magazine, opened it and stared at the glossy, perfect, naked tits of the smiling woman. He continued to smile. He'd just have to start without Carole Ann.

Charles Gardener slumped in his armchair. He was too dejected to do much. He did have some legal work to catch up on but he'd drunk too much wine at lunchtime. Nina had cooked a decent joint

69

of beef with all the trimmings and now she'd gone out to see some woman who'd come out of prison recently. A convicted murderer. He didn't approve of Nina's prison activities; they took up so much of her time, but he preferred that to her having a career. Some of his colleagues had wives with careers. They had scratch meals, hardly entertained and were permanently tired. Nina always had bags of energy. Just lately she had seemed rather busy and pre-occupied but, as she said, 'If I was at home all day, darling, I'd be so bored. I don't play bridge and I'm not sporty. I do have to *do* something.' She was a little younger than him, of course, she was forty-two, he was fifty-six or as near as damn it. And he was jaded. A lifetime in the legal profession had seen to that.

He'd begun to doze when the doorbell rang.

'Hello, is Nina in?' asked the soft-voiced woman at the door. Soft-voiced, a trace of a London accent and very attractive.

'And you are?'

'Carole Ann Forbes.'

He hadn't met a murderess before, not at such close quarters. He'd been in court and seen murderesses in the dock but they hadn't looked like her. She had a full sensual mouth, lovely deep blue eyes with long lashes, her skin, though pale, was perfect. The dress almost sheer, seemed to float around her. High firm breasts jutted out proudly above a neat waist and her full womanly hips rounded nicely into long, long legs.

'You'd better come in,' he said. 'I'm sure Nina will be back soon; she did go off to visit you about an hour ago.'

'That's a coincidence,' said Carole Ann.

In the sitting room he asked, 'Tea? Coffee?'

She shook her head. She sat on the sofa watching him, waiting for him to speak.

'I hear you've just moved to Fowchester,' he said.

She smiled and nodded.

'Why Fowchester?'

'Nina knew of lodgings that would take ex-prisoners and she said she'd help me find a job.'

He smiled. 'I see,' he said jovially. 'My wife's to blame, is she? I'm sure she'll do her best – about the job.'

There was an awkward pause. Charles longed to ask her about the murder, but he felt to do so might breach his wife's trust. It wasn't often she talked about her 'prisoners' but something about

70

Carole Ann Forbes had induced Nina to discuss her, albeit in scant detail. Now he'd met her he could see the interest, at least from a male viewpoint.

After dredging his mind for a suitable question he managed to ask, 'Did you drive here?'

'Not exactly,' she said, with a charming smile. 'I hitched a lift.'

'Somewhat foolhardy, I should have thought.'

Carole Ann shrugged. 'Everything's a risk these days. One good thing about the last ten years is there's more women on the road. I started walking and, hey presto, someone stopped.'

'A woman.'

'No, it was a big, hairy man. Gentle as a lamb. He dropped me off on the main Magham Green road. I wasn't really sure where the house was.' She paused and looked round the room. 'It's a terrific house.'

Charles smiled. He was no DIY man but he wasn't going to tell Carole Ann that. 'It was a shambles when we moved in fifteen years ago but we're both pretty well satisfied with it now. It took a great deal of planning and a considerable amount of patience. The garden was a virtual forest of weeds but that too has been tamed.'

'I've never had a garden.'

'Never?' queried Charles in disbelief.

'No, never. Unless you count prison. I was in charge of the vegetables and the flower beds. I read the right books. One of the screws – the prison officers – said I was a natural.'

'Would you like to look round my garden?'

'I'd love to,' she said, seeming genuinely pleased. 'Thank you.'

Charles noticed how her eyes sparkled. Her delight at his suggestion was charming – almost childlike. He offered her his arm and led her out through the french windows to his horticultural domain.

He took his time in showing Carole Ann his roses, his garden pond, his lilies and dahlias, his rock garden. They were *his*. Nina wasn't a garden person. She liked to sit in the garden occasionally but she didn't like to get her hands dirty. She was a very fastidious woman in some ways.

Carole seemed entranced by the garden. She asked questions about soil and compost and the best positions for certain plants. Charles hadn't enjoyed himself so much in ages, so much so that it was Carole Ann who looked at her watch and said, 'It's nearly four. I've been here for ages. It doesn't look as if Nina is coming back, does it?'

'Strange, that,' said Charles thoughtfully. 'I hope she hasn't had an accident. She didn't say she was going on to ... one of her friends.'

'Perhaps it was a spur of the moment decision,' suggested Carole Ann.

'Hmm,' said Charles thoughtfully. 'You could stay. I'll make some tea. If you leave now I'm sure she'll be here any minute. It's a shame to miss each other. Please don't worry about getting back to Fowchester – I'll give you a lift.'

'I'm not sure. My landlady serves supper at six.'

'I'll ring her. Plenty of time yet.'

Carole Ann laughed. 'I won't be missing much. So don't worry. On Sunday night it's either egg and sardine salad or egg and cheese, followed by fruit jelly and evaporated milk.'

Charles laughed. 'We do slightly better than that. After Nina's gargantuan Sunday lunch we can only manage something light in the evening, smoked salmon or some homemade soup and crusty bread.'

Carole Ann agreed to stay. Charles made tea and managed to find some almond fingers at the bottom of the biscuit barrel. He was aware, as he prepared the tray, of how much he was enjoying himself. But where the hell was Nina?

It was over an hour later when Nina's car drew up outside the house. Charles stood waiting for her in the hall.

'Hello, darling,' she said breezily. 'Sorry I've been so long but there was so much to talk about.'

'With Miss Forbes?'

'Yes, Charles. I told you I was seeing her.'

At that moment Carole Ann appeared in the doorway and said, 'Hello, Nina.'

Nina blushed slightly. 'There you are,' she said, feigning surprise badly, 'I did call—' She broke off to look at Charles. 'I'm sorry, darling – I went to see that friend of mine, Adele. I know you don't really approve of her so I told you a little fib.'

Charles could feel his mouth tightening. 'I wouldn't say I exactly disapproved of her – it's more her lifestyle I object to.'

Nina's eyes flickered back to Carole Ann. 'Has Charles been looking after you? He can be quite entertaining at times, can't you, darling?'

72

'We've got on famously – haven't we, Miss Forbes?'

'I knew you two would get on,' said Nina. 'You will stay, won't you, Carole Ann?'

'I'd love to.'

'Good. You come into the kitchen and we can chat while I fix some supper for us.'

Charles felt dismissed. He wandered out into the garden and into the conservatory, and from that vantage point he watched the two women chatting together side by side in the kitchen. His shoulders set rigid, he clenched and unclenched his fists. He was very angry. He had to control himself. Nina had had the grace to blush but he'd known she was lying. He always knew when she was lying. The anger never really left him. One day he knew he would explode. It was just a question of when. And, of course, of getting the evidence. He had to have evidence. It seemed somewhat demeaning to have to start following her. But then he'd done it before and he could do it again. His public school motto had been: Semper Fidelis. And that was a precept he had continued to live by.

After some time he allowed his shoulders to relax and began to water his plants. The venus flytrap looked particularly healthy. Its vice-like leaves were closed at that moment. He moved a finger closer to it. As the leaves opened, he muttered, 'You naughty girl.'

Seeing the spade propped up near the door, he caressed the spade handle for a few moments, then, taking the spade firmly in his hand, raised it high above his head and, hesitating only briefly, he smashed it down on the living plant. Just for a second he thought he heard it scream. That gave him satisfaction. He continued to wield the spade until the pot and plant were smashed beyond recognition.

He felt much better immediately. He even smiled as he began sweeping up the battered remains of Little Venus, as he'd called her. As he collected the soil and what was left of Little Venus into a large dustpan, he murmured, 'You shouldn't have been so promiscuous. You should have kept your leaves closed. You had it coming, my darling.'

Chapter Eleven

Nina insisted on driving Carole Ann back to Fowchester. Now that they were alone and not in the confines of a prison, Carole Ann felt the balance of power had changed. She'd been grateful to Nina in prison, had regarded her as a paragon, someone steady and reliable, someone she could rely on. She saw now that Nina Gardener had problems of her own. That inside the composed outward appearance was a person greatly at odds with her own image. Nina was taking Charles for the proverbial ride. And someone else was riding Nina.

'You've guessed,' said Nina after a few minutes of silence. 'I knew you would. It's all been getting a bit hairy lately. Charles can be pretty dull-witted but sooner or later even he will guess.'

'Guess that you've a lover?' said Carole Ann.

'I wish it were that simple, Carole. I am fond of Charles but passion isn't his forte. He's a good man, a good provider, and I know he's fond of me. But it's not enough. Perhaps if I'd had a proper career—' She broke off to negotiate a tight bend.

Once on a straight road, she said, 'I can't keep talking about my problems, I really must get you fixed up with a job.'

'Charles mentioned you need someone to take care of the garden.'

Nina smiled. 'You worked in the prison garden, didn't you? Are you any good?'

Carole Ann shrugged. 'I'm strong, I enjoy working in the open air and I can read and follow instructions.'

'I'll talk to him,' said Nina. 'I'm sure he'll agree.'

Nina followed her into the Braithwaite house. There was no sign of Enid, just the familiar sound of old CR belting out another pop song. 'Oh dear,' said Nina as she paused in the hall. 'That's rather unfortunate, isn't it?'

In the bedroom Nina sat on the bed, watching as Carole Ann rolled a cigarette. 'It's pretty ghastly here,' observed Nina, casting her eyes round the rather drab room. 'It won't be for long, dear heart, so don't despair.'

Carole Ann began to feel slightly uneasy. What was Nina doing sitting on her bed? Was there anything more to say? They watched each other warily until Nina said, 'I'm sorry, Carole, I know you're wondering why I'm here.'

Carole Ann puffed on her cigarette, thinking back to those prison visits when she'd done all the talking and Nina had listened. Now the roles were reversed. Carole Ann had nothing to say and Nina wanted to talk. In fact she seemed generally nervous; her hands fluttered on the candlewick bedspread and her eyes appeared anxious.

'This is confidential, Carole. I'd be grateful if it didn't go any further.'

'Of course.'

'It's about the murder of Alan Lattaway.'

Carole Ann murmured, 'Yes?'

'I think I may have been the last person to see him alive.'

Carole Ann felt the words hit her like a remembered blow. She could feel her heart beating faster – those were the words the police had used. 'We have reason to believe you were the last person to see Michael Summerton alive.' She took a deep breath.

'You couldn't have been, surely? Wasn't he found on the river bank?'

Nina stared at her unflinchingly. 'Yes. I sometimes met him there in the summer. He used to go fishing often then.'

'Why are you telling me?'

'Carole, I'm telling you because I want you to provide me with an alibi.'

'Me? Why?'

'Charles was at a Round Table meeting that night till very late. That's one of the reasons I nipped out to meet Alan. We only talked. I wanted to end it. I tried to convince him that it would be best all round. But he got rather upset. We had a slight contre-temps and I left him about half past eleven.'

'You may have to tell the police the truth.'

'I can't do that. I've always been discreet. Poor Charles has a reputation to keep in the town.'

75

Carole Ann felt like saying she should have thought of that before, but she resisted the urge and said instead, 'What do you want me to say?'

'You'll do it?' cried Nina in surprise. 'Thank you, Carole, thank you.'

'If the police find out I'm here,' said Carole Ann softly, 'and I'm sure they will – they'll probably suspect me anyway. It wouldn't be just your alibi then – it would be our alibi.'

Nina beamed. 'I hadn't thought of that. A mutual alibi. I like the sound of that.'

'I don't like the sound of any of it.'

'Don't worry, Carole, I'll just say I came to have a chat with you about eleven. I'd become rather bored and I drove over here just on the chance of seeing you. We drank tea and I stayed until about 1 a.m.'

'You seem to have it all worked out,' said Carole Ann dully.

'We have to get our stories straight. And, as you say, we could both be in the firing line.'

They talked some more, adding a few details, making sure they got the times just about right – to be too exact about times might seem concocted – and once Nina was convinced Carole Ann would say the right things she stood up to leave.

'Be quiet going down the stairs,' warned Carole Ann. 'Mrs B. bolts the door any time between eleven and midnight. If I go out Dave unbolts it for me. She doesn't stir during the night. I think she's a bit deaf anyway.'

'All that loud pop music, no doubt,' said Nina disapprovingly.

For some time Carole Ann lay on her bed unable to sleep. She had known Alan Lattaway, but she was fairly sure no else knew that. It came as a surprise that Nina Gardener was the woman in his life. Strange, how life flung its surprises. Nina, glamorous, sophisticated and surprisingly desperate. A woman she had thought the epitome of respectability. Not that she could blame her, Alan was – had been – a very attractive man.

She smiled to herself in the darkness. After years in prison it wasn't surprising most men looked attractive. Although, of course, no one could compare with Michael. He'd been very special. Even now, so many years on, she couldn't believe she'd killed him. And the question always remained – *why*?

At Fowchester police station O'Neill eagerly awaited the pathologist's report. When it came it was something of a disappointment. Death by stabbing, two upward thrusts into the chest. The wounds themselves were indicative of a medium-bladed knife, possibly a kitchen knife. O'Neill sighed at that. Who in Fowchester hasn't got a medium-bladed kitchen knife? He read on: the blood alcohol level was quite high but the stomach was empty. Time of death was estimated at between 1 a.m. and 3 a.m. but there was some leeway as the night had been so warm. Alan Lattaway had been a fit young man, of medium height. There was no evidence of disease. *That* piece of information wouldn't have been much consolation to anyone, of course, but the pathologist had to keep to the format.

He handed the report to Fran and waited for her to finish reading it.

'It's not very helpful, is it?' she murmured.

'It's about as helpful to us as a flea wearing a truss,' said O'Neill. 'But we'll be not downhearted, Fran. Let's look at the photos and the drawing and the list of his belongings.'

The photographs had been pinned on the notice board. The list of belongings was next to it. The items themselves had been sent to forensics and the results could take weeks. O'Neill stared at the list: one small black leather wallet containing two ten-pound notes, plus a white business card and a packet of three unopened condoms.

'The motive wasn't robbery and obviously he hadn't had a sexual liaison with anyone.'

'But was he on a promise?'

O'Neill smiled. 'If he wasn't, he was hopeful.'

After staring at the photograph for a few idle moments, O'Neill said, 'His blood alcohol levels were high and where he drank the alcohol is the first question we have to answer, and with whom he was sharing his tipple is the second.'

'Should be easy,' said Fran.

'Sure to goodness my bagman – we'll go and see how easy.'

The fishing gear was listed, the fishing rod had been found. There was just one thing missing: the bait – no maggots, nothing. This indicated quite clearly to O'Neill that Lattaway meant to meet a lover and the fishing was purely incidental. The missing bait he intended to follow up. He jotted the word 'bait' on a piece of scrap paper and placed his paperweight on top.

The Wanderer pub was doing a fairly brisk lunch-time trade. So brisk that O'Neill wondered what was going on. He'd intended to interview the bar staff but six men were lined up at the bar waiting to be served drinks and there were obviously others waiting to be served with meals. The regulars, mostly retired, stood around looking nonplussed, the office and shop workers – all two of them – waited with an expression of wary resignation for their meal numbers to be called out.

'Shall we come back later, boss? asked Fran.

'We will not. I don't believe in walking out of a pub without either a drink, a meal or some information. You'd be wasting my time, Fran, if we did anything but stay.' His eyes drifted towards one of the bays. Fran followed his glance – to the two cameras on the floor being guarded by a young woman.

Fran whispered to O'Neill, 'Look at that.'

He frowned in reply and said, 'I'll be finding out what's going on. I'll have a word with the landlord and you find a seat well away from the bar.'

O'Neill saw Roger advancing along the length of the bar, his wife Connie squashed herself to accommodate him, grimacing as he passed. Luckily he didn't boom out O'Neill's rank, he merely said with a big smile, 'Hello there? Is this business or pleasure?'

'Both. Let me guess who that lot are.' O'Neill indicated the tables that had now filled.

Satisfaction lit Roger's small eyes. 'Press from London. *Daily Mirror* and the *Sun*, I think. According to them, all the papers will be down soon.'

'Why's that, Roger? Our little murder can't have created that much of a stir.'

Roger grinned, 'Come off it, Mr O'Neill, with a released murderess on your patch, known to use a knife, it's quite likely the press would take an interest.'

O'Neill could feel himself grow tense. He was angry but he tried not to show it. He fought the desire to order a drink, ordered two coffees, smiled at Roger's surprised expression as if he hadn't a care in the world, walked back to Fran's table and then scowled.

'What's the matter?' asked Fran. 'You look like a man who's just had an almighty—'

'Sure I've had a shock,' he said before she could finish. 'It's a shock when a local landlord knows more about police matters than we do. I think Ringstead has deliberately withheld information from us, the bastard. I'll swing for him. I will!'

'What information?'

O'Neill looked across at the press men queuing up for more drinks. 'It seems,' he said slowly, 'that a woman has been released from prison and is living in Fowchester.'

'Well, that must happen all the time. Unless they're on licence I can't see that we would necessarily know.'

'We should have been told. This woman, according to Roger, is a murderer and used a knife.'

'Oh, I see. What's her name?'

'If I knew that I'd have been telling you, Fran,' he answered irritably.

'Shall I find out from the press crowd, boss?'

O'Neill shrugged. He knew he shouldn't take out his moods on Fran and he felt a bit calmer now as he watched her walk away. He saw her lips move but could not hear what she said. Her dark hair swung easily across her face; she was wearing a skirt today and his eyes dropped to stare at her legs for a moment. A woman like her could be his salvation, he knew that. Fran came back a few minutes later, smiled with satisfaction and sat down.

'Well, and what did you find out?'

'I found out they're from *Today* and the *Sun*.'

O'Neill managed to smile. 'I knew that. Come on, tell me the rest.'

Fran couldn't help feeling more cheerful. When O'Neill smiled it lifted her spirits. She tried not to care about him but she did. He was vulnerable and always a little sad but she was sure he was a man who had the capacity to enjoy himself once he found solace in something other than drink. What he needed, of course, was a woman. Maybe she could find him someone . . .

'Fran, a man could die sitting here waiting.'

'Sorry. The woman's name is Carole Ann Forbes. It seems she likes to be known as Carole Ann and not just Carole. She was convicted ten years ago of the murder of her lover, Michael Summerton. Death by stabbing. At the moment she's lodging in Fowchester with a Miss Enid Braithwaite, I've got the address.' Between gritted teeth, O'Neill said, 'Jasus, I'd like to grill Ringstead on a barbecue. He must be knowing.' He paused. 'By the way, how did you find out?'

Fran laughed, 'I told them my boyfriend was in the police and for the right price I could probably get them an interview with Carole Ann.'

O'Neill shook his head, 'You shouldn't have said that, Fran, they'll not leave you alone now.'

'They will when they find out I'm on the case.'

'You shouldn't mess with that crowd,' he said. 'But well done, Fran. At least we know. We'll get round there now, come back here in the evening. I don't suppose for one minute she murdered Lattaway but we'd better check her out and warn her the press are on her trail.'

'Why don't you think she might be the murderer?'

'Just an Irish hunch, that's all, just an Irish hunch. And the knowledge that in this life nothing is that easy.'

Fran laughed. 'Never mind the hunches, boss. It's lunch I want, I'm starving. I could—'

O'Neill put his hand to her mouth. 'Sh, will you. I'll get you some sandwiches, we can eat them in the car and tonight I'll personally cook you something decent.'

'Vegetarian decent?'

'Of course.'

Fran realized she had fallen nicely into that one but somehow she didn't mind. A meal cooked by someone else was always a treat. 'Can you cook yet?' asked Fran.

'Cook! I'm brilliant, although my recipes are a bit limited. But you'll enjoy it.'

They left by the back door of the pub, carrying sandwiches, and Fran ate as O'Neill drove.

'I'm surprised she didn't change her name,' murmured Fran between mouthfuls.

'I suppose she thought no one would find her in Fowchester,' answered O'Neill.

At the house Miss Enid Braithwaite opened the door. She reminded Fran of a fat pigeon, all pouting chest and tiny legs. After the introductions Enid said, 'If it's about that murder, Miss Forbes hardly ever goes out. She's as good as gold. I don't want you upsetting her.'

'We won't be doing that, Miss Braithwaite. We just want to warn her the press are on their way here,' he reassured her.

Miss Braithwaite was not reassured; her chest heaved dramatically. 'Vultures!' she said, 'they're just vultures. That girl has suffered enough. Something ought to be done. Can't the police move them on?'

O'Neill shook his head, 'Only if they cause an obstruction to the road or commit common affray or incite people to riot. I suggest you just keep your front door closed and refuse to speak to them on the phone.'

'Of course,' said Miss Braithwaite primly. 'Shall I tell her you're here?'

'You be telling us which room and we'll find our way,' said O'Neill, flashing her one of his most winning smiles.

Enid Braithwaite was not easily won over. She sighed deeply and then nodded towards the stairs. 'Oh all right then, upstairs, second on the left.'

The knock on Carole Ann's door produced an immediate 'Come in.'

Carole Ann stared first at O'Neill then at Fran.

'Police,' she said, as if it were printed across their foreheads.

For once O'Neill seemed at a loss. He'd noticed her amazing blue eyes, her rounded high breasts, her perfect skin. She wore a blue cotton dress that flared from a slim waist.

'You'd better come in,' she said.

Once in the room, Fran noticed how neatly bleak it was. This room was more soulless than some prison cells she'd seen. The one armchair, with wooden arms and a thin foam seat, sat in front of the black and white TV. A paperback book lay open on the rumpled pink candlewick bedspread.

'You'll have to sit on the bed,' said Carole Ann.

O'Neill perched on the edge of the bed, Fran sat beside him. They both waited for the inevitable question: 'Why have you come?' or 'What's it about?' Neither came.

After a short silence O'Neill said, 'We're coming here to warn you, Miss Forbes, that the London press are in Fowchester and on their way to this address. They seem to think you newsworthy.'

'They must think I killed that man,' she murmured, looking straight at O'Neill. He stared back, mesmerized by the luminous blue of her eyes. 'Perhaps,' said O'Neill. 'But I'm sure you'll be wanting to tell me all about it.'

'No.'

Fran tried not to smile. O'Neill looked quite taken aback. His line usually worked. He tried again. 'We'll be wanting to fend off the enquiries about you, Miss Forbes, so I'd be appreciating some cooperation.'

'Why, Chief Inspector?' she asked coolly.

O'Neill began to finger his tie. 'Right, I'll be coming clean with you, Miss Forbes. We need information to state categorically that you had nothing to do with the death of Alan Lattaway.'

'I didn't have anything to do with his death,' she said.

'Good,' said O'Neill with a smile. 'We're making progress. Did you know the man?'

'I didn't know him,' she said, looking away from O'Neill.

Fran watched O'Neill's face for his reaction, because if he hadn't realized she was lying through her teeth he must have been dazzled by her blue eyes.

'So you never met Alan Lattaway?'

'No, I never met him.' She crossed her legs, showing some thigh and a shapely ankle. The voice was soft, almost childlike. This time she looked into his face. Fran saw O'Neill smile as if he believed her. But Fran knew a liar when she met one. And she was certain Carole Ann Forbes was manipulating O'Neill with as much skill as a matador with a red cloak. And if she didn't stop him he'd go down like the bull.

Chapter Twelve

O'Neill relaxed back on the bed, observing Carole Ann. 'Let's be starting from the beginning, shall we? When did you arrive in Fowchester?'

'At the beginning of May.'

'From which prison?'

'Middleton Grange.'

'Other prisons?'

'I moved around, Chief Inspector. I've lost track. I was in Holloway at first.'

There was a slight pause while O'Neill indicated to Fran that she should take over.

'Tell me, Carole, about—' she began.

'I like to be called Carole Ann, if you don't mind, sergeant.'

'Call me Fran and I'll call you Carole Ann.' Fran caught the look of surprise but carried on with her question. 'Tell me about the man you did kill.' Again the change in expression, from surprise to slight shock. After a pause, Carole Ann said softly, 'Michael.'

'Yes, Michael Summerton.'

Carole Ann's face softened. 'He was the love of my life,' she said.

'Yes, but it seems you stabbed him to death.'

Her answer was hardly above a whisper and Fran had to strain to hear her. 'I don't know why. I've never known why.'

'But you were convicted and sentenced to life imprisonment. You must know why.'

'I don't.'

Carole Ann's mouth had set in a determined line. Fran tried another tack. 'Try to tell me about him as a man. What did he do for a living?'

'He was an artist and a potter. He was really talented.'

'Did he earn much money?'

'A pittance, but we were happy.'

Fran smiled encouragingly. 'How long were you together?'

'From the day I left school at sixteen. We lived with an aunt of his.'

'So you met as children?'

Carole Ann nodded thoughtfully. 'When I was twelve. He was in my class at the new school.'

'Why a "new" school?'

'I was put into care when I was twelve and I had to change schools.'

'And you liked him right from the start?'

'Oh yes . . . I loved him right from the start.'

Carole Ann was smiling now, happily remembering. Fran realized that this was something she wasn't lying about. She really had loved Michael Summerton. But had it been a normal sort of love?

Fran was just wondering if she should continue with this line of questioning when the loud knocking on the front door began. O'Neill sprang to his feet and looked out of the window. The press had decamped and some were hanging about by the front gate, others were in the front garden. He scowled slightly at the interruption.

'Fran, you go downstairs and see them off. Tell them that in a few days we'll give them a press conference.'

Fran sighed inwardly, knowing that the small mob outside were more likely to take notice of a male officer than a female officer; life shouldn't have been like that, but it was.

Miss Braithwaite, looking faintly Russian, stood by her kitchen door with arms akimbo, as if defending the Winter Palace against marauding Reds. 'Blooming cheek,' she muttered angrily. 'I'm going to write to my MP about this.'

A lot of use that'll be, thought Fran, but she smiled reassuringly and said, 'I'll get rid of them.'

As she opened the front door the suddenly noisy group surged forward. In a loud voice Fran said, 'I'm Detective Sergeant Wilson. My boss, DCI O'Neill, has asked me to ask you, politely, to leave *now*. We will be giving a press conference, to which you will all be invited, in a few days' time.'

There was a momentary silence. Then the jeering and calling out began. 'Is Forbes guilty?' 'Is she under arrest?' 'Come on, love, give us a clue.'

Fran straightened her back. 'No comment,' she said loudly. More quietly and with slow emphasis she repeated, 'No . . . comment.' Still they carried on shouting questions, moving forward as if they would like to trample over her. 'Right,' she said. 'I've got only one thing more to say and when I've said it I hope you'll take notice because you *are* disturbing the peace.' She paused; they waited expectantly, silent now. She took a deep breath. 'Just . . . *piss off*!' With that, she slammed the front door shut, walked towards the stairs, gave Miss Braithwaite a cheery wave, who nodded and said, 'Well done, dear, you told them,' and then made her way back to Carole Ann's room.

O'Neill and Carole Ann stood each side of the window so that they couldn't be seen.

'They're going,' said O'Neill. 'Well done, Fran. What did you say to them?'

'It was my last well-chosen phrase that did it, boss.'

'And that was?' he asked.

'Piss off.'

For a moment he looked vaguely disapproving, then he smiled. 'I'll be remembering that in future.'

He turned then to Carole Ann, who seemed to be shivering slightly. 'I'll just ask you again, Miss Forbes. Did you know Alan Lattaway?'

'I did not,' she replied as she gave him the full benefit of her crystalline eyes.

'We'll be leaving it at that for the moment,' he said. 'But I'd be asking you to stay indoors for a few days, just until the press weary of the story.'

Carole Ann's composure began to fail. Her eyes filled with tears. She said nothing. O'Neill's face, he knew, registered his disquiet. He'd condemned her to yet another period of captivity and he hated to make a woman cry. He patted her on the shoulder. 'We'll soon find Alan's killer and then they'll be losing interest in you.'

She still remained silent but looked at him pleadingly.

It was only as they were at the bedroom door that she spoke. 'Please,' she said, 'get me back in prison.'

'You don't mean that,' said O'Neill.

'I do.'

'I'll tell you what,' he said slowly. 'I'll make every effort to get the press off your back but if you're worried or they come back here – just ring me any time and I'll come here. Perhaps we could even convince them you've left Fowchester.'

'Would you do that, Chief Inspector? Would you really?'

'Sure I would.'

For a moment Fran thought she was about to run forward and kiss him but she didn't. Carole Ann stood stiffly as if trying to control herself. Then she said, 'Thank you – thank you both.'

Fran was glad to be out of the house and back in the car. O'Neill seemed hardly to notice her presence and he didn't speak until they arrived at the police station.

'I'll be seeing Ringstead now,' he said as he slammed the car door shut. 'You can go through the first batch of PDF's.'

'Thank you kindly, boss,' said Fran, mimicking Carole Ann's voice and wide-eyed expression. O'Neill was not amused.

Ringstead was behind his office desk as usual. He looked up at O'Neill with a slightly pained expression. 'You've heard, I take it.'

'With . . . respect, sir' – O'Neill placed great emphasis on the 'sir' – 'I don't like looking a complete and utter berk in front of my staff or, for that matter, the local press. Because the local press probably alerted the London boys. I'd like some sort of explanation.'

'Calm down, O'Neill. You're getting paranoid. We didn't know she was in the area. I found out about three hours ago when the local rag rang me. It'll be all over the papers in the morning. Have you seen her yet?'

O'Neill nodded.

'What did you think of her?'

'I thought . . .' – what did he think? – 'I thought she was a bit pathetic. And I certainly don't think she had anything to do with the murder.'

'Good-looker, is she?'

'What's that got to do with anything?'

Ringstead gave one of his nasty, knowing grins. 'I guessed she was. Just be careful, O'Neill, you do have a penchant for a pretty face.'

O'Neill knew his boss was deliberately trying to rile him. Ringstead was racist, sexist and a man who thought the meaning of political correctness was voting Tory.

'Yes, sir,' O'Neill replied. Then after a meaningful pause he added, 'Most men do.'

Ringstead squirmed in his seat. His wife was not renowned for either looks or charm. 'Get this one cleared up quickly,' he said irritably. 'I know we're short of manpower but you'll have to forgo any off duty until it is. Make sure Wilson does her bit too. She needs taking down a peg or two; don't take any chances with her. Do it all by the book. Cock up on this one, O'Neill, and you'll wish you'd never left Ireland.'

Outside the office door O'Neill swore under his breath, wondering if that crack about off duty was meant to mean no cricket – there was a one-day game on Sunday and he was going to be there if he had to be doing interviews between overs.

Fran was in the office, scanning through a pile of PDFs. She looked up as he entered. She didn't need to ask if Ringstead had been his usual obnoxious self, it was written all over O'Neill's face. 'A lot of people knew Alan Lattaway, boss,' she said. 'He'd built up his insurance business over a few years and it's going to take ages to interview all his clients.'

'Any disgruntled ones?'

'A few. I'll use coloured stickers to mark those on the front of the forms.'

O'Neill managed a smile. 'You're a dab hand with the stickers, Fran. It's a pity you're not so good with computers.'

'One day I'll be forced on a computer course, boss, and then you'll miss my stickers,' she replied. 'And anyway, I've excelled myself. I've rung the chief reporter on the *Fowchester* and he's promised to find anything he can for us on the Carole Ann Forbes murder case. Says he'll get stuff faxed from London for me from the posh papers too.'

'How did you manage that? I've always found him a miserable old git.'

'He's not that old.'

'He's over forty.'

'He's forty exactly.'

'So you know all about him. And what did you promise him in return?'

'It's none of your business, Connor.'

'Everything you do is my business.'

'Not in my own time, it isn't.'

O'Neill let it go at that, although he wasn't at all happy about Fran being indebted to Simon Goodwin, the local Lothario. He guessed she'd promised to go out with him and it made his stomach churn just thinking about it. Goodwin had been married twice and seemed to be able to charm women, especially young women, with nauseating ease. Unfortunately, O'Neill knew, it would be useless to make objections too clear to Fran; she'd do what she wanted anyway.

She continued reading through the forms and making neat piles. O'Neill watched her, she looked pale today and tired.

'Don't you forget, Fran, we're going to the Wanderer pub this evening and then I'll be cooking you a great meal.'

'I hadn't forgotten.'

He noticed the very slight peeved note in her voice. He'd ignore it, he decided. He'd make the evening special, then maybe she wouldn't want to go near that shark Goodwin.

It rained that evening for the first time in days. Great sheets of rain that bounced from the roads and, like magic, made everyone disappear indoors.

From Fran's cottage it wasn't far to the pub, but rather than get soaked O'Neill took a minicab, left the cab door open, told the driver to sound his horn, and as Fran opened her front door he hurried her the few steps into the cab. Even so, rain trickled down their faces, but it was summer rain and refreshing after the 'drought'. Somehow the rain – or was it Fran – made O'Neill feel cheerful.

The Wanderer pub was half empty. Those who had braved the rain gave off a damp smell. In the games room loud laughter and cheers occasionally erupted and the clicking sound of billiard balls being knocked about seemed particularly loud.

O'Neill again ordered coffee for two and felt virtuous on a personal level but vaguely unpatriotic, knowing full well a real man of Eire would never drink coffee in a pub.

As Roger served him the coffee somewhat reluctantly, O'Neill asked him if Alan Lattaway had been in the pub on the night of his murder.

'I've already been asked that,' said Roger. 'I tell you, Mr O'Neill, I knew the bloke; well, he came in here quite often but I can't remember seeing him on Friday night. It's this warm weather we've been having, brings people out like flies. It's a big room and if someone sits round a corner you can't see them from the bar.'

'All right if I take a look from behind the bar?'

'Yeah, no problem. Come on through.'

From behind the bar O'Neill could see it was an entirely different perspective. Only the eating area of the bar could be seen clearly and if the bar front itself had been busy Roger, who was about five feet eight, wouldn't have been able to see over the customers' heads.

'What about the other staff or your wife?' asked O'Neill.

'I'll give her a yell.' He opened a door by the side of the optics and shouted, 'Connie, get yourself down here.'

Moments later Connie appeared. 'You don't give me any peace, do you?' she said as she was met by him at the small doorway. He scowled at her and took her by the arm. O'Neill saw her wince slightly.

'The Chief Inspector wants a word,' said Roger, moving aside so that she could get past his bulk. 'And where's that Julie?'

'She's in the kitchen cooking,' replied Connie, giving her husband a scathing look. 'She can't be everywhere at once.'

Roger went looking for Julie and Connie smiled at O'Neill. 'You look at home behind the bar.'

'I don't feel it,' he said. 'I've been asking your husband if he remembers if Alan Lattaway was in the pub on Friday night.'

Connie gave a husky smoker's laugh. 'Bless you, Chiefie, all he notices is big breasts and how much is going in the till and whether his old cronies are in or not. The other punters are – well, a blind man would notice more.'

'What about you, Connie? You look like a woman who'd be noticing most things.'

She smiled and looked at him sideways. 'To be honest, I'm not sure. I know he was in Thursday, but Friday was so much busier. The trouble is, if there are two men drinking or a group, maybe only one will buy the drinks. If they're sitting at an alcove it's difficult to see them – you can't see from the bar.'

'Sure I noticed that. What about the food section?'

'What about it?'

'You serve meals every evening.'

'We've only just started doing meals on Sunday evening. We've always done Sunday lunches, plain roasts, but now we're doing a few meals on Sunday evening – chips with everything, because that's what the punters want. Mind you, we haven't been doing all that well so far, not in the evenings – wrong time of year, I suppose.

People just want nice cold drinks and a packet of crisps on warm evenings.'

'And what about Julie?'

At that moment Roger appeared, looking slightly breathless and seriously puce in the face. 'Guess where I found her – in her room writing letters and smoking. She'll have to go. I've had enough—'

'Don't go on, Roger, not in the bar. She's a good girl and a good cook. You'll be glad of her in the winter, she'll bring trade in then.' The thought of increased trade had its effect and when two men approached the other end of the bar Roger edged his way, crab-like, towards them.

O'Neill came to the side of the bar he felt most at home on, sipped his Guinness and remembered Fran was somewhere in the pub. 'Connie, I'd be grateful if when Julie comes down you'd send her over to us – we're in the alcove near the door.'

'Will do, Chief Inspector.'

When he found Fran she wasn't alone. A tall guy was sitting next to her and they were deep in conversation.

'This your boss?' said the man getting up.

Fran nodded.

'Lucky devil. See you again, Fran. Take care.'

'Bye Austin.'

O'Neill muttered as he left, 'What sort of name is that?'

'He seemed a nice bloke,' said Fran. 'He lived for a while in Birmingham. He's a flying officer with the air force.'

'I don't care if he's the chief air marshal, Fran. You shouldn't pick up strange men in pubs – you should know better.'

'Come off it, boss, if I waited to be introduced like some sweet old-fashioned girl I'd never make any friends. You know how I'm treated at the station. I'm ignored.'

'I'm telling you, Fran. You should have been interviewing him not chatting him up.'

Fran took a deep breath. 'He wasn't in here Friday night, he didn't know Alan Lattaway. What more can I say, boss, unless you wanted me to bring out the thumbscrews?'

'There's no need to be sarcastic. Drink your coffee.'

'What did you find out, boss? You were gone so long I thought you'd deserted me.'

'Precisely nothing.'

They were sitting in silence when Julie approached. She was,

O'Neill supposed, in her mid-twenties, short, about five feet two, with spiky reddish-brown hair, slim, but with fairly muscular arms and legs. Her eyes were dark brown and she had a solemn expression. He smiled to himself. With Roger being so fat he probably choose his barmaids by size; only small ones would get past him.

'I'm Julie Johnson,' she said, looking only at O'Neill.

'Hello, Julie, DCI O'Neill, DS Fran Wilson.' There were nods all round. 'Sit down, Julie,' said O'Neill. 'We won't keep you long.'

She half smiled in response,' I wouldn't mind if you did. Anything's better than cooking chips. I smell them all day.'

'It's about Alan Lattaway,' he explained. 'We wondered if you'd seen him.'

'I've been thinking about that. I'm not positive and I couldn't swear to it on the Bible or anything, but I think I caught a glimpse of him in the games room on Friday night. No one wanted food so I came out of the kitchen and just then I saw him going into the games room.'

'What time was that?'

'Early, about eight, I think, but I'm not too sure.' She frowned, trying to remember.

'Was he alone?'

'He may have been but someone walked in after him.'

'Could you describe him?'

She shrugged. 'I'm not very good at this. It was only a glimpse.'

'Just try to remember anything at all about him – height, the way he walked—'

She paused, turned her head towards the games room and said excitedly, 'I do remember, I do. He wore green wellies and one of those padded waistcoat things.'

'Thank you very much, Julie, you've been a great help.'

'My pleasure,' she said with a smile.

After she'd gone O'Neill said, 'Are we going back to Hadon Lodge now or in the morning?'

Thinking only of how hungry she felt, Fran said tentatively, 'In the morning?'

'Sure,' said O'Neill cheerfully. 'We'll be there bright and early in the morning.'

Chapter Thirteen

Carole Ann pulled her bedroom curtains shut and sat stiffly in her armchair. She sat very still, unaware of the passage of time. Only the voice of Enid Braithwaite stirred her with her 'Come and get it' shout up the stairs. Slowly Carole Ann walked downstairs.

Her meal was already on the table – minced beef and potatoes with processed peas and cabbage. A typical prison meal. Enid, her chief screw, stood by the kitchen door, folded arms resting under her bosom while Dave Reynolds sat already eating. His head was low over the plate but he lifted his eyes when she walked in and she knew from that furtive sort of glance that he lusted after her.

The clock on the mantelpiece seemed to tick more loudly than usual. Enid appeared with bowls of jelly and ice cream and set them down. 'I'm a bit tired tonight. I've done the pots; will you two do the dishes?'

They nodded in unison. She began undoing her apron then waddled away, and a few moments later they heard the sound of her sitting-room door shut.

'Wait for it,' said Dave. They waited but all was silent.

'Perhaps she's gone off him,' suggested Dave. The silence made them both edgy. The routine had changed. Dave began to drum his fingers on the table.

'You should eat your pudding,' said Carole Ann in an attempt to break the unnerving quiet. They had grown to expect the sound of Cliff Richard singing cheerily and however much it irritated them it had become the norm, part of their new institution.

The meal was still to be finished but Carole Ann pushed both plates away. She'd eaten a few mouthfuls of each but swallowing was difficult; she felt she might choke.

'What's up?' said Dave. 'You missing ol' Cliff?'

Carole Ann shook her head. 'Reporters have been round here today, and the police asking questions.'

'What did you say?'

'I told them I didn't know him.'

'Did you?'

She didn't answer him.

'They'll soon get fed up,' said Dave and then added with a sly smile, 'Could be to your advantage, though.'

'What do you mean?'

'You could sell your story.'

'What story?'

'Don't be thick, woman. How you killed your fella.'

'I don't remember anything about it.'

'Come off it. You can't kill someone and not remember.'

Carole Ann's head drooped. She wanted to cry. If he kept on she would cry. 'I don't remember,' she said.

'You lost your memory?'

'I was drunk,' she said. The misery of finding Michael's body next to hers was as vivid now as it had been then, perhaps more vivid, because then she'd been in shock and couldn't speak with the horror of it all. 'I don't want to talk about it.'

Dave shrugged. 'Have it your way, love. I'm going out for a drink. Do you want to come with me?'

She shook her head and bit her lip to try to stop the tears. 'The press might see me. The police think it best I stay in for a few days – until they're gone.'

'Please yourself, love. You think again about the press. You could make a packet.'

'I've got nothing to say.'

He stood up, stared at her for a moment and then muttered, 'Right, see you later.'

Back in her room, Carole Ann moved her armchair in front of the TV and allowed the programmes to wash over her. The pictures moved, the voices spoke but she neither heard nor saw. She just sat, oblivious.

When she tired of just sitting she undressed and lay on top of the bed. The rain had stopped now but it was still warm and humid. She wondered if Trish and some of the others were asleep in prison yet, or if they were tossing and turning and thinking of how things might have been, just as she had done on many summer nights in prison. She felt yet another wave of home sickness for prison, any prison, all prisons. 'Good night, Michael,' she whispered into the darkness.

She was still awake when the bedroom door opened. She could see the shape of Dave Reynolds by the door. He stood there for some time. Then he said, 'You awake, love?'

'I'm awake, Dave,' she said. He closed the door quietly and turned the key in the lock. She watched his shape moving in the dark, undressing. She pulled back the covers and he slipped in beside her. She closed her eyes and thought of Michael.

O'Neill showed Fran into the lounge. He'd tidied carefully, dusted and polished, aware that the last time she'd seen the house it had been a tip.

'Make yourself at home, Fran,' he said. 'Put your feet up. I'll just be performing a miracle out here.' He handed her a large glass of wine and closed the kitchen door.

Fran glanced round the room. It was neat and tidy now but still a little soulless, or maybe it was womanless. She noticed the book-case in one corner which contained a selection of cricket books, one or two spy novels, a few books on Ireland. The coffee table was bare, the pictures on the walls were of stark Irish landscapes or white cottages set below glowering clouds. They hadn't been his wife's choice, of that Fran was quite sure. In the corner by the window was a small round table and, on it, a tall pottery vase decorated with painted flowers. How long since the vase had held fresh flowers? she wondered.

She stared at her watch. She'd been sitting for ten minutes, she'd drunk half her wine and there seemed to be little activity going on in the kitchen. It was at moments like these, halfway between regret and anticipation, that she most missed a cigarette. It had been a year now since she'd given up and she still occasionally desired a cigarette as a social crutch, a way of getting through difficult moments. Although she knew she was more confident in her work – she'd even got used to the masses of paperwork, she liked working with O'Neill – nothing helped the aching loneliness she felt in Fowchester. People were born here, lived out their lives, some of the older ones had never ventured as far as London or Birmingham. It was the sort of town where people kept their friends from school and lived in the next road to their mother's.

She envied that closeness but it made being a stranger that much harder to bear. And deep down she believed she'd always feel like a foreigner.

O'Neill reappeared just as Fran had stood up and decided to go searching for him. 'I've come to top up your wine,' he said, refilling her glass.

'I can't smell anything cooking,' she said. 'Let me give you a hand.'

'That's not necessary,' he answered. 'It's all under control. You don't get any smell with my cooking, I've got one of those extractor fans. Put the TV on if you want – just relax.'

'Connor—' she began uneasily.

'Yes.'

'Connor, I'm here for the food – and your company of course – but nothing else. It's not that I don't—' she broke off again, realizing she was going to say 'fancy you'.

'Sure, Fran, I understand. You don't have to explain.'

His expression seemed to convey slight disappointment, or was it her imagination? Or did she hope, deep down, that he really was disappointed?

He returned to the kitchen, shut the door, and Fran, by now feeling a little lightheaded with hunger, drank the wine quickly in an attempt to line her stomach with something.

It was ten minutes later that the front door bell rang. She couldn't really hear what was being said but she did hear O'Neill mutter some sort of thanks, which probably meant it wasn't a work call.

Moments later he announced the first course was ready and would she like to come through to the dining room. The table was laid sparsely, just cutlery on a white cloth and a lone chrysanthemum in a tiny glass vase. There were no candles, just a lit lamp with a cream shade on the sideboard. The room was small but far more cosy than the lounge.

The first course was a selection of mushrooms in a garlicky sauce with tiny slices of fried ciabatta bread. The main course was tagliatelle with a pesto and pine nut sauce and a mixed salad. She hadn't been eating long before she realized – O'Neill wasn't responsible for this meal, Luigi Bonaventure was. The Bonaventure restaurant was the town's newest restaurant and Fran had eaten this very meal there one lunch time.

95

'Connor, this is absolutely delicious and I have no complaints but I wish you'd come clean.'

'About what?' he asked, trying to force an expression of innocent indignation on to his face.

'This pesto didn't come out of a bottle. I think Luigi had a hand in it.'

O'Neill raised his hands in mock surrender.

'Sorry, sarge, it's a fair cop; you've got me bang to rights.'

Fran laughed. 'I thought perhaps you'd learned to cook. I would have cooked if I'd known.'

'Now don't be insulting me, Fran. I can cook. I can fry. But I was a bit put out by the thought of vegetarian cooking. I rang Luigi and persuaded him my credibility with a colleague was at stake. He asked if you were beautiful and I said "very". And he agreed to deliver it. Anyway, I've made the pudding.'

Dessert was strawberries and cream. Fran, by now, had drunk one more glass of wine; a combination of the good food and wine had really cheered her. She was still amused by his deception and flattered that he thought she was worth it. Even so, she was relieved when he began to talk shop.

'I had a bit of a showdown again with Ringstead this afternoon,' said O'Neill.

'What about?'

'This and that.'

'Is he happy with the way the murder investigation's going?'

O'Neill's responsive laughter made her laugh too. 'Is it likely, Fran? Is it likely?' And they both laughed together as though they'd heard a great joke.

When they did finally talk about the case O'Neill suggested they only had one real suspect and that was Ian Bishop. Fran disagreed. 'I think our Carole Ann is mentally disturbed.'

'Rubbish,' said O'Neill. 'Anyway, what would be her motive?'

'She doesn't need a motive if she's disturbed.'

'Give me two reasons you think it's her.'

'One, she's done it before; two, she's extremely odd.'

'Compulsive killer or impulsive?'

'Don't get technical, Connor, I'm awash with wine.'

'I don't think she's odd at all,' he said with a smile. 'I think she's been institutionalized and I think she's vulnerable, even a bit pathetic, and, in my experience, she's a one-off killer.' He paused to give Fran more wine. When she said no, he began to urge her: 'Come on now, Fran, the night is young – we're young and we're having a good time, aren't we?'

She nodded. 'Oh all right then, just one more.' As she sipped it she told herself she should have more self-control. But it was good wine and she was happy, so what the hell. She'd almost forgotten now where they were in their conversation, then she remembered. 'Now as for lover boy, why do you think he's our man?'

'Easy – he was seen with Alan, yet said he didn't know him, he had the opportunity, and motive. And I think he knows how to kill. These types with shotguns and green wellies always do.'

'Julie only gave us a very vague description, Connor. Lots of men wear Barbours and green wellies round here. If Ian's alibi for the early evening hadn't checked out we would have heard by now.'

Fran had made a very good point and O'Neill was perfectly well aware that the description could have fitted almost any country male. He suspected neither Ian Bishop nor Carole Ann. Not having a real suspect was beginning to irritate him. O'Neill observed Fran's face in the half-light for a few moments. 'You saw the dead man's expression. He didn't fight back because he was taken completely by surprise. He was killed with two quick jabs in just the right place.'

'You don't think you could be prejudiced in Carole Ann's favour just because ... well, because she's so attractive? We don't know anything about her.'

'Not yet,' said O'Neill. 'But we will. And shame on you, Fran, for saying such a thing. I admit she's a good-looking woman but why on earth would she kill a stranger? She said she didn't know him. Even if she's lying, and I concede she might be, she hasn't been in Fowchester long enough to work herself into a murderous state. For a woman to murder it usually takes considerable provocation.'

'That's if she's sane to start with.'

'We'll be finding all that out, Fran, and when we do and I'm right, you can cook me a meal and I shall expect a great big steak.'

'You'll be lucky,' said Fran. 'You know I don't eat meat and I don't cook it either.'

'You're a hard woman,' he said, smiling, not meaning it.

It was after midnight when he saw she was wearying. 'I'll walk you home, Fran,' he said. He knew she wouldn't stay on but he still felt a sense of disappointment that she so quickly stood up ready to leave.

Chapter Fourteen

Nina Gardener stared into her wardrobe wondering what to wear for the day. She was prison visiting so she wanted to look neither too glamorous nor too severe. In the end she chose a pleated cream skirt and navy blouse. She wore small pearl earrings and her second-best rope of pearls.

Charles had just bathed and was changing in his adjoining dressing room. She could hear him moving about. If he was in a good mood he hummed as he got dressed but lately she hadn't heard him humming; in fact, he seemed quieter than usual, almost subdued.

She was applying her make-up when he walked in.

'Where are you off to today, darling?' he asked from the doorway. She didn't turn round, she continued to apply her mascara. Once she was satisfied, she said, 'Ferndale Open today. A new prisoner requested a visitor.'

'You'll be home when I get back from the office?'

'Of course, darling.'

'Any plans for the weekend?'

She swivelled round to face him.

He was wearing a dark grey pinstripe suit with a silk waistcoat. His hair was freshly washed and he smelled of expensive after-shave. He was unsmiling, stiff. Nina smiled, 'Don't look so glum, darling. I haven't invited anyone, although we are due to visit my mother soon.' He didn't need to groan, his expression said it all. His mother-in-law lived in Cornwall and he hated Cornwall in high summer. He loathed the crowds, the steep hills, the claustrophobic villages filled to overcapacity with milling holiday-makers and screaming children. Luckily the boys were staying at a villa in Spain for several weeks so at least he didn't have the irritation of them lounging about and demanding he dig forever deeper in his pockets.

After a few moments' pause he said, 'So we'll be having the weekend to ourselves, then?'

'Unless something crops up, darling.'

'Such as?'

'We may get an invitation, Charles.'

'Who had you in mind?'

Nina turned back to her dressing-table mirror and began to brush her hair.

'I thought Lawrence might invite us to dinner.'

'Why should you think that?'

'Just reciprocating our invite, darling, that's all.'

In the mirror Nina could see her husband's face and the top half of his body. His lips were set in a grim line, his hands clenched by his side. In that instant she knew that he knew, but what exactly he knew she wasn't sure. She had noticed, over the past few days, Charles being quieter, perhaps even a little morose. Had he actually guessed or was he merely a touch suspicious?

'If he does invite us, darling,' she said soothingly, 'and you don't want to go, we could always say we'd already made arrangements.'

'We'll see what happens,' he murmured as he walked out of the bedroom.

Over breakfast he drank two cups of coffee and ate two slices of toast in silence whilst reading *The Times*. He was particularly quiet and Nina felt a little tremor of anxiety. It was as if he were sulking, but he didn't usually sulk. Had he found her empty gin bottles? Had he found her full ones?

'I'll be home at seven, darling,' he said as he kissed her cheek. She watched him go to the garage and waited till he'd driven away, then she sat down, poured herself another coffee and began reading *The Times*. On the second page was an article devoted to Carole Ann Forbes and a discussion of the rise in violence by women towards men. No wonder Charles had been so engrossed over breakfast. He had met Carole Ann and agreed that she could do some work in the garden. Would it be a mistake, though, to have her here? Especially if the police thought her a prime suspect.

It was just after ten when Nina saw her cleaner walking slowly up the path. The poor woman was well into her sixties but she was thorough, even though she had to sit down frequently.

Mrs Marriot let herself into the kitchen. She was slightly breathless and paused to use her inhaler. Nina noticed her blue rinse was even more blue today, matching her blue Crimplene dress; her thin face seemed a little more pinched but was enlivened by round patches of red blusher. God forbid I should ever sport a blue rinse, thought Nina, or wear a Crimplene dress, but the niggling doubt was there that one day she might.

'Nice morning, Mrs Gardener,' said Mrs Marriot after she'd slipped her inhaler back into her brown shopping bag and donned a plastic apron. 'Do you want the usual today?'

'I would like the bedrooms given a good hoovering and if you could dust the guest bedrooms.'

'You having people for the weekend, then?'

'Not as far as I know but it's always a possibility.'

Mrs Marriot nodded sagely. 'Right then, I'll start in the kitchen.'

Nina watched her working for some time. She had most of the morning to get through before she went on her visit. She made tea for Mrs Marriot, who enjoyed a regular cuppa along with her short rests. She placed the tray of tea and biscuits on the kitchen table and they sat opposite each other. 'How's the family?' asked Nina.

'So so,' she answered glumly. 'My son's not too good. He's still unemployed and now he's having marriage problems as well.'

'Are they still together?'

Mrs Marriot managed a wry smile. 'Well, you could call it that. They don't spend much time in the house. He's always out somewhere. Does a bit of fishing summer and winter, drinks when he's got the money, plays a bit of football.' She paused. 'Terrible about that poor man on the river bank. Whatever is the world coming to? He was the chap who came here, wasn't he?'

'Did he?' murmured Nina. She watched Mrs Marriot's grey, rather sunken eyes for any hint of maliciousness in that question. She seemed to know she was being observed closely and continued to hold Nina's gaze as if willing her to answer.

'Oh, I *do* remember,' said Nina, trying to sound nonchalant. 'Yes, he did call by once, to try to persuade me to buy some insurance. I'm surprised you remembered.'

Mrs Marriot smiled, or was it a smirk? 'I knew him. He sold my daughter a policy. Said he was a financial adviser but they're only insurance salesman, aren't they? Still, he seemed a nice enough man; tried to flog me a policy as well. But I couldn't afford it and anyway I've got a funeral policy out.'

Nina could feel her heart beating faster. Did Mrs Marriot know?

If she'd seen him once, could she have seen him on other occasions? 'More tea?' she asked.

She shook her head. 'No thanks, I'd best get on. Did you buy one from him, by the way?'

'One what?'

'An insurance policy, Mrs Gardener.'

Again those grey eyes bored into hers. 'A small one. My husband has me very adequately insured. I just thought it would be a gesture to insure my own life – for Charles's sake and the boys'.'

'I expect the police will be visiting you at any time, then,' said Mrs Marriot, picking up her duster and polish.

'Why should they?'

Mrs Marriot looked at her sharply. 'Ohh,' she said with an equally sharp intake of breath, 'they'd be bound to. I expect they'll interview everyone who knew him—'

'I didn't exactly know him,' interrupted Nina, hoping she didn't sound too defensive.

'No, but if you had a policy out with him they'll be going through the names and addresses, won't they?'

'Yes, I suppose they will. I wouldn't be able to tell them much, of course.'

'That's as maybe, but you know what the police are like. They have to do a proper job.'

This time Nina knew she wasn't imagining things. There was a note of triumph in her cleaner's voice. She'd always thought her harmless. Now she wasn't so sure. If she did know about her affair with Alan Lattaway, who else knew? Did her son know? Carole Ann Forbes knew and now her cleaner. How long before Charles found out? She didn't want to lose him. He had his faults and his good points, his wallet being one of them. Without him she'd be destitute. And she feared poverty more than anything else. If Charles reacted badly he might ask her to leave. And then she'd probably have to buy a poky little cottage somewhere in a dull ugly village.

She rested her hands on the side of her head and slumped forward slightly. She needed to think clearly. How on earth was she going to deal with Mrs Marriot? She had to keep her quiet, she really had no choice. But how?

Charles had driven fast towards Fowchester. He really wasn't in the mood for women drivers doing the school run. He wanted fast clear roads and a clear mind. He was angry, he'd been angry for days. He'd hid it well, he knew that, but he couldn't keep it up for ever. One of these days when he lost his temper he was going to do more than smash a plant. Nina's little games just couldn't go on. He guessed she had embarked on another little 'fling', She tried to cover her tracks of course and she always lied, eloquently in the circumstances, but he knew when she was lying, the tone of her voice changed, perhaps imperceptibly to others but not to him. He was used to the nuances, he was accustomed to the lies.

At his office in the High Street he parked the BMW in the office car park and sat for several minutes staring into space. How many other people knew about her affairs? Did his colleagues know? Were they laughing at him, saying 'poor old duffer' or perhaps worse, thinking he condoned her infidelities or was too blind to see what was happening? He'd managed, by various means usually involving money, to get rid of one or two of her lovers quite successfully and now he just had to keep tabs on his new partner, Lawrence. He'd noticed what they'd been doing under the tablecloth. Nina had played the same game with him once.

He glanced at his watch; it was 8 a.m. Time to go in. As he walked into his office he resolved to shelve his worries – at least temporarily, he didn't want the practice to suffer or people to observe that he wasn't quite his usual self.

Once in his room, he noticed he hadn't tidied his desk properly the night before. Files were still piled high, his pen and diary were not side by side, staples and elastic bands lay scattered in what should have been a bare expanse of polished mahogany. The two spider plants on his windowsill drooped through lack of water. In his private cloakroom he collected water in a jug and watered them immediately. Then he rearranged his desk, took his most urgent file and started work.

At eight-thirty other staff began to arrive. He found the noise quite reassuring; it meant the day had begun. At nine exactly, his secretary Sally Blake brought in his first coffee of the day.

'Good morning, Mr Gardener,' she said softly. Her soft voice was one of the reasons he'd employed her, and of course her timidity. Timid secretaries worked harder, said little and didn't get involved in office politics. She was pretty too, in a doll-like way, with a roundish face, wide blue eyes and a small neat mouth. She barely reached five feet and he had to admit that she had an equally small brain, but all he required from a secretary were nimble fingers and the ability to spell. Sally, with her soft voice, quiet tread and a propensity to speak only when spoken to, soothed him.

The morning wore on with almost nonstop calls from demented clients who wanted, demanded even, progress reports on their house purchase. Charles found himself growing increasingly irritated. If he had any news he'd be ringing them. By the time he'd notched up the twentieth call of the morning, the last one being an hysterical woman for whom completion day loomed as dramatically as judgement day itself, he knew he'd have to have a drink.

He didn't usually go into the Wanderer pub – he preferred the Crown Hotel – but he felt like a change and he knew via the office gossip that it seemed the last place Lattaway had been seen was the Wanderer. It gave the Wanderer pub a certain interest and made it a place in which he might find some business.

Julie, helped by Connie, was busy cooking the lunches. Julie was growing rapidly disillusioned with the customers of the Wanderer. The 'specials' for the day were skate with black butter and gherkins, a home-made chicken curry, and a mushroom and vegetable bake. There had been one order, for the chicken curry – with chips!

The heat in the kitchen was already making Julie irritable. The smell of frying chips never seemed to leave her. As three more orders came in and Roger started to yell from the bar that he wanted Connie out of the kitchen, Julie started to undo her overall.

'What are you doing, Julie?' asked Connie.

'I'm off, I've had enough. I like cooking but this isn't cooking, it's being a chip fryer and I can't take any more.'

Connie touched Julie's arm. 'Please don't go, think about it. I'll get Roger to give you more money—'

Julie's face remained angry and implacable.

'Please, Julie – just for me. Don't walk out now. I know you need a break; you go in the bar and I'll carry on cooking. Please—'

Julie hesitated and Connie knew she was winning.

'Tonight, Julie, we'll get smashed, just you and me. Or if you like, we could go to a club in Birmingham I know that doesn't close till three.'

Julie smiled grimly, shrugged her shoulders and said, 'Forget clubbing. I'll go on the bar.'

At that moment Roger yelled another order through the hatch: skate in black butter, new potatoes, broccoli, mushrooms and peas.

'I'll do that one,' said Julie. As she prepared the meal she smiled and thought, someone in fucking Fowchester recognizes a good meal when they see one. Twenty minutes later Connie had given in to Roger's demands and returned to the bar, leaving Julie carefully arranging the meal on a plate.

At the doorway she called out loudly: 'Fifty-six!' Number fifty-six was a middle-aged man in a pinstriped suit sitting alone in one of the booths.

'That looks wonderful,' he said. 'Thank you.'

Julie went back to cooking chips but she'd calmed down now. The new potatoes, sitting on the plate, white and virginal, had cheered her up a little.

She consoled herself with the thought that she had a decent room overlooking the river, that she managed to send some money home and that her dad had seemed a little better when she last visited.

Julie had promised herself she'd stay for a few months and she always kept her promises.

Chapter Fifteen

O'Neill's next visit to Ian Bishop didn't prove very successful; he was out.

From there he'd driven with Fran to the Lattaway house. Stephen's last outburst had ended in tears and O'Neill had to admit he hadn't given much credence to Stephen's condemnation of the lovers. He'd seen this sort of reaction before. The bereaved often needed a scapegoat for their anger. Sometimes it was a hospital, sometimes a GP or maybe an ambulance that didn't arrive in time. More often, though, there was some deep-seated guilt – the 'if only' syndrome. 'If only we hadn't gone out', 'If only we had caught the train', 'If only we hadn't had the row'. All the 'if onlys' in the world couldn't turn back the clock, and when that realization came the pain started its second wave.

Stephen was alone in the house. He stood sullen and pale at the front door.

'Mum's at work,' he said.

'It was you I wanted to speak to, Stephen,' said O'Neill. 'May we come in?'

Stephen nodded and led them through to the lounge, where a horror video blared out. He made no attempt to turn it off but stood, hands stuffed into jeans pockets, looking miserably defensive.

O'Neill was about to ask why he wasn't at school, then he remembered that the school holidays had already started.

'How are things?' asked O'Neill, knowing there was no real answer.

Stephen shrugged.' OK.'

'How's your mum?'

'All right.'

'Turn off the video, Stephen. I want you to sit down and tell us about the night your daddy died.'

Stephen didn't move, just stared at O'Neill with his father's brown eyes for a few seconds; then, sighing, he moved across the room slowly and switched off the TV set.

'Be sitting down, Stephen.'

O'Neill sat next to the boy and Fran sat opposite in an armchair. She smiled encouragingly at Stephen but he didn't smile back.

'Now just be telling us, Stephen, about that evening. Your mum went out about eight, she says. Was your daddy in the house then?'

Stephen opened his mouth but no sound came. He blushed with embarrassment.

'Just be taking your time,' murmured O'Neill.

Eventually Stephen said in a rush, 'Mum went out; Dad was working – he does a lot of work in the evenings; people are home from work then. He came in about nine, said he was staying in for the evening. We watched TV for a while and then the phone rang about ten-thirty and he said he'd decided to go fishing. I asked him if I could come and he said no . . . we had a row. He went to the garage, got his fishing gear and left. He didn't say goodbye—' He broke off, his voice choked, his eyes glistening with tears. 'I—'

'Go on,' urged O'Neill.

Stephen turned slightly to look O'Neill straight in the face. 'I went to the fridge a bit later for something to eat and I saw his maggots. He keeps them – he kept them – in the bottom of the fridge in a plastic container. So I thought I'd take them to him . . . he wasn't very pleased to see me. He was waiting for someone. He didn't plan to do any fishing. We had another row and I threw the box of maggots into the river . . . I said stupid things. I said I was in the way . . . I said no one wanted me. Dad told me not to be stupid, that this woman was just a fling, it wasn't serious. My dad put his arm round me . . . and said . . . he said he still loved Mum and that he loved us both and that one day we'd be a proper family again.'

Stephen slumped forward, rubbing furiously at his eyes.

'One more question,' said O'Neill. 'I know it's painful. Did your mum know he'd gone fishing?'

Stephen shook his head and slowly let his hands drop. Tears streaked his face. He looked up. 'No. I knew and that woman he was going to meet knew. She must have killed him. Mum wouldn't have killed my dad. She was fond of him really, that's why she let

107

him stay. I shouldn't have said those things. I felt bad because I left him there – if only I'd stayed maybe I could have saved him.'

'And maybe not,' said O'Neill.

'I hate Bishop,' said Stephen. 'I hate him for being alive and for not being my dad.'

There was no answer to that and O'Neill and Fran left shortly afterwards.

A week later Brian Phelps was jogging along the towpath. It was 6 a.m. and the air was warm and balmy. Brian had lost his early enthusiasm for the dawn run after the first twenty minutes. Now he was sweating and puffing, his legs ached and he was longing to get home to a cool shower and a few mugs of hot sweet tea. You're too fat for this lark, he told himself as he rounded the bend in the river. He stopped by the bushes and sank down on to his haunches to catch his breath. This is going to be the death of me, he thought, as a pain shot through his side. He stayed in a crouched position until the pain left him and then he breathed a sigh of relief that it hadn't been a heart attack.

He was forty-five, he was unfit, drank, liked his food too much and had a beer belly that made him look six months pregnant.

His eyes drifted out to the river. It ran still and clear and he had the urge to take a quick dip. He walked forward on to a path between the nettles and weeds and stared down into the greenish shallow near the river bank. He saw a couple of small grey fish swim by.

Now that he'd stood there for a few minutes the sweat had begun to cool on his body and he shivered. He gazed upwards and saw that great grey billows of cloud were moving across the sky. It was bloody well going to rain. The first drop hit his forehead, then another, then another, like an orchestra warming up; only he wasn't warming up, he was chilling down. He began to jog again, on towards the park and the estate. He was nearly there when he saw the down-and-out sitting by the tree. He assumed he was a down-and-out because in the summer the alcoholics sometimes came down to the towpath to drink their cans of strong lager. It's a bit early, thought Brian, but perhaps he'd been there all night, so paralytic with drink that he didn't feel the rain.

He was nearly level with the man and the tree when his eyes alerted him – even before his brain had time to decode what he was actually seeing, he knew something was very wrong – and he felt a nauseous fear creep over him. The man, head slumped, was the wrong colour. Brian stopped jogging. He stood still. The rain was heavy by now and his socks were soaked. Even now he wasn't sure. He called out, 'You all right mate?' He didn't really expect an answer. He walked closer. He could now see that blood had seeped from the man's chest – a sticky mass on a navy blue sweatshirt, the white emblem of crossed cricket bats spotted with blood.

Brian had never seen a dead body before and the thought crossed his mind that he might not really be dead – maybe in a coma or something. He steeled himself then to do something he feared. He planned to touch the man. He took a deep breath, bent down and lifted the man's chin. The eyes were still open. The rain bounced off his waxen face. Brian knew there was no doubt the man was dead. The eyes told him that. The extra shock came not when he realized death was a certainty but when he realized he knew this man.

Brian Phelps didn't jog towards the main road, he ran as fast as he could. He ran without noticing his legs or his breathing. He ran with a purpose. There was no one about in the High Street but he was oblivious to where he was or who was there – he simply had to get to the police station.

He ran into the car park, across the forecourt and into the main entrance. Only when he was inside the building did he realize how ill he felt. He could hardly breathe, let alone speak.

'Take your time, sir,' said a young constable at the desk. Brian leaned forward, his hands on his thighs, trying desperately to control his breathing. 'I think you'd better sit down.'

Once on a chair, Brian said, 'A body . . . I've found a body . . . by the river—'

'And your name is, sir?'

'Brian Phelps . . . I'm telling you . . . there's a body. I know him—'

'Address, sir?' asked the constable.

'For God's sake, man,' burst out Brian, 'don't just stand there.'

'All in good time, sir. Your address?'

Brian sighed. 'Fourteen Chater Avenue.'

'Right, sir, thank you. You just sit there and I'll get someone from CID to speak to you.'

The call came through to O'Neill just before his alarm clock went off at 7 a.m. He'd been awake since six, just lying on his back listening to the rain and staring at the ceiling.

'I'm on my way,' was his only comment on the phone. But as he dressed quickly he began muttering 'Jasus' repeatedly until he felt better. He rang Fran as soon as he was dressed; she muttered sleepily, 'I don't believe it.'

'Believe it,' said O'Neill. 'Be getting a move on, Fran, everyone's been called out but I want to be on the scene first.'

Uniformed police had already gathered by the river but the rain was so heavy there were no keen dog-walkers or near-neighbours taking an interest. O'Neill noticed the ground was already turning to mud. The rain whipped into the river and the river responded by flowing faster. The sky was overcast and grey as death itself. Shivering as the rain trickled down his neck, he pulled up the collar of his black raincoat and began walking alone towards the corpse. He couldn't help feeling relieved when Fran appeared beside him. She wore a navy anorak, black jeans, and carried her purple umbrella.

'Is that thing big enough?' he asked.

'You'll be glad of it, boss,' she said, noticing how wet he already was. O'Neill took it from her so they could both shelter under it and they walked slowly towards the dead man.

The body reminded Fran of a puppet with broken strings. The rain had beaten against his bloody chest, diluting the blood, and some had pooled on to the ground on his right side.

O'Neill tried to remain detached. The head was slumped on his chest; he had a full head of dark brown hair, the palms of his hands were uppermost, unmarked by age or defensive wounds.

'What are you thinking, Fran?' he asked.

Fran, too, had been studying the body. 'I don't think this victim put up much of a fight either.' she said slowly.

O'Neill bent down, still holding the umbrella, forcing Fran to crouch down too. He lifted the man's chin and found the close eye contact hard to take. The pupils of the eyes were blank and fixed. As he let the head drop back the jaw opened slackly.

Sitting back on his heels, O'Neill crossed himself and whispered the Prayer for the Dead. Then he leaned forward and felt in the man's trouser pockets for any ID or belongings. The left pocket was empty, in the right were two cubes of a soft indescribable consistency. 'Christ!' muttered O'Neill. 'What the hell is this?' He withdrew the cubes and held out his hand so that Fran could see.

She grimaced. 'What is it?'

O'Neill stared at the two pinkish squares in his hand for a moment before realizing what they were. 'It's Spam.'

'That tinned meat stuff?'

'Sure that's what it is. Anglers use it sometimes as bait. But if he was fishing, where the hell's his rod?'

They found the rod in the nettles a few minutes later, plus a small box seat. Their search was interrupted by the arrival of the police surgeon and the Scene of Crimes team, who arrived in big boots and yellow plastic macs. Behind them strode Ringstead, carrying a large black umbrella. The rain still poured.

'Same method?' asked Ringstead, looking over to the tree where the corpse sat and where the team were now arranging a yellow plastic protective tent over the body. He nodded briefly at Fran and said, 'This is all very good experience for you, isn't it, Sergeant?'

She nodded in reply and hoped the rain would rot the soles of his expensive black shoes.

'It seems it's a stabbing,' said O'Neill.

'Don't you know for sure yet, O'Neill?'

'I know he's well and truly dead, sir, and I don't think he died of a stubbed toe.'

'There's no need to be flippant, O'Neill. If you've seen all you want you'd better get round to his next of kin.'

'I'll be waiting for an estimated time of death from the doc before I do that, sir.'

Ringstead shrugged. 'And O'Neill,' – he paused for a moment to survey the scene – 'I want that Forbes woman in the station for questioning, pronto. The trial transcript has come from the Home Office. I've read it and I don't think there's much doubt that she's involved. All you have to do is prove it.'

As O'Neill moved away he swore under his breath.

'Don't take any notice, boss,' said Fran in a whisper. 'He's probably a Mason and it's addled his brain.'

O'Neill smiled tightly and sighed. 'Come on, Fran, let's be getting this over with.'

Later, they stood outside the white painted door of the terraced house in Bushland Avenue and waited for someone to reply to their knocking. Eventually they heard the sounds of footsteps descending the stairs and of a baby crying. The woman who answered the door looked no more than twenty to O'Neill. She was short, a little plump, with brown curly hair and hazel eyes. She wore a red T-shirt and jeans. Her left shoulder was wet where the baby had dribbled. Now she held the large-faced baby, who looked male, on her right hip and his cries halted at the sight of them. 'CID,' said O'Neill solemnly before showing his warrant card and introducing himself and Fran. 'Are you Mrs King?'

She nodded and half smiled. 'What's he done now?' she asked.

'We'll be coming in, Mrs King, to explain.'

O'Neill could sense she guessed something was wrong, seriously wrong, because as she led them through to the living room she kept up a running commentary. 'He didn't know that TV was nicked, honest he didn't; and, I mean, that drink driving offence – he wasn't much over the limit and the insurance—' She broke off as the baby began to wail as if he also sensed something was wrong.

'Let my sergeant hold the baby, Mrs King, and you be sitting down,' said O'Neill. With only slight reluctance Mrs King handed over the baby to Fran. The baby stared at Fran and was silent.

O'Neill cleared his throat. 'It's my sad duty, Mrs King, to tell you that we have reason to believe that . . . that a man's body found near the river has been identified as that of your husband, Patrick King.'

'What are you saying? What are you saying?' she screamed. She half rose from the sofa and then slumped back.

'I'm saying, Mrs King,' he said softly, 'that your husband is dead.'

'No. I don't believe it. He's gone fishing. He went last night. He'll be back. He will.' Her eyes had become wild and staring. 'He will,' she repeated again and again, as if by saying the words she would make them become fact.

O'Neill moved across to sit with her and signalled for Fran to take the baby into another room. 'Listen to me now,' he said quietly. 'I'll be wanting your doctor's telephone number and the number of a relative. You'll be needing someone to be with you.'

'I don't believe you. Who said it was my husband? How would they know?'

'He was very definite, Mrs King. Now you be getting me those numbers.'

She stood up unsteadily, walked through to the hall table and picked up her phone book with trembling hands. 'I don't believe you,' she said, but the tears welling in her eyes and the tremor in her voice told O'Neill that she was beginning to believe him. And he would have given his right arm for it not to be true.

Once O'Neill had telephoned her GP and her sister, he still had to ask the same questions, when what he would have liked to do was give her, and himself, a stiff drink.

'Fran, make some tea,' he called.

Fran, who wasn't used to babies, already had a seriously squashed arm. The baby weighed a ton. She guessed he was about six months old, and he alternated between smiling at her, trying to find her left breast and, then, realizing she wasn't his mother but a complete stranger, screaming fit to burst her eardrums. Motherhood, she decided, was not for her.

It was difficult, with the baby on one hip, trying to make tea but she managed it eventually and took in a cup for Mrs King, who sat blank-faced and pale, eyes awash with tears that she couldn't seem to shed.

'He needs a bottle,' she said dully.

'I'll do it,' said Fran as she handed her a mug of hot sweet tea. The baby flapped his arms towards his mother but she ignored him, holding the hot mug between her hands for comfort. Fran could no longer ignore her aching arms or the screams and, handing the baby to O'Neill, she said, 'Here, you take him; I'll fix his bottle.' The baby's screams stopped, his mouth opened as if to recommence screaming, then he stopped and smiled in absolute delight. O'Neill couldn't help it, he felt a wave of pure pleasure and in those few seconds forgot the reason for his visit.

The moment quickly evaporated when he heard Mrs King gulp and he became aware that she was staring at him with dull, lost eyes. Just to break the silence he said, 'What have you named him, Mrs King? He's a beautiful baby.'

'He's Robert. His dad likes the name Robert but I call him Robbie ... oh God ... please tell me it's not true. He'll come through the door soon, won't he?'

O'Neill didn't answer and was relieved when Fran appeared with Robert's bottle. Mrs King showed no sign of wanting to feed her baby and as the baby seemed more settled with O'Neill, Fran handed him the bottle.

'It's not too hot, is it?' asked O'Neill.

'I'm not that stupid, boss,' muttered Fran.

113

The baby sucked greedily and O'Neill became engrossed in feeding him. It was the first time he'd ever fed a baby, and with a shock he realized that at this moment he understood why Jenny had been so desperate to have children. That realization compounded his feelings of guilt that he had neither shared her desire for children nor realized just how much it meant to her. He was grateful when Fran spoke to Mrs King.

'What's your first name, Mrs King?'

'Lisa.'

'Lisa, I want you to think back carefully and tell me when you last saw your husband.'

Lisa bit her top lip, trying desperately not to cry. 'We'd a row – a silly row about the usual—'

'The usual?'

'Money. We only ever row about money. He said he wanted a new fishing rod. I said we couldn't afford it. Then he let it slip he'd won some money on the horses. And I said he'd promised to give me some money for the kids.'

'Kids?' queried Fran.

'I've got another one – Danielle. She's still asleep – she's a bad sleeper at night, she always sleeps on in the morning.'

'When did you have this row?'

'Most of the evening. He wouldn't tell me how much he'd won and when I went on and on he just walked out saying he was going fishing.'

'What time was this?'

'About eleven, Danielle was still awake and whingeing; the baby had just woken up and he said, "I've had enough of this, I'm going fishing." '

'Did he often go night fishing?'

'He loves it. Not so much in the winter but at least once a week, perhaps more, in the summer . . . oh God—' She stopped, as if remembering something.

'What is it?'

A slow tear began to trickle down down her face. 'He used to say . . . he used to say he could happily die by the river bank . . . he must have fallen in – he couldn't swim.'

'It wasn't that, Lisa. I'm afraid he was murdered.'

'No . . . that couldn't be true . . . he didn't have any enemies. Who would kill . . . my Patrick?'

This time the tears flowed and she sobbed, great racking sobs. The baby paused and his face began to pucker at the sound of his mother's distress.

To both O'Neill's and Fran's relief, at that moment anxious relatives turned up, surrounding Lisa King with a sea of tearful faces.

'We'll ring, Lisa, before we come,' explained O'Neill. 'But you will need to make a formal identification either today or tomorrow.'

'Today,' she said firmly. 'I want to see him today.'

'Fine. We'll come at three o'clock. Just one more question – did he have any money on him?'

Lisa frowned and brushed her hand over her forehead. 'His winnings, I think. I don't know how much; he didn't say.'

'Can't you leave her alone?' said one of the males converging around her.

Just as they were leaving, the child they hadn't seen wandered into the room in a pink nightdress. She was at first puzzled and then, as she realized the atmosphere was strange, she wailed her anxiety: 'Where's my daddy, I want my daddy.' One of the group scooped her up and O'Neill and Fran left unnoticed.

When they were outside the house O'Neill said, 'I'm having a drink, I don't care what you say.'

'I'm not arguing, boss, I want one too, but the pubs aren't open yet.'

'What a bloody country,' said O'Neill. 'We'll be going to the betting shop first, then. After that we'll have a drink.'

The Fowchester betting shop was at the other end of the High Street, with blocked-out windows and steel-reinforced doors. Inside the dim interior a few men stared at the TV screen or scanned the *Racing News*. The shop smelled of stale tobacco and pine disinfectant. For some reason it reminded Fran of an old-fashioned public toilet.

There wasn't much of a queue of people waiting to place bets and the teller seemed to know O'Neill. 'Won't keep you a minute, Connor,' he said cheerfully.

'Don't tell me you bet as well,' said Fran.

'I have been known to, on a sure thing and if it's an Irish horse.'

Having parted the men from their money, the teller said, 'How can I help you two? Because I can tell you haven't come to place a bet, Connor, not with that face on.'

O'Neill managed a slight smile. 'I'm surprised you remember me, Bill, it's been a long time.'

Bill nodded. Fran was somewhat taken aback by Bill's appearance. His shiny head was hairless but his ears sprouted hair as energetically as if it were weeds. He wore a gold earring in each sprouting ear and the hair from his eyebrows had also gone, presumably to take up residence in his ears.

'It is a serious matter, Bill – a murder enquiry.'

'You'd better go through to the back.'

In the back room, Bill lit a cigarette after he'd been told of Patrick King's death. 'Christ,' he said, 'I can't believe it. He was in here yesterday and he won.'

'We'll be wanting to know,' said O'Neill, 'how much he won.'

Bill played with the hair on his ears and inhaled deeply on his cigarette. 'It was a good win. The best for years—'

'How good?'

'A thousand pounds good.'

Chapter Sixteen

O'Neill drove out of Fowchester towards a village pub – any village, he didn't care which one as long as they could get a meal and a drink there. It had stopped raining now and the sun was beginning to shine. The dampness caused a faint haze over the fields and the air smelled of wet grass.

He was pleased with himself. At least he'd managed without a drink so far, and especially just after meeting Lisa King. He tried not to think about her predicament; it reminded him all too painfully of his own experience—

'Boss?'

'Yes, Fran.'

'Aren't we supposed to be back at the station reading the trial transcript?'

'Sure we are, Fran, but all in good time. We've got the formal identification at three and we're deserving some lunch before then.'

'What do you make of Patrick King winning a thousand pounds?' she asked. 'Do you think robbery was the motive?'

O'Neill's eyes didn't leave the road. After a moment or two he said, 'I don't think the motive was robbery. He wouldn't have left the house carrying a thousand pounds.'

'In a fit of pique he might,' suggested Fran.

O'Neill shook his head. 'He could have stuffed it under the mattress. But what puzzles me is why he didn't tell her the amount or give her some of it. A fishing rod wouldn't cost anything like that.'

'I wouldn't know, boss,' said Fran. 'The nearest I've got to fishing was winning a goldfish at the fair when I was about ten.'

'How's the mouse, by the way?'

'He's brilliant. I'm training him.'

'What for?'

'I haven't worked that one out yet, boss. I thought, sniffer dogs being so expensive, I could train a mouse or two to do the same thing.'

O'Neill laughed. 'You've only got the one mouse.'

'That is a worry to me, boss. He may have sexual problems. Perhaps that's why he's such promising material on the sniffer mouse stakes. He can smell a mere crumb from under the floorboards.'

'Sure he's a genius among mice, I've no doubt of that.'

They both laughed then, loudly and together, and in a strange way it seemed to confirm that if they both found the idea of the sniffer mouse funny, then they were both alive. That another's death hadn't engulfed them or made them sour.

But, for O'Neill, it wasn't enough just to share a laugh to reaffirm life itself, he wanted to make love to her. His hand strayed to her knee.

'Don't, Connor,' she said. That was all. He removed his hand and said lightly, 'You're breaking my heart, Fran.'

'Look, there's a pub,' said Fran, pointing to a pub sign which read 'The Hen and Feathers'.

Once inside, O'Neill soon realized that the Hen and Feathers was the sort of pub that seemed to subsist on two old men in a corner playing dominoes and drinking half pints. The seating arrangements were of round tables and hard seats, and the landlord seemed to think that a hunting horn and six horse brasses was all that was needed to create the right ambience. The landlord himself was grey-faced and miserable-looking.

O'Neill was about to order something alcoholic when he thought better of it, so he ordered two coffees. The landlord, with some disdain, shook his head. 'I could perhaps get the wife to make you a pot of tea.'

O'Neill nodded. Could he keep this up, he wondered. He asked then about food, although he already had the feeling that food here might be as rare as truffles in the desert.

'We can do you a roll, sir – of your choice—' Before O'Neill could answer, the landlord added, 'Ham or cheese?'

'Let's not be too flamboyant,' said O'Neill. 'We'll have the cheese and two packets of crisps – plain.'

The landlord's mouth, which previously had set in a grim smile, now gave up all pretence of trying and, with a scowl, he disappeared into the kitchen.

Fran sat on her rigid-backed chair listening to the exchange and trying to keep her face straight. 'Dump!' said O'Neill as he sat down. The cheese rolls and tea took ten minutes to arrive but they were delivered personally by the landlord, who said, 'You from Fowchester?'

He made it sound as if Fowchester were the next stop to Katmandu.

'We are,' they said in unison.

'I hear you've had a murder down that way. I read about it in the papers. Some maniac of a woman. She been arrested yet?'

'Not yet,' said O'Neill tersely.

'Bloody police, bloody useless they are. They have a murderess right under their noses and they haven't arrested her.'

Fran gave O'Neill a light kick under the table as a warning to say nothing he would regret later and answered sweetly, 'I'm sure you're right. The police don't need evidence these days, do they, they can just force confessions out of people.'

'Now, I never said that. But I mean, personally I think they should bring back hanging. If they'd hanged her years ago she wouldn't been able to kill again, would she?'

O'Neill could keep quiet no longer. 'That's very perspicacious of you, landlord.'

The landlord, not recognizing the sarcasm, smirked gratefully. 'You enjoy your meal,' he said.

When he'd gone O'Neill said, 'It's not funny, Fran,' as she tried not to laugh. 'That's just the sort of attitude Ringstead has. And we're definitely up shit creek. This new murder puts us back to square one—'

'We never got to square two, boss. In fact, I can't see we've made any progress at all.'

'Don't be depressing me, Fran. We haven't had forensic back on either of them yet. Maybe the post-mortem will turn up something.'

Fran wasn't convinced. 'What suspects do we have, anyway?'

He shrugged. 'Don't be asking me questions like that, Fran. One murder's serious, two is an epidemic.'

'What about a connection between the two victims?'

'It's a possibility, it's a small town. What are you thinking, Fran?'

'I'm not sure, a dodgy deal, a hit man – anything.'

'O'Neill smiled, 'I don't think this is big-league stuff. It's more like revenge—'

'Not hot-blooded, though, not frenzied.'

O'Neill was forced to agree. 'Two men both die late at night in the same place, in the same way – both anglers, one with no bait but a pocket of condoms, one divorced, one married. What does it sound like? Apart from being a bloody mystery.'

Fran was at a loss. After a long silence she said, 'It could have been a homosexual meeting ground.'

'Or they could have been meeting a woman?'

'The same woman?'

'Now there's a possibility – a jealous husband knowing where they were likely to be meeting and lying in wait.'

'What about a peeping tom or a flasher?'

O'Neill nodded, but doubtfully. 'We'll check the known sex offenders living in the area but I'd have thought he might have watched the action and become aroused and then . . . no, that line of reasoning doesn't hold. The same woman gets away twice? It doesn't seem likely.'

'Different women then, boss. They both see a murder and run off. Don't tell a soul because they're married. Maybe he raped them and they're too afraid to come forward.'

O'Neill sighed. 'Fran, your thinking is confusing me. Suddenly we have two rape victims as well. I can't cope with it.'

'It was only a suggestion.'

'What worries me is both men seemed totally unprepared for the attack.'

Very quietly, Fran said, 'Do you think Carole Ann Forbes's lover put up much of a struggle?'

He frowned at her. 'I'll not be knowing that, Fran,' he said crisply, 'until we've read the transcripts. And we won't be doing that until we've taken Lisa King to the hospital mortuary. But whatever we find out, you're not going to convince me Carole Ann committed two murders.'

'Two more murders,' corrected Fran.

'Don't get clever, Fran. What motive, anyway?'

'She did say she wanted to go back to prison.'

O'Neill tensed. He was beginning to get annoyed with Fran, and although he didn't want to say anything he'd regret later, he wanted to stay in control of this investigation. 'Come on, Fran. We've got work to do.'

Fran stifled a retort, and as they walked out of the pub the landlord called out, 'See you again.'

'Not till Ireland suffers a total drought,' muttered O'Neill.

After the formal identification O'Neill and Fran returned to the station in a subdued mood. Lisa King's recognition of the fact that the waxy, white shell lying to attention on a mortuary table had, only the day before, been her husband drew forth an anguished squeal of pain and uncontrollable weeping. Now she had actually seen his body she would never again experience any real hope of seeing him again. But O'Neill knew that one day in the town she'd catch a glimpse of someone and for a split second her breath would catch and hope would rise, only to fade instantaneously as today's memory came flooding back. He knew that it would be best to leave her alone for a day or so. He longed to find out about the thousand pounds but for that he would need her cooperation, and at the moment she was in no condition to be interviewed.

In the meantime a large team, mostly borrowed from other forces, would still be out collecting information from friends, neighbours and colleagues of Alan Lattaway. The information collected on the Personal Descriptive Forms was then collated and put onto computer. Suspicious of anyone, they asked more questions. Should they then fail to satisfy, the names would be referred to O'Neill, and Fran would put her stickers on the forms just in case they missed anything. So far, on Alan Lattaway there had been nothing. The one or two disgruntled customers had been dealt with by the team and had alibis, and they weren't murderously disgruntled anyway; but someone had been. It was strange, thought O'Neill, that they hadn't found anyone with a real grudge, maybe a scorned woman, because he had the feeling that Alan would have been seriously looking for a woman.

In the first year after Jenny's suicide O'Neill had taken out and bedded several women, as if by doing so he could recapture Jenny in some way. It hadn't worked, it had just made his loneliness more acute, made him miss her even more. He'd calmed down in the second year and now it seemed he'd set his sights on Fran. You bloody eejit, he told himself, you're just setting yourself up for more misery.

On his desk sat the trial transcript, a great thick tome. He looked over to where Fran was busily typing.

'What are you typing, Fran?'

She glanced up, 'Just a list, boss.'

'Shopping list?'

She sighed. 'No, of course not. Just a list of names.'

He noticed the slightly triumphant look in her eyes. 'And?'

'And there's one name that crops up twice.'

She continued to type.

'Don't be keeping me in suspense, Fran.'

'It's a woman and she's married.'

'Just be telling me now,' said O'Neill.

'Okay, boss. How does this grab you? Nina Gardener.'

'You're sure?'

'I'm sure.'

'In what connection?'

'One, she was mentioned by Carole Ann. Two, she was on Alan Lattaway's list of customers. He got a hefty commission on her policy. Could just be a coincidence. Mind you . . . has she already been interviewed?'

'Not yet,' said O'Neill.

'Do you know her?' asked Fran.

'I've spoken to her husband once or twice. He's genial enough, but stiff. You know the type – you'd be half suspecting he was wearing women's underwear under his pinstripe. He's the town's main solicitor, in fact he's my solicitor for my house sale.'

'What about his wife?'

'Ah, she's a good-looking woman. I've only seen her in the car with him, never spoken to her.'

'Young?'

'Younger than him. He's in his fifties, she looks about thirty-five.'

O'Neill stared into space for a while, then he said, 'Alan Lattaway was a good-looking man—'

'And so was Patrick King.'

'One murder victim at a time, Fran.'

'Do you think she's the type, boss?'

'What for? Having an affair?'

Fran sighed. 'I didn't mean that. I meant clandestine meetings on the river bank. She sounds like a night-in-a-four-star-hotel type to me.'

'Perhaps she's just very discreet. Or she likes the open air.'

'You'll be telling me next she likes fishing, boss.'

'I'll be telling you no such thing, Fran. We'll see her tomorrow.'

'And there's another name that keeps cropping up, boss.'

'Surprise me, Fran.'

'Dave Reynolds. He's been seen in the Wanderer pub on a couple of occasions.'

'We could be saying that about the whole population of Fowchester. I read his crime record – I'm not supposing he's not capable of murder, but there'd have to be profit in it for him. He was only violent when someone trapped him or tried to have a go. Even then, as far as professional criminals go he was fairly restrained.'

'Worth a go though, boss. Pete Preston interviewed him and did his PDF.'

'And?'

'Well, he did have an alibi. Miss Braithwaite heard him come in at eleven-thirty, actually spoke to him, and then she bolted the door at twelve and said she was awake most of the night and would have heard if he'd gone out again.'

'OK, so we speak to him as well, although I can't see he would have anything to gain from killing Lattaway—'

'Perhaps he was paid, boss.'

O'Neill nodded, annoyed with himself that that thought hadn't immediately sprung to mind. He thought about it, raked his hand through his hair and said slowly, 'A paid killer for Lattaway – maybe. I can't see it for King, though, can you? He worked at Catcher & Co. as a surgical instrument maker. At the moment we have to presume he had a happy marriage.'

'He could have been killed by mistake, or just as a ploy to throw us off the scent.'

'What scent would that be?' said O'Neill with a hint of a smile.

He turned then to the trial transcript but was immediately interrupted by a call from the pathologist, Edward Foster.

'O'Neill, it looks like the same killer. Stab wounds to the front of the chest, good aim, three thrusts. I've compared the photographs of the wounds and I'm as sure as dammit that the knife is the same. Otherwise he was a healthy young man. I estimate time of death as being between twelve and one-thirty. Oh, and there's one more thing – a small mark on his chest worried me. A V-shaped mark. I think the murderer tried to make one more stab at him and the tip of the knife broke off. The blade is, as good as I can estimate, about ten inches long with a narrow tip. He didn't have time to put up a fight, the first wound would have rendered him dead almost immediately. Angle of the wounds indicates a right-hander, but . . . I could be wrong.'

'You aren't usually,' said O'Neill. 'Thanks a million.'

O'Neill was about to put the phone down when Foster said, 'Oh, and by the way, there was no evidence of recent sexual activity.'

He relayed the gist of the report to Fran and said, 'Come on, we'll be taking another look along that river bank.'

It was, by now, six o'clock and Fran could see no end to the day. What she really wanted was a cool shower, a long fruity drink and a spell staring at the TV. It seemed she wasn't going to get any of it.

Just as they were leaving, the phone rang again. It was Lisa King's brother to say he'd found Patrick's money, nearly a thousand pounds, in the garage, stuffed into a plastic bag.

'How nearly the thousand?' asked O'Neill.

'Fifty quid short.'

'Well, that's that,' said O'Neill to Fran, who had begun tidying her desk. 'He wasn't robbed, at least not of a thousand quid. It strikes me the poor bastard may have just—'

He stopped abruptly as a thought struck him. He noticed Fran's quizzical expression but didn't say any more.

Two uniformed men stood guard at the park end of the river. The tent-like structure still covered the place where Patrick King had been found, but the inch-by-inch search was obviously over; there were no other police personnel in sight. The river bank was deserted, in the distance he could see the lights of the Wanderer pub. The nettles had been squashed by the feet of the police team, the late evening sun seemed to cast a pinkish glow on the river.

'Why exactly have we come down here, boss?' asked Fran.

'I wish I knew,' murmured O'Neill. Now that he was here, he couldn't quite put his finger on the disquiet he felt.

Chapter Seventeen

At the Wanderer pub Roger watched, with some satisfaction, the punters at play. The news of the murder of Patrick King had, Roger noticed, spread even before the poor sod had developed rigor mortis and Roger, who took an interest in such things, had played his part in passing on the news. He'd had a couple of extra drinks so he felt quite cheerful, just the opposite of Connie, who looked as miserable tonight as if he'd been part of the family.

'Roger, I'll have a pint of your Bateman's,' called out a regular from the queue that had suddenly enveloped the bar. Roger took one of the fast disappearing pint glasses and lowered the Bateman's pump.

Someone by the bar said, 'Terrible news . . . poor old Brian . . . he found him. He's in a state of shock.'

Another voice said, 'Yeah, but they weren't friends, were they? I mean, last time I heard, they were having fisticuffs outside the pub.'

'Nothing in that . . . just a row about some old banger Patrick had sold Brian. They got it sorted.'

Connie appeared then from the other end of the bar and Roger patted her backside with his free hand. She glowered at him, trod on his toe, his left big toe, the one with the ingrowing toenail, and then murmured, 'Sorry, dear.'

Roger watched her as she served more punters. For the past few hours the thought had festered in his mind that Patrick King and Connie were more than just a little friendly. King had always chosen the right time to approach the bar, a time when Roger was serving someone else. He'd seen the way he'd looked at her breasts and watched as she moved down the bar. And now she was as miserable as sin. It all added up and after closing time he'd have it out with her. She wasn't going to make a fool of him again.

Connie wished she'd trodden harder on Roger's foot, wished she'd done enough damage to keep him incapacitated for a week. Julie had a night off, unfortunately, so it meant that just she and Roger had to cope with the influx of curious ghouls who came to the pub just because it was the nearest hostelry to the murder site. Connie had known Patrick and Alan and had liked them both, but neither of them, of course, had fancied her. Roger manufactured jealousy like a production-line commodity, although Connie was astute enough, and knew Roger well enough, to know he enjoyed fantasies of her being with other men and that he rationalized that by acting like an outraged husband. One day he might go too far but at the moment she could cope with him. He was really quite stupid and if a man overtly flirted with her, Roger took that at face value. He didn't notice the quieter, shyer ones, like Alan and Patrick. Both of them had just needed someone to listen to their woes and she'd done that. After all, no one would confide in God-zilla – mine host – or in Julie, who, while she could flash a smile, managed to remain aloof from the customers in a way that Connie couldn't quite fathom.

The press had come back in force and were busy buying drinks for anyone who'd ever said 'Good morning' to either man, and after she heard Roger being pressed to have yet another drink she wondered if he was responsible for tipping them off after Alan's murder.

At that moment he was standing by the optics pouring himself another Glenmorangie and telling a reporter, 'Yes. I knew him well.'

'Lying toad,' she muttered, loudly enough for the reporter to hear. Roger's expression hadn't altered, so she assumed he was too busy enjoying his whiskey to be able to hear at the same time. The reporter, though, copy-sharp of ear and eye, sidled quickly away from Roger towards Connie.

'Now, you look like a woman who knows what's going on around here' he said. 'Let me buy you a drink.'

Connie stared at the little man with the bald head, dark blue shirt and loud striped tie, then, ignoring him, turned away from him, and said, 'Next!' in a loud voice.

'Bitch,' he murmured, but without passion or emphasis, picked up his pint glass and walked away to find a more receptive person, or a grateful drinker.

126

O'Neill and Fran stood at the entrance to the lounge bar, saw the reporters and hesitated. 'Perhaps this wasn't one of my better ideas,' said O'Neill. 'I'll stay off the booze or I might take a crack at one of those . . . pariahs!'

Fran smiled up at him. 'I'm impressed with the description, boss.'

O'Neill shrugged, 'I'm trying to control my language and my temper. But Jasus, just seeing them is enough.'

'Let's go, then,' said Fran. O'Neill didn't answer, his eyes scanned the pub as though looking for someone. 'I'm looking for Julie,' he explained. 'She's more the age group for the two men. You never know, she could have been having a flirtation with one – or both.'

'She didn't strike me as the type.'

'Why not?'

'She smiles at men all the time but it's a bit fixed, as if her heart's really elsewhere.'

'I hadn't noticed,' said O'Neill. 'I'll be speaking to Connie, we'll come back tomorrow before opening time. Speak to all of them, try and jog their memories a bit.'

Fran watched him walk to the bar and she watched one of the reporters watching O'Neill. After a few seconds of conversation Connie moved towards the optics – she was obviously going to give O'Neill a drink.

The reporter had picked up his camera from the floor. Fran walked forward quickly past men holding pints, she didn't have time to be polite, she just pushed herself towards the table. There, a man with a blue shirt and bald head was aiming his camera straight at O'Neill, who was just about to accept a glass of whiskey from Connie. Fran lurched forward so that she sprawled across the reporter's raised camera arm. She fell so heavily the camera loosed from his grasp and slipped noisily to the floor. The whole pub seemed to share the moment – in complete silence.

'You bloody idiot,' he shouted at her.

O'Neill was, by now, at her side helping her up. 'Are you hurt?' he asked.

'No, I'm fine. Let's get out quickly.' She could hear the buzz starting up in the pub, heard the words 'police' and 'CID' and knew by the way the bald reporter now cradled his camera and stared at her vindictively that he had guessed it was no accident. 'If my camera's broken you can bloody well pay for it,' he snarled.

O'Neill stared coldly at the man. 'That's providing you can prove you didn't deliberately trip up my DS. Can you be proving that?'

There was no answer. O'Neill still had his arm around Fran and as they walked away someone from the same table said, 'Some pigs have all the luck – I bet he's shagging her tonight.'

O'Neill stopped in his tracks. Fran could see that he was furious. 'Leave it, boss, leave it,' she said.

'Wait for me outside, Fran. I'll deal with them.'

Fran made no move to go and O'Neill pushed her towards the door. 'Just get outside and don't argue.' Fran had never seen him like this before. Reluctantly, she left the pub.

A few minutes later he reappeared and strode off towards the river. She had to jog to keep up with him. They walked briskly in silence, he held up the yellow tape for Fran to go underneath and they walked on. It wasn't dark yet and they could see a uniformed constable standing by the murder tree, the yellow tarpaulin tent still in place. As they passed, O'Neill nodded at the constable and walked on.

'Are you going to tell me what was said?' asked Fran.

O'Neill stopped and smiled. 'Let's just be saying, Fran, I made him an offer he couldn't refuse.'

'And that's all you're going to tell me?'

'It is indeed, but thanks for stopping him taking that photo, Fran. Ringstead wants me off the case – one more cock-up and I'm finished on this one.'

'You didn't say he came on that strong, boss.'

'At this moment our Carole Ann Forbes should be in an interview room. No, that's an understatement – according to Ringstead, who's read the trial transcript, she should be back behind bars.'

'What are you going to do?'

O'Neill frowned. 'I'm staying up all night to read it.'

'Do you want any help?'

'That's a grand offer, Fran. In that case it might only take half the night.'

As they neared the park Fran saw them. A group of teenage boys gathered round a lamppost. The same five. One of them stepped forward, throwing an empty can of lager in their path. 'It's "melons" again. Hello, darling.'

O'Neill gave Fran a sidelong glance then said, 'Police. You've got by the time I count to five to clear off.'

The obvious leader had stepped forward, the rest apparently waiting for something to happen.

O'Neill carried on counting. 'We're ever so scared of the police, ain't we, lads?' said the ringleader.

One of them laughed, 'Fucking terrified.'

'O'Neill said, 'Five,' and the group, as if by some joint consciousness, all ran off laughing and jeering and once out of the light of the lamppost were just dark figures running in the distance.

'You should have told me about that crowd,' said O'Neill later as they sat in their office.

'I thought they were relatively harmless, boss,' said Fran, feeling irrationally that she was somehow to blame for the whole incident.

'Don't be thinking too much, Fran, and next time tell me. And why exactly were you walking on the river bank alone at night?'

'It wasn't late, it was still daylight.'

'I don't care what the bloody time was – you're a police officer, you should be having more sense.'

Fran was about to agree when she realized she was falling into the victim trap, taking the blame.

'Hang on one minute,' she said angrily. 'I shouldn't have to worry about where I walk in the town I live. Being in the police has nothing to do with it—'

'Sure it has—'

'No it hasn't.'

O'Neill paused, aware now that he might be about to say something he'd regret. 'Just don't be arguing with me, Fran. Let's get on with reading this trial transcript, unless of course you want us both to lose our jobs.'

O'Neill chose to read the actual trial and handed Fran the social and psychological reports, and he wondered if in the morning they'd be driving round to arrest Carole Ann Forbes.

They both read silently, engrossed. The town hall clock struck eleven and they were both still reading. Fran eased her position as she grew stiff but she didn't stop reading.

O'Neill read on, growing more incredulous as he turned each page. The paucity of the actual evidence appalled him and the investigation seemed less than rigorous. Trained monkeys could have done a better job.

He longed to read aloud some of the exchanges but Fran was

still wading through the social and psycholgical reports, so he controlled the urge to interrupt her and went to get coffee and sandwiches from the canteen.

Fran murmured, 'Thank you,' as he placed the coffee and carefully chosen egg and cress sandwich in front of her, and carried on reading.

At twelve Fran looked up, stretched her arms above her head and yawned.

'Well?' said O'Neill.

'Sad background,' said Fran.

'Do you think she murdered Michael Summerton?'

Fran sighed and frowned, 'To be honest, boss, I don't know.'

'Tell me what you found out, Fran?'

'All of it?'

'Just a précis of the main facts.'

Fran kept the report in front of her, glancing at it from time to time. 'Carole Ann was born in 1961 to Margaret Forbes, aged sixteen, single and unemployed. They lived in a village in Hertfordshire in Margaret's mother's house quite happily, until Carole Ann was seven. The grandmother died of cancer at the age of fifty.

'After this Margaret seemed to go off the rails. Well . . . to sum it up she sold the house and spent the money, or at least started to spend the money. She did have help. She moved into a rented flat with Richard Dixon, known as Dick. She'd known him for six weeks. That was when Carole Ann started having problems. For the very first time she was often left alone at night. She began having problems at school and home. She starting wetting the bed, something she'd grown out of long before, she began having night terrors and Richard Dixon was not a patient man, especially when he was violent. Margaret was often reduced to locking Carole Ann in her room for her own protection.'

'Poor kid,' murmured O'Neill.

'It gets worse,' said Fran. 'The money ran out and Richard threw them out. They lived in a hostel for a while, but eventually they were given a council flat and for a while things were a bit happier for Carole Ann, except that Margaret grew steadily more depressed, she couldn't find a job, had no money, no relatives and she got desperate and started bringing different men home.'

'On the game?'

'Carole Ann doesn't think so, she said they were boyfriends but they didn't last very long. One night when Carole Ann *margaret* had gone to the pub promising she'd only be half an hour, one of these boyfriends called; it seems he was special to Margaret. Carole Ann let him in. He sexually assaulted her. When Margaret returned Carole Ann appeared very distressed and Margaret, in a fearsome rage, went to find him. She searched him out, found him in a pub, smashed a glass and ground it into his face. He was pretty badly hurt, nearly bled to death, and when it came to court the judge, of course, heard from the prosecution about her managing to get through several thousand pounds, and the "boyfriends", and her being in the pub when the alleged assault happened. And meanwhile Carole Ann said nothing. Carole Ann refused to be examined and Margaret refused to give consent.'

'The mother didn't call the police at the time?'

Fran shook her head. 'The only mitigating circumstances brought forward in the mother's case were that she was drunk at the time and that it was a first offence. By the way, boss, this isn't Carole Ann's version of events; the social workers found all this out from Carole Ann's records when she was placed with foster parents. At the time it was hoped Margaret would get a light sentence. It wasn't murder, after all, but it seems the defendant, still horribly scarred and blind in one eye, swayed the court with his protestations of innocence. He admitted only to knocking on the door and being told by Carole Ann to go away. To his credit, the judge did ask for information about Carole Ann, but the disturbed behaviour at school and the fact that the head mistress said "she was inclined to bend the truth" didn't do much to persuade him she had actually been assaulted. Anyway, it didn't really seem to matter what was said; Margaret had pleaded guilty anyway.'

'How long did she get?' asked O'Neill as he stared thoughtfully out of the window to the High Street below.

'Three years.'

'Where is she now?'

'Dead. She hanged herself in prison just before she was due for release.'

O'Neill sighed.

'She wrote to her daughter every week but her daughter never replied.'

'Why not?'

Fran smiled. 'Carole Ann wouldn't comment on that. The report

131

does mention she seemed willing to talk about Michael at length, but any traumatic incidents she simply refused to discuss. She met Michael at school and they became inseparable. When they were sixteen they ran off to London together, lived rough, lived in squats. Didn't get into any trouble. When they were eighteen someone from social services helped them find an attic flat in a run-down house in Belsize Park, North London. Michael earned money here and there doing odd jobs, he even sold a few water-colours, and according to what's known they were quite happy.'

'No history of violence on either side?'

'Not according to this. They did go out drinking quite a bit, but when drunk seemed quite good-natured. At least, that's what Carole Ann said.'

O'Neill nodded. 'What reason could she have for killing him, Fran? That's the question. By all accounts she's unwilling to discuss traumatic events but there's no evidence of violence in her past.'

'Her mother was violent,' said Fran softly.

'I'm not wanting to start a heredity debate, Fran. I don't think she murdered Michael Summerton. But I think we may have to bring her in.'

'Why?'

'Eventually the press reports will get to her, they'll start dragging up her past life and her mother's. I'm worried it may send her over the edge or make her be doing something that will ensure she goes back to prison.'

'Maybe she's already done that, Connor,' said Fran.

Chapter Eighteen

O'Neill grunted in reply. 'It could just be coincidence, Fran, that two men have been killed in the same way, but I've been reading the post-mortem report on Michael Summerton. The knife wounds are almost identical: to the chest, with upward thrusts. The victim taken by surprise—'

'Well, he would have been taken by surprise,' interrupted Fran. 'It seems he was asleep and drunk at the time.'

'That's not the point, Fran. What I'm saying is that the nature of the stabbings points to the same killer.'

'What about the knife?'

'That's a bone of contention. A kitchen knife with blood on it was found at the scene. In fact, under questioning . . . come over here and read this with me. This is the "knife section".' Fran walked across to his desk, moved a chair, sat down, and together they began to read part of the prosecuting counsel's – Alexander Myles's – questioning:

Myles: How do you explain, Miss Forbes, that the knife, exhibit A, was found on your bedroom floor?

Forbes: I threw it there.

Judge: Would the defendant speak up, please, I can't hear you. Repeat your answer.

Forbes: I threw it there.

Myles: Did the knife belong to you?

Forbes: I think so.

Myles: You think so? Perhaps you'd like to examine the knife.

Forbes (examines knife – exhibit A)

Myles: Is this one of your kitchen knives?

Forbes: Yes.

Myles: Why did you throw your kitchen knife across the room?

Forbes: I don't know.

Myles: Come now, Miss Forbes, you must know. I suggest it was because you were horrified by what you'd done and wanted the knife out of your sight.

Forbes (no reply)

Myles: So you were horrified by what you'd done? Yes or no?

Forbes: I was horrified – by his death.

Myles: Is it true that on the evening in question you had both been drinking in a public house, had arrived back at your flat inebriated and had then smoked cannabis?

Forbes: Yes.

Myles: Would you say that because of your overindulgence in drink and drugs you were more likely to be violent? Yes or no?

Forbes: No. I'm not a violent person.

Judge: Please speak up, Miss Forbes.

Myles: Miss Forbes, would you like me to repeat the question?

Forbes: No. I heard the question. I'm not a violent person.

Myles: We've heard evidence that you and Michael Summerton came back to the house just after midnight, that you both were laughing and happy, but later one of the other residents of 14 Orchard Terrace heard raised voices. Were you in fact arguing?

Forbes: No. We went straight to sleep.

Myles: You deny you had a row?

Forbes: Yes.

Myles: I submit to you that you did have a row and that row ended, but was not resolved, because Michael Summerton fell asleep. And while he slept you crept into the kitchen, picked up the knife from the drawer and viciously stabbed him to death. Furthermore, I also submit that you knew exactly what you were doing and that your intention was to kill your lover, Michael Summerton.

Forbes: Why would I do that?

Myles: You ask why, Miss Forbes? I suggest to you that you were pathologically jealous, that the seeds of the row were set in the public house Jack Straw's Castle. That you saw him flirting with another woman and in a jealous rage you killed him.

Forbes: I didn't see him flirting.

Myles: But you did kill him?

Forbes: I don't know.

Myles: You don't know? Come now, Miss Forbes. You must know.

134

Forbes: I must have done it, I suppose. I was there.

Judge: Thank you, Mr Myles. We'll adjourn for lunch.

'What are you thinking so far, Fran?' asked O'Neill as he flicked over the pages.

'I think she's not trying very hard but what's the actual evidence against her?'

'Solid evidence is her fingerprints on the knife. And, of course, the fact that she was there, beside the body.'

'Did she phone the police?'

'The landlord, Joseph Peters, found them. They were a week behind with the rent. He came up to their room on Saturday morning about 9 a.m. to collect. He knew they were in, he lived in the basement flat and he kept tabs on his tenants. When there was no reply he used his key. He found Carole Ann moaning and rocking herself backwards and forwards on the bed. Summerton was lying on his back, bloody and very dead. Carole Ann's face and hands were covered in blood.'

'What did she say when the police arrived?'

'She said, and I quote, "He died in my dreams." After that she didn't speak for a day. The police surgeon saw her and recommended a psychiatric opinion.'

'What about the investigation?'

O'Neill sighed. 'About as comprehensive as a search for a lost bike. I'm thinking they thought there was no point. They had a suspect, they had evidence, no doubt someone checked her background and found out about her mother. Carole Ann wasn't denying anything very strenuously – so why should they spend time and trouble?'

'Motive?'

O'Neill smiled. 'That's something you worry about when you haven't got a suspect.'

'You've read the trial transcript, what do you think?'

O'Neill paused. 'If I'd simply read the transcript I would have thought her guilty too. And if I'm honest I'd have been keeping the investigation to a minimum.'

'So what now?' asked Fran as she stared at the clock on the wall that showed 1.30 a.m. Now that she knew the time she already felt more tired. She yawned. Her eyelids seemed suddenly more heavy and itchy. From being a warm night, she realized, the temperature had dropped and she began to shiver. The only sound outside was the occasional car passing along the High Street or the sound of voices as the few men on duty passed by at the front door. The only sight was the orange light from the streetlamps and the black sky glinting with the silver pinpricks of stars.

'Wear my jacket,' said O'Neill, handing her his brown cord jacket from the back of the chair.

'I'm OK. I'm not cold.'

'We'll not be packing it in yet, Fran, so don't think you'll be going home to bed.'

'Did I say I wanted to go home, boss?'

'You yawned; I thought you were giving me a hint.'

Fran slipped the jacket round her shoulders and murmured, 'I wouldn't have been that subtle.'

O'Neill flicked through the psychiatric report and said, 'Come on, Fran, be explaining it to me in plain English.'

'I'll do my best,' said Fran. 'The psychiatrist, Frederick Wieldstein, saw her when she was on remand one month after the murder. And judging by her answers she seems to have talked to him quite a bit – except for the childhood assault, which she refused to discuss. It seems the period of her life when she lived with foster parents was miserably unhappy and she missed her mother very much.'

'Was she giving any reason for not writing to her mother while she was in prison?'

'She said she didn't know why. Wieldstein seems to think that she felt guilty that her mother was in prison.'

'You don't agree?'

Fran shook her head. 'I think she was angry with her mother, felt abandoned – she was very young, after all.'

'What does he think about her sanity?'

'Wieldstein uses lots of scales – the Impact of Event Scales, which judges the impact of events, and avoidance scales, et cetera.'

O'Neill sighed. 'Be getting on with it, Fran. Was she sane or not?'

'Sane, yes, as opposed to raving – but depressed, anxious and showing all the signs of being guilt- and grief-stricken.'

'Guilt because she'd killed him?'

'No, guilt because she hadn't died too.'

O'Neill said thoughtfully, 'She changed her plea, you know. From not guilty. And I can't help wondering why.'

136

'Could it have been because a not guilty plea would have made it a bit sticky for her in court?'

'You mean because her defence counsel might have tried to find out more about Summerton?'

'Or just asked too many questions?'

'About what?'

Fran shrugged, she was getting too tired to think any more. The whole case was beginning to be one big blur. 'Maybe she was so much in love with Summerton that she didn't want his memory tarnished. Perhaps that was more important to her than her freedom. Wieldstein did comment that – hang on, I'll find the quote' – she flicked through the pages – 'Here it is:

' "Carole Ann Forbes's love for Michael Summerton seems to border on the obsessive. She saw him as being an amalgam of mother, father, lover, friend, and she could see no faults in him. To her he was perfect. The onus was on him to maintain his 'perfection'. Her mother had 'failed' her. There had been just the one long-term male figure in her life – Dixon – and he had failed her. Although she refuses to discuss this traumatic period of her life in any detail, she does admit to both hating and fearing him.

"In contrast she saw Summerton as her total "family" and she does exhibit signs of jealousy, bordering on the pathological. She recalls searching through his pockets, examining his clothes for lipstick marks, questioning him at some length if he went out without her. This is markedly at odds with her avowed love and trust of him, which is vital to her mental wellbeing.

'In conclusion, I would say that if Michael Summerton actually broke the trust by which she held such great store and which was the key to her sanity, then she could become unbalanced in her actions. Her mother, she felt, had "betrayed" her by going to prison. Thus she punished her mother by not visiting or answering letters.

'Carole Ann has not admitted to me that she killed Michael Summerton, but the trauma of killing the man she loved would have been sufficient to have created an amnesiac "blocking" of events. She could well have committed the murder in a state of "automatism", which is a prolonged period of abnormal behaviour and impaired awareness, her subconscious only allowing her to remember events after Summerton's death. One memory which she does have and which she has not disclosed to the police is that she remembers wetting the bed and she also remembers that in her dreams Summerton was dying and she was powerless to help him. The effect of alcohol on her I am unable to establish but as this was combined with smoking cannabis, she could have been experiencing the effect of a "black out" and this physical phenomenon is common and, usually, irreversible. Her blood alcohol level was high when taken two hours after arrest and, in my opinion, high enough to conclude that she would indeed have suffered an alcohol-related amnesia and that she would be highly susceptible to suggestions she had killed Michael Summerton.

'Since the death of Mr Summerton, Miss Forbes reports disturbed sleep, distressing dreams that wake her up leaving her sweating, shaking and very fearful. Equally distressing to her is the fact that she does sometimes wet the bed. This brings back other disturbing memories which she finds hard to cope with and which she prefers not to discuss. Occasionally during waking hours Miss Forbes has recurrent and fearful recollections of the event. Some situations remind her of the night of Michael's death and she experiences tightness in the chest and a subsequent choking feeling.

'On our first meeting she had very little recall either of prior events or of the arrival of the police. On our subsequent meeting she had better recall.

'In general, I feel that Miss Forbes is suffering from a newly recognized psychiatric disorder, PTSD – post-traumatic stress disorder – and according to the various American scales I have used she reaches the higher levels. Her psychiatric condition before the event is hard to judge, although her main anxiety seems to have revolved around Michael Summerton leaving her for another woman. According to her recollections of her life since she met him, she was sleeping well, eating well and managing to hold down a waitressing job. Only occasionally does she recall feeling particularly anxious and irritable towards him and this usually coincided with the third week of her menstrual cycle.

'In my opinion, it may take two or three years for her to recover and I would suggest counselling therapy and a course of anti-depressants.'

'He's sitting on the proverbial fence, isn't he?' said O'Neill, annoyed that it all seemed so inconclusive. 'And the judge's final words are very brief – I'll read it to you' – he flicked through the pages quickly – 'Here it is,' he said after a few moments. ' "Miss Carole Ann Forbes, you have pleaded guilty to murder. Although you killed Michael Summerton in a state of drink and drug intoxication, this is no defence in law. I have no course open to me other than to sentence you to the mandatory sentence of life imprisonment", et cetera.'

'She could well have done it.'

'She could, but she didn't,' said O'Neill. 'And for some reason she only spent ten years in prison. Perhaps someone at the Home Office had their doubts too.' He felt more sure now that she hadn't done it. But why he felt so certain he didn't know.

'Connor, I know you want her to be innocent but it all points to her being a killer. I know she's attractive and seems docile but she may not be quite what she appears.'

'Her looks have nothing to do with it,' snapped O'Neill.

Fran smiled. 'If she was piggy-eyed and thin as a stick with a scar down one cheek and an aggressive nature, would you feel the same way?'

O'Neill, annoyed that Fran had perhaps got a point, said, 'Two strange men didn't betray her, did they?'

'They may have done,' murmured Fran. 'Or perhaps she was premenstrual at the time.'

'I wouldn't know about that,' said O'Neill uncomfortably.

What he should have said to Fran was that he didn't understand women as well as he would have liked. He'd had no sisters and he hadn't understood his wife's mood changes until it was too late. He stared out into the darkness knowing that in the morning he'd have to bring Carole Ann in for questioning. What unnerved him about that was that maybe she'd confess. Confess to two murders he was damned sure she didn't commit.

'Do you mind if I go home now, boss, just to get a couple of hours sleep?'

'I'll drive you.'

'There's no need, I can walk.'

'You'll not be walking,' he said with a smile.

Fran shrugged wearily, she didn't really mind if she had to fly home on his back as long as she got to her bed.

On the short drive home he said, 'We're needing some feedback from the prison service, Fran. She spent two years in Holloway. You can start there. I'll bring her in for questioning and you'll have to be going to London on your own. Ringstead couldn't cope with the two of us away from Fowchester – especially together.'

'You mean tomorrow, boss?'

'That's what I'm meaning.'

It was 3 a.m. when Fran finally got to bed and the tiredness left her the moment her head hit the pillow. She lay with her eyes closed, her brain scrambling information into random slots. And none of it made sense.

The knife figured largely in her thoughts. A knife that had broken. An old, well-used knife or just a cheap knife that broke under the strain? Had Carole Ann borrowed a knife from Enid Braithwaite's kitchen and had anyone thought to ask?

Chapter Nineteen

The Governor of Holloway prison, Mrs Elizabeth Thornton, greeted Fran with tea and biscuits in a small sitting room that adjoined her office.

'If we talk in the office we'll be disturbed all the time. This is my retreat and woe betide anyone who comes in here.' She laughed cheerfully. 'Often if I'm going out I change in here, which is one of the reasons no one comes in.'

Mrs Thornton was, thought Fran, with a certain amount of envy, one of those women who managed to be charming and feminine and yet have an air of confidence and authority. She was tall, at least five nine, wore a soft green trouser suit with a white blouse; her understated make-up gave her a youthful look, and although she was too angular to be called pretty, she was certainly chic. Her dark hair was plaited at the back to sit neatly on her head, and with shrewd brown eyes she managed to observe Fran even as she poured the tea.

'I've only been at Holloway for two years so I don't know Carole Ann Forbes personally, but I do have her records. I hope they'll be of some help.'

Mrs Thornton began flicking through a dossier on her lap. 'It seems that Forbes was very depressed for a year after admission. She saw the prison doctor several times – mostly about sleeplessness, which of course is very common here. One of the senior officers managed to get her interested in gardening and her mental state improved after that.'

'So she was never in any trouble?'

'It doesn't appear so from the records.'

'What about visitors?'

'She didn't have any. Though in her second year she did request a prison visitor.'

'Nina Gardener?'

Mrs Thornton shook her head. 'No . . . let me check.' She hurriedly turned the pages. 'No, as I thought, Hilary Markham.'

Fran felt at a loss. 'No visitors at all?'

'I'm afraid it is common for some prisoners to have no visitors. Either their friends or relatives abandon them or they didn't have anyone in the first place. Happy stable home lives are, I'm afraid, a rarity among the prison population. But according to this she did have regular letters.'

'Who from?'

'A Josephine Price. A penfriend.'

'Penfriend?'

'Yes. It happens. Someone on the outside reads the case in the paper and decides to get in touch.'

'Why?'

Mrs Thornton smiled. 'I'm not sure – identifying with the prisoner in some way. Either with the crime or the person's background or just their looks. There does seem to be some element of . . . attraction in general.'

'You mean lesbian attraction?'

'In some cases. Sometimes after an exchange of letters the penfriend makes an application to visit.'

'And you allow that?'

'Yes. As you know we censor all post so we do have some idea of the nature of the letters.'

'Would that be recorded?'

'I'll look.' After a few moments of searching through the dossier Mrs Thornton smiled. 'There's no comment made on the letters so you can presume they were entirely innocent.'

'Are some not . . . innocent?'

'Censoring letters is very much resented by the women here, as you can imagine. However, it does protect many of them from hate mail and death threats.'

'Is that common?'

'With certain crimes, yes. It's particularly associated with crimes involving children. More recently, as society seems to have become more violent, we do seem to have more prisoners convicted of murdering husbands or lovers. Then the hate mail is predominantly from men.'

'Or men writing as women?'

Mrs Thornton frowned thoughtfully. 'Yes, that's a possibility.'

Fran finished her tea and chewed on a biscuit and then said, 'Does it seem odd to you that this Josephine Price didn't visit?'

'Not at all. I think most penfriends remain just that. Perhaps an actual meeting might destroy a few illusions, and of course many people don't wish to enter a prison, under any circumstances.'

As Fran was about to leave, Mrs Thornton said, 'If it would help, I could introduce you to the senior wing officer, Joan Norman, she's one of our longest-serving staff and I think she got to know Forbes quite well.'

Fran thanked her and Mrs Thornton accompanied her to B wing. Holloway reminded Fran of a run-down school, more so when she saw how young some of the prisoners were. Her senses were almost overwhelmed by the smells and the noise. The corridors seemed to emit the odour of female bodies and cheap scent, all overladen with cooking smells and disinfectant. As she walked on, it began to remind her more of a hospital; trolleys trundled, keys jangled, noisy footsteps paced up and down. Occasionally the far-off sound of raucous laughter circulated and seemed to bounce off the bare walls. Then came a piercing scream and the sound of sobbing, and raised voices, and Fran wanted to be out of it. It suddenly all seemed so oppressive, a tight little world on its own. A world of unhappy troubled women . . .

'Here we are,' said the Governor at the entrance to the B wing office.

Joan Norman was plump and grey-haired with a ready smile but rather sad blue eyes. On her navy uniform, hanging from a chain around her waist, was a huge bunch of keys. Mrs Thornton shook Fran's hand. 'I'll leave you in Joan's capable hands, Miss Wilson. Good luck with your investigation.'

'Come on in, love,' said Joan Norman. 'Take a pew.'

The office comprised a desk, a padlocked filing cabinet, a few chairs, a potted fern and a tiny barred window high up in the wall. On the desk were an overflowing ashtray and an untidy array of used mugs and scraps of paper. 'We all use this office – it's always a mess. Do you want a cigarette?'

Fran nearly answered yes. She did want one. She swallowed hard, took a deep breath and said, 'I gave up.'

'Well, good for you. I'll give up as soon as I retire from this job. Now, I believe you want to know about Carole Ann Forbes.'

Fran nodded.

'I got to know her quite well,' said Joan, pausing to caress an unlit cigarette between her fingers. 'She was in a bad way at first. I thought she might have to go with the "dollies"—'

'Dollies?'

'We call them that – those who shouldn't really be here. The disturbed ones – cutting themselves, screaming, crying, head-banging, that sort of thing.'

'Was she violent?'

Joan shook her head. 'Funny that, she was here two years and I saw her provoked on several occasions – she never rose to the bait. She was quiet and passive. If you told her to stand on her head for half an hour she would. They can be a worry, the quiet ones. I prefer them with a bit more spirit – it's more normal.'

'Did she form any relationships?'

'You mean lesbian?'

'Friendships?'

Joan lit her cigarette and thought for a moment. 'There was one woman she took to – Trish. Trish had a great sense of humour, always in a good mood although why she was so cheerful beats me. She was a lifer – set fire to her mother's house with her mother in it. Lucky she didn't get Broadmoor.'

'Is Trish still here?'

'No, she was transferred some years ago. She's still doing time.'

Fran had to ask the question now that she hadn't asked the Governor. 'Joan, do you think Forbes murdered her lover? You've had years of experience and must have known many murderers in that time.'

Joan smiled. 'Hundreds, love, but I'll tell you this – sober she wouldn't have done it. More than half the women here have committed crimes under the influence of drink and drugs. Alcohol affects everyone differently but I'll tell you this – there aren't many it makes a better person.'

That was it, thought Fran, no one would hazard a real opinion. There was only one thing she could do. Go back to the scene of the crime. See the room where it happened. Talk to as many people as possible. Find some evidence either way.

Belsize Park was much leafier than the Holloway Road. It had a certain faded grandeur. The houses along the avenue were tall, at least five storeys, but on many the white paint had become grey, the window frames had begun to rot and large families no longer lived in them. They were inhabited by ones or twos living their lives in expensive bedsits, paying for the privilege of more trees and slightly less traffic. Fran had once lived in a multi-occupied dwelling. It had been like living in a house of ghosts – people came and went but you never actually spoke to them.

Number 14 was so run down that for a moment Fran thought the whole house leaned slightly. The five steps up to the porched front door were crumbling; an empty hamburger packet lay alongside a crushed can of strong lager on the second step down. The front door had the benefit of an intercom system but it didn't look as if it needed a system, the wood was rotting and a hefty shove from anyone of reasonable strength would have allowed entrance.

Fran guessed the blank nameplate at the bottom corresponded to the basement and she rang the bell.

'Who is it?' said a male voice.

'CID. Detective Sergeant Wilson.'

There was no reply, but after a few minutes Fran could hear footsteps and then the door opened. The man at the door was unshaven, with greasy black hair, and wore a black armless vest and blue jeans with a fat frill of gut jutting above his leather belt. His arms were muscular and hairy and he smelled strongly of fried food and body odour. Fran supposed he was in his late forties. She vaguely hoped he wasn't the landlord of yesteryear but she had a strong suspicion he was.

'Mr Joseph Peters?' she queried.

He nodded. 'You got some ID?'

She nodded and showed him her warrant card.

'What's it about?'

'It's about one of your tenants of ten years ago.'

'What have they done? Still in arrears with their poll tax?'

Fran scowled at Peters, hoping to look faintly intimidating.

'No,' she said tersely. 'Carole Ann Forbes.'

'Oh, her!'

'Yes. I'd like to ask you some questions.'

'Christ Almighty . . . not again. I thought that was over years ago.' He stared at Fran with a semi-leer on his face. 'You'd better come in. At least you're better looking than the other cops who came.'

She followed him down the dark stairs to the basement. As they got to the bottom the naked light bulb died.

'It's on a timer,' he explained. 'Makes the inmates get a move on when they come in.'

The basement room was a room for all seasons, and all of them winter. It was dark, there were bars at the window, from which came only a faint stream of sunlight. In one corner was a state-of-the-art TV showing Sky news to a bucket-shaped black leather armchair. There was a mini-bar set out on a round table and a full ashtray on the floor. The air reeked of cannabis.

'You'd better sit down,' he said as he pulled a pine chair from beside a gate-legged table and placed it by the side of the armchair. He sat down, crossed his legs and said, 'Get on with it.'

Fran's unease increased now that she had sat down. She wanted to tell him to switch off the TV but she almost feared being in a silent room with him. She now knew what people meant when they called their TV 'company'.

'I believe you were the owner-occupier when Carole Ann Forbes and Michael Summerton lived here.'

'That's right.'

'What were they like as tenants?'

His small brown eyes narrowed and he smirked. 'They weren't bloody angels. Especially at weekends, that's when they went out boozing.'

'Were they noisy?'

'Only when they came in. That bloody front door opens and closes at night every five bloody minutes. Drives me daft.'

'Do you live here alone?'

'I do now. My wife buggered off about six years ago with a half-blind piano tuner. Good riddance to both of them.'

'How did you get on personally with Miss Forbes?'

There was a long pause and again that leery smile. 'All right as long as she paid the rent.'

'And the night of the murder?'

'What about it?'

'Did you hear anything?'

'I said at the trial – I heard them come in laughing and joking. I heard them go up the stairs—.'

'You're sure it was them?'

'Are you bloody joking?'

Fran shrugged and said lightly, 'Just testing.'

'I went up in the morning for the rent. They paid weekly then, now it's monthly. I knocked on the door, banged and banged. I thought they were trying to pull a fast one so I used my master key and let myself in. And there she was all covered in blood, and shaking. And he was dead as a dodo.'

'Did she say anything?'

He shook his head. 'She was well out of it.'

'You mean she was in shock?'

'I was in bloody shock. I didn't think she was the type.'

Fran stared at him. 'Why wasn't she the type?'

He shrugged. 'Well, she was a quiet sort really. I know she liked a drink, but she was never stroppy. And anyway, Summerton was the boss; she'd do anything he said. Anything – get my drift?'

Fran wasn't sure that she did. 'Could you expand on that? What do you mean exactly?'

'If they were short of money she'd . . . work extra hours. She did lunch-time waitressing at a place in Hampstead . . . and—' He broke off, looking uncomfortable.

'Mr Peters, if you don't cooperate I shall nick you anyway.'

'What bloody for?'

'Using cannabis, keeping an unruly house, anything you like.'

He blustered a bit more, looked at Fran with pure hatred and then said, 'OK. Trial's long gone, isn't it? They can't do me for perjury now – mind you, I only didn't tell the whole truth because I didn't want her to go down. It didn't make much difference anyway, did it?'

Fran nodded. 'She would have gone down anyway – she pleaded guilty. What could you have said that would have helped her?'

'Nothing much, only that Summerton bloke wasn't the angel she made him out to be. She was dead loyal right to the end.'

'Just tell me.'

He held his head on one side as he spoke and Fran felt his eyes flickering over her body.

'In that last year before he copped it they had trouble paying the rent. It was only her wages they lived on and it wasn't much. One day she came down here when my wife was out. She said Michael had sent her. She had her rent book in her hand, she seemed all nervous, like, and tearful. After a bit of a rigmarole she tells me that Michael says she's got to pay the rent.'

'So?'

'You're not quick, are you? She was offering herself as rent money. Well, I couldn't refuse, could I? She was beautiful.'

Fran felt her stomach heave. 'Did it happen again?'

'No, worse luck. After that they seemed to find the rent, until that morning. I like it paid on Fridays, see, before they spend it on booze.'

'Do you think Summerton was her pimp from then on?'

He shook his head and laughed. 'Shouldn't think so. She was bloody useless. She cried all the way through.'

'How do you think they paid the rent, then, after that?'

'He was selling, no doubt about that.'

'Selling what?'

'Anything he could get his hands on – cannabis, heroin, uppers, downers, LSD. You name it, he sold it.'

'Do you think she knew?'

An expression passed across his face which made him look less cocksure. 'I do think she was a bit slow on the uptake about some things. I don't mean she was thick, but he'd tell her he'd sold another painting and she believed him. Well, like she said at her trial, she loved him – silly bitch.'

'But she smoked cannabis?'

'A lot of people did, even more now. He only smoked cannabis, he wasn't daft enough to take anything stronger.'

'Why didn't you say this at the trial? And don't give me that crap about worrying about Carole Ann.'

Taking a cigarette from a pack on the floor, he lit it and stared at her through the smoke. 'This place then was full of cannabis and other drugs. Now it's clean apart from my bit of cannabis but you have to look after yourself, don't you – no other bugger will. At that time I just wanted to keep the police off my back.'

'Is that how you acquired this place? Looking after yourself?'

'No need to start being clever,' said Peters with a sneer. 'It was all quite legit. A relative left it to me. I expect he bought with the proceeds of crime but I wasn't going to ask any questions, was I?'

Fran sighed inwardly and struggled to be polite with the creep. 'Thank you for your help. Before I go I would like to speak to anyone else who lived here at the time.'

'You won't get much out of them. There's two of them. One's daft as a brush, the other's a bit deaf. On the ground floor, adjacent to each other's rooms – 2 and 3.'

Fran walked back up the dark stairs with the knowledge that Peters was watching her. Poor Carole Ann, no wonder she cried and how desperate things must have been to make her have sex with the landlord from hell.

As she waited for the occupant of the door marked '2' to answer her knock, it crossed Fran's mind that maybe in a drunken state Carole Ann thought she was stabbing not Michael, but her rotten landlord.

'Hello, Sofia,' said a high-pitched voice as the door opened. The voice's owner was about four feet ten and was wearing a long blonde wig. Round her tiny shoulders a purple shawl was pinned with a huge black brooch. Her face was pinched and wizened, her grey eyes furtively looking to the right and left of Fran.

'I'm not Sofia,' said Fran. 'I'm Fran Wilson, police.'

The old lady stared at her through round gold-rimmed glasses. 'You look like Sofia,' she said. 'Come in, come in and talk to me.'

The large bedsitting room was swathed in purple: purple curtains, lavender walls, a purple tablecloth, even the plants ranged along the windowsill were purple-flowering African violets.

'Drink, Sofia?'

'I'm not Sofia,' repeated Fran.

'Yes. You told me. Police. But you look like Sofia.'

'Who is Sofia?' asked Fran, thinking she should get this straight from the beginning.

'She's my daughter. She's so pretty. She's just like you – lovely dark hair. Have a drink . . . I'll pour you a drink.'

'No thank you,' said Fran, but the old lady took no notice and began pouring generously from a decanter into two huge wine glasses.

'There you are, Sofia. It's good sherry, your favourite.'

Fran took the offered glass and sipped. It was good.

'Now come and sit down, dear.' The two armchairs, complete with purple throw-over covers, were facing an unlit electric fire. There was no television or radio. The only signs of a 'hobby' were an empty embroidery frame that lay forlornly on the cream candlewick bedspread covering the single bed and a pile of *National Geographic* magazines that lay in a pile near the front bay window.

Once they had both sat down, Fran said, 'You're very kind, Mrs—?'

'Dorothea Hawkins. But I'm called Dotty.'

I'm not surprised, thought Fran. 'Can you try to remember back to ten years ago?'

Dotty laughed a high-pitched, slightly maniacal laugh. 'I can remember back to seventy years ago – wonderful days. I was a ballerina, you know. Just look at my legs' She lifted her long black skirt to well above the knee to show a leg a sparrow would have been ashamed of.

'Splendid legs,' said Fran approvingly. 'But could we just go back a few years to when Carole Ann Forbes and Michael Summerton lived in the attic room?'

Dotty took a huge swig of sherry and fixed Fran with a steady gaze. Her glasses had slipped further down her thin nose and Fran had to look away.

'Sofia, you mean,' said Dotty with a slight note of aggression in her voice.

'No,' said Fran firmly. 'Carole Ann Forbes – fair hair, very pretty.'

'Of course I remember her. I'm not stupid. I used to be a ballerina.'

Fran waited and watched Dotty's glasses as they slipped still further down the nose. 'Did you say you were from the police?'

'I'm a detective sergeant.'

'I was a ballerina.'

Fran fixed a smile on her face and tried again. 'Carole Ann Forbes – you do remember her, don't you?'

'She's in prison.'

'She's out now.'

Dotty smiled. 'Well, I am glad. Sofia was a lovely girl.'

'Sofia?'

'I called her Sofia. I call everyone I like Sofia. She's my daughter.'

Fran began to feel she wasn't just losing the battle, she was fighting with matchsticks against swords.

'Carole Ann Forbes – tell me about her, Mrs Hawkins.'

'Call me Dotty.'

'Dotty – tell me. Did you talk to her?'

Dotty grinned lopsidedly, 'Of course I did. She liked my sherry. She was a nice girl.'

'What about Michael?'

'I liked Michael too. He used to give me stuff.'

'What stuff?'

'You know,' said Dotty with a sly smile.

'Tell me.'

'He used to give me smokes.'

'Cigarettes?'

'No, cannabis.'

'He sold it to you?'

'No, he gave it to me.'

Fran nodded but she found it hard to believe, although looking at Dotty anything was possible. 'Did you like it?'

'I didn't smoke it. I don't approve of smoking.'

'What did you do with it?'

'I sold it, dear, of course.'

Of course, thought Fran. How very normal for an old-age pensioner! 'Tell me, Dotty, did you hear anything the night Michael died?'

Dotty suddenly leaned forward to peer closely at Fran's face. 'That's what the policeman asked me.'

'And what did you say?'

Dotty grinned and then laughed. 'Nothing. I didn't like him. He had a big list of questions with him – he wouldn't sit down and he wouldn't have a sherry. I couldn't trust him. You can't trust someone like that. I tried to tell him that I'd been a ballerina but he wouldn't listen, so I said I couldn't remember—' She laughed at the memory.

'So you did hear something?'

'I saw them. I peeped through the curtains and I saw them. They were drunk, fooling about.'

'And that was all?'

'I didn't say that was all, did I? I watch people coming and going all the time. I don't need television.'

'So you heard something else?'

'I didn't say that, did I?'

Fran waited.

Dotty stared at Fran's empty glass and said, 'Have another sherry, Sofia, and I'll tell you.'

Dotty seemed to totter slightly as she walked over to the sherry on the sideboard, but she poured another large measure and with a steady hand carried it back slowly and carefully.

151

'You can see how graceful I am, can't you, dear? It's in the blood, you know.'

Fran looked around for somewhere to get rid of her latest drink. She sidled towards a potted fern and when Dotty looked away poured most of it into the compost. 'We were talking about the night before Michael Summerton was killed,' Fran said firmly.

'So we were, dear, so we were. As I said, I didn't hear any more but I did see something.'

'What did you see?' Fran tried to keep both the excitement and the impatience from her voice.

'Someone followed them in. They left the door open and I saw someone follow them in.'

'What did he look like?'

'It wasn't a he, dear. It was a woman.'

Chapter Twenty

O'Neill was surprised by the early morning phone calls. The first was a breathy-voiced individual – a man, definitely, but trying, with not much success, to sound like a woman. The message, though, was quite clear. 'Nina Gardener is a lying, two-faced bitch. Ask where she was on the night of the murders.'

'Sure I will,' said O'Neill calmly. 'And thank you for calling . . . sir.'

He'd hardly had time to digest that call before Ringstead rang.

'Today, O'Neill. Bring her in today! This is your last warning. I'm off to a meeting in Birmingham today and when I come back I want to see her name on the holding list.'

'I'll have to be arranging for a police matron to come in.'

'Arrange for Mother Teresa to come in. I don't bloody care. Just bring her in.'

O'Neill smiled to himself, knowing that Ringstead's face would be puce and sweating by now. 'Certainly, sir, she'll be in today. Wilson's gone to London, by the way. She's tracking down . . . let's just say she's helping the cause.'

Ringstead slammed down the phone.

O'Neill took his spare shaving gear and spare shirt from his locker and went into the cloakroom. As he shaved he thought about the first call. He bet himself a fiver it was Dave Reynolds.

He'd already looked up Reynolds' criminal record. True, he'd held up a few building societies, and in one exchange a six-feet-three ex-marine had rugby-tackled him and Reynolds had lashed out with a chair leg masquerading as a shotgun. He'd gone down for GBH because the marine had needed stitches, but in the annals of violent crime it could have been termed self-defence. Once charged with GBH, Reynolds could hold his head up in prison and O'Neill knew that was important in the criminal fraternity. Certain crimes had status, made you a man to be reckoned with, sometimes challenged by a 'harder' man but, nevertheless, not to be despised.

Before 8 a.m. O'Neill was on his way to Magham Green and the home of Charles and Nina Gardener. The early sun was soft and hazy and the day promised to be hot. The imposing house, isolated about half a mile from the village, was set back from the road by a winding path bordered by trees and bushes and a bank of wild flowers and weeds. The lawn in front of the house was neat and weed-free. Various surrounding trees gave a bower-like feeling to the house and a small stream overhung with a weeping willow ran to the right of the house.

Charles was driving out of the garage as he approached. He stopped the car immediately, got out and stood waiting for O'Neill.

'Chief Inspector. What brings you here so early this fine morning?'

O'Neill smiled. 'It's a grand day, all right, Mr Gardener. I've just come to have a chat with your wife, about . . . Carole Ann Forbes. Your wife was her prison visitor, I believe.'

Charles nodded. 'I'd like to be present, if you don't mind.'

'That's fine by me,' said O'Neill amiably.

Charles let himself into the house by the front door. It felt cool inside and the scent of fresh cut flowers hung in the air.

'Nina's upstairs somewhere; I'll give her a shout. Nina!' he called loudly.

When there was no response Charles showed O'Neill through to the study. On a large mahogany desk facing the window was a word processor and one leather-backed chair. The walls were lined with book shelves and O'Neill noticed Charles's reading taste didn't extend much beyond law books and Greek myths.

'Nina!' Charles shouted again.

O'Neill heard her call out, 'Have you forgotten something, darling?'

'The police are here,' Charles shouted back as if the whole of Fowchester police had arrived.

Moments later Nina appeared. She was dressed in white cotton slacks and a blue and white striped cotton top. She looked fresh and unconcerned. She smiled at Charles. 'Why the study, darling? There's nowhere to sit.'

Charles shrugged and introduced O'Neill.

'Come through to the kitchen, Chief Inspector,' said Nina with a

154

friendly smile. 'It's very pleasant there in the summer and you get a wonderful view of Charles's flower beds, of which he's very proud – aren't you, darling?'

Charles didn't reply and O'Neill caught a scent of tension in the air as pungent as the smell of flowers.

The kitchen was large and rustic, a new Aga sat in what had once been a large fireplace, the floor was quarry tiled and in the centre of a long pine table was a blue ceramic pot filled with white stocks. The morning sunshine drifted in through the window and O'Neill lost his desire for a bachelor flat and decided he wouldn't mind playing the country squire . . .

'It's lovely, isn't it? My favourite room of the whole house,' said Nina as if she'd guessed what he was thinking.

'You'll have coffee, won't you? What about you, darling, aren't you going to the office?'

'All in good time,' said Charles.

O'Neill noticed that Nina swallowed nervously and kept her back towards them as she made coffee in a percolator.

'You haven't asked, Nina, what the Chief Inspector is here for.'

She turned then. 'I guessed, Charles. He obviously wants to know about Carole Ann.'

'How long have you known her, Mrs Gardener?'

Nina's eyes left the percolator for a moment and she smiled prettily at O'Neill. 'About two years or so. When she transferred to an open prison she requested a new visitor.'

'What did you talk about on your visits, Mrs Gardener?'

She shrugged and ran a hand through her hair. 'Anything and everything, really. A mixed bag.'

'Leave the coffee for a moment, Nina, and come and sit down,' said Charles. With a reluctant last look at the percolator Nina sat down at the top end of the table.

'And what did you make of her?' asked O'Neill, gazing at her steadily.

'I liked her. She was sometimes depressed and a little excitable but we did have a certain rapport. I shouldn't have got involved with her at all, but I did. I felt sorry for her. It was a mistake.'

'I wouldn't have said she was excitable,' said Charles.

'You only met her once, darling.'

Nina's voice, O'Neill noticed, had become a little snappy and nervous.

155

'I'm quite a good judge of character, Chief Inspector,' said Charles, glaring at his wife, 'and I found her, on the one occasion I did meet her, to be rather charming and quiet.'

'That was only because she admired your garden and she needed a job.'

O'Neill could see in Nina Gardener's face the realization that she had disclosed her feelings too easily. She began to backtrack. 'I really don't mean to sound bitchy but she seems to think I can produce a job for her from thin air. I actually don't have that many contacts. Charles is the one with contacts.'

'Don't underestimate yourself, darling,' said Charles. 'Your contacts with the criminal world are legion.'

Nina pursed her lips and O'Neill noticed that small wet patches had begun to show underneath her arms. The kitchen was warm, but not that warm. She stood up. 'Coffee's ready,' she said.

While Nina was pouring coffee Charles said, almost casually, 'You knew that chap that was murdered, didn't you, darling? The first one – Alan Lattaway.'

The cup chinked loudly in the saucer and after a moment's pause she said, 'I told you, darling, he called by one day wanting me to buy some insurance.'

'And did you?' asked O'Neill. Nina carried the coffee towards him, her hand trembled slightly but she managed to set the cup and saucer down quite gently.

'Answer the Chief Inspector, darling. I'll see to the other coffees.'

Nina's eyes flickered towards her husband as he stood up.

O'Neill realized it wasn't police reaction she was concerned about; she seemed wary of her husband, even scared. She put her hand to her mouth and then said softly, 'He spoke to me about life insurance in general. I said I'd think about it but my husband was more than adequately insured.'

Charles walked back, put down the coffee and stared straight at his wife. After a momentary expression of unease she looked away.

'Do you deal with all household bills and financial matters, Mr Gardener?' asked O'Neill.

'Of course,' said Charles, as if he'd never contemplated his wife doing such a thing.

'And do you have a private income, Mrs Gardener?'

She shook her head.

'Why do you ask?' demanded Charles.

O'Neill stared at Nina. She coloured slightly under his gaze. Then she turned to look at her husband. 'He's asking, Charles, because he knows I took out a small policy with Alan Lattaway.'

'What sort of policy, Nina?' asked Charles coldly.

'A combined life and pension plan, darling. Something I could have afforded from the housekeeping.'

'Why didn't you tell me, darling?'

O'Neill sat back in the chair and watched them. Charles, with straight back and seemingly in control, was, O'Neill noticed, clenching and unclenching his fists. The tension showed in his jaw; his words were clipped and his eyes glittered with anger. Nina, too, was tense but she showed this mainly in the slight flush of her cheeks and the occasional fluttery hand movements she made.

Eventually she said, 'I didn't tell you, darling, because I didn't think you would approve, especially as he wasn't our usual broker and as he came to the door.'

'And as he was good-looking?'

'I didn't notice.'

Charles smiled coldly. 'Must be the first time, darling. You know you have a very discerning eye.'

'Please, Charles, not now. The Chief Inspector doesn't want to hear us squabbling.'

'Later then, darling,' said Charles with a smile that could only be described as menacing.

O'Neill began to feel uneasy, wondering if Nina was actually safe in the house. But he had a job to do and questions to ask, and what could he actually do about it? Could he separate them?

'Mr Gardener, I would be appreciating it if you would allow me to speak to your wife alone. You're both seeming a little stressed at the moment.'

'I'll stay, Chief Inspector. This is my home. And I've left my wife alone with too many men in the past. Nina can't help it – she's a predatory woman and I have to think of your safety as well.'

'Charles, how could you—' Nina's eyes began to fill with tears of humiliation.

'You could be coming down to the station to make a statement, Mrs Gardener,' suggested O'Neill.

Nina made obvious efforts to control herself. She took a deep breath, changed her position in the chair, sipped at her coffee. 'No, I'll stay here. I've done nothing . . . wrong. I bought the policy. I saw him again after that twice. Once on signing and once when he brought me the actual policy.'

'And what did you think when you heard he had been murdered?'

'Think? What do you mean?'

'I mean, Mrs Gardener, do you suspect anyone?'

'No, no, of course not. Why would I suspect anyone? I didn't know him well. I knew nothing about him.'

'You knew he liked fishing. Men who like fishing talk about it.'

'I . . . suppose so, but that doesn't mean—'

'That you killed him?'

'This is ridiculous, Chief Inspector,' said Charles. 'My wife may have her little . . . flings. But she's no killer – that's unthinkable.'

'Is it, sir? Perhaps your wife would tell us both where she was on the night of Alan Lattaway's death.'

There was a slight pause before Nina said, 'I was at home, of course.'

'All evening?'

'Yes . . . of course.'

'And you, Mr Gardener?'

'Me? Surely you don't think—'

'Where were you on the night in question?' persisted O'Neill.

'At a Round Table dinner, a men-only do.'

'What time did you come home?'

Charles straightened his tie. 'I suppose it was about one, maybe quarter past one.'

'Did you drive home?'

'Yes, I only drank two glasses of wine the whole evening so I wasn't over the limit.'

'And was your wife in when you came home?'

'Yes, of course.'

'She was in bed?'

Charles looked towards Nina. 'When I come home late I sleep in the spare room so that I don't disturb her.'

'I see,' said O'Neill. 'So, in fact, you didn't see her.'

'Not exactly. But you were in, weren't you, darling?'

'Of course I was, Charles. I had an extremely boring evening.'

'And you were alone, Mrs Gardener?'

Nina's eyes sparkled angrily. 'I thought I'd made that quite clear. Of course I was alone.'

'No phone calls?'

'No one phoned me, I can assure you, Chief Inspector.'

O'Neill paused. 'Where was the Round Table dinner, sir?'

Charles frowned. 'The hotel on the main road. The Moat House.'

O'Neill nodded. 'About five minutes away from Fowchester, in fact.'

'Yes, I suppose so.'

'And did you leave the dinner party at any point?'

'What for? What exactly are you getting at?'

O'Neill stared directly at Charles. 'I'm trying to eliminate you from my list of suspects.'

'For God's sake, man, do you really think I would risk my career to murder some man because he sold my wife an insurance policy?'

'That does sound far-fetched, sir, but jealousy is a strange emotion capable of making fools of us all. And we all know this is about more than just an insurance policy.'

Charles looked about to respond angrily but instead stayed silent and glanced across to his wife as though she could help him out in some way.

O'Neill stood up. 'I shall be back, sir. I'm off now to interview Carole Ann Forbes.'

Charles Gardener's relief was obvious and in a show of solidarity with his wife he came to the front door with his arm around her shoulders. O'Neill noticed, though, that Nina wore a worried frown. At the front door she said, 'Chief Inspector . . . I—' She broke off.

'Goodbye, Chief Inspector,' said Charles firmly as he shut the front door.

O'Neill stood in the porch wondering what she had been about to say. He had to admit he was none the wiser. He was sure Nina had been having an affair with Alan Lattaway, but that didn't prove murder. Charles may well have slipped out of the Moat House Hotel that night, but how could he possibly know they would be meeting on the river bank – unless he'd followed her there before? That didn't explain why Patrick King had been killed. Unless he'd seen something that night and had to be silenced.

He was about to move away when he heard the raised voices

from inside the house. He couldn't hear what they were saying until Charles shouted loudly, 'You disloyal bitch.' The sharp crack of a slap followed and then the sounds of sobbing and footsteps running up the stairs. O'Neill stood there. Should he bang on the door? Or should he just ignore it? He'd interfered once before but that hadn't been a great success.

So he waited, telling himself that if there was a scream or more raised voices he might be forced to play the foolhardy hero again. But there was no sound and after a few minutes he left the porch and began walking towards his car.

Chapter Twenty-One

Fran paused outside the room marked '3'. Was talking to a deaf woman going to be much help? As far as she could see from the layout of the house this room also looked out on to the road, but if she was deaf she wouldn't have heard anything.

The tall woman with grey hair who opened the door wasn't quite what Fran expected. She was prematurely grey with the thick curly hair and unlined complexion of someone only just into their forties. She wore tight blue jeans and a navy T-shirt.

'I'm Fran Wilson, Detective Sergeant, Fowchester police,' she mouthed loudly and carefully.

The woman smiled. 'And I'm Ruth Baker. Resident of this dump. And not as deaf as you think. Come on in.'

The room was untidy and strewn with papers and brown manila envelopes. 'I look disorganized,' said Ruth. 'But I have an organized mind. What can I do for you? Do sit down if you can find a chair anywhere.'

Fran perched on the arm of the sofa – his time she didn't plan to stay long. 'I'm making enquiries about the death of Michael Summerton ten years ago.'

'Are you indeed?' she replied softly. 'There's no need to raise your voice, Sergeant. Two years ago I had an operation, a stapedectomy – my hearing is pretty good now. I was one of the lucky ones.'

Fran smiled. 'Your landlord seems to think you're still deaf.'

Ruth's generous mouth smiled back. 'I just pretend; the man's an absolute pig. Would you like a coffee? I'm just having a break. I need a break, I mark GCSE papers and A levels.'

It seemed churlish to refuse, and in a few minutes Ruth had produced coffee and chocolate biscuits and had scooped up some of the papers from the floor, table, sofa and chairs.

'Fire away, then, Sergeant. What info can I give you?' she said.

'Did you know Carole Ann Forbes?'

Ruth's blue eyes seemed to darken slightly. 'As much as any poor demented soul who lived here then. She was a nice girl, friendly, pleasant.'

'You thought she wasn't capable of murder?'

'I still don't. I've been writing to the Home Office for years to say that there has been a miscarriage of justice. But to no avail.'

'She's recently been freed, so perhaps your letters did have some effect.'

'Really! That's wonderful. I'm so pleased.' Ruth seemed genuinely delighted, but after a few moments said, 'The crafty devils. You know what they've done – released her early just to save a retrial. Friends of mine wrote too. Women are treated so unjustly in this country. A man would only have been tried for manslaughter.'

'Why are you so sure she didn't do it, Miss Baker?'

Ruth sipped at her coffee. 'I'm a night owl. It's true I didn't hear them come in that night. But in those days I had a cat – behind the landlord's back, as it were. Around midnight I let Tommy out – only in the summer months, he liked to wander when the air was warm. He'd be there on the doorstep in the morning. Anyway, that night the front door was slightly open. People often did that. The door's been patched up a bit since then. But in those days it needed a really good slam. I often felt the vibration.'

As Ruth Baker talked, Fran began taking notes.

'Anyway, for some reason,' continued Ruth, 'I looked up the stairs and caught a glimpse of someone. It was dark inside – because he fixes the timer so that people don't reach the top before the light goes out – but I saw someone. I wasn't to know what would happen and I must admit I wasn't concerned because so many people come and go and one doesn't know if they're residents or not. But it seems that Carole Ann and Michael came in moments before I opened my door – other residents heard them. And no one admitted to coming in after them.' She broke off, then said, 'I'm not going too fast, am I?'

Fran shook her head and smiled to encourage her flow.

'In the morning I opened the door and there was no cat. I got dressed immediately and went searching for him. I had no joy. When the police came calling I was very upset and I must admit, to my shame, I forgot about the figure on the stairs. I remembered later, of course, but because I was so deaf and because it was such a fleeting glimpse, I don't think they paid my statement much regard. I never found my cat and I missed him dreadfully. I didn't mention the cat to the police. I didn't want *him* to find out. I thought that in the future Tommy might return or I'd get another cat.'

'I'm sorry about your cat,' said Fran. 'Could you tell me one thing? Did you think the figure you saw was male or female?'

Ruth shook her head. 'I'm sorry. A shape in the darkness is hard to genderize. The clothes were dark, maybe black, but I did notice something – a trace of perfume in the air, but of course it could have been aftershave.'

Fran smiled ruefully. 'Is that the only reason you're convinced Carole Ann didn't kill Michael Summerton?'

'Not quite. She came in for a chat quite often just after she got back from work, before Michael came back from wherever he'd been. She had real patience – it's very lonely being deaf, you know, and so many people haven't got the time. Anyway, I digress, we did communicate one way or another, sometimes we talked by note. This particular day, she told me she thought someone was following Michael. It was obviously worrying her.'

'Did you tell the police after his death?'

'I did, but I don't think they believed me, I was somewhat well known by the police for being rather vocal on human rights issues. I'm not a popular person with the boys in blue.'

'Did Carole Ann have any idea who might be following Michael and why?'

'If she did, she didn't tell me.'

'Did you visit her in prison?'

Ruth shook her head. 'I wrote saying that I would come but she wrote back saying she would not appreciate my visiting.'

'Did she say why?'

'I knew why.'

'Why, Miss Baker?'

Ruth Baker stared at Fran and said slowly and carefully as though Fran were deaf, 'I'm surprised you haven't guessed, Detective Sergeant. I was in love with her.'

Fran was a little taken aback but she smiled and said, 'Just one more question, Miss Baker. What did you think of Michael Summerton?'

163

There was no hint of a smile now. 'I think, to be brutally honest, he was a lying little shit.'

'And why was that?'

Ruth paused for a moment to sip her coffee. 'For one thing, he had lots of visitors when she was at work, mostly women. For another, he was lazy and workshy. He was also dealing in drugs, but I don't think Carole Ann guessed it went beyond mere cannabis. I didn't tell her. She was in love and blind to his faults.'

'Did you mention all this to the police at the time?'

'I tried. But I think that it was far too much trouble to trace his contacts and, anyway, from what I've heard Carole Ann kept changing her plea. I think the police convinced her she'd done it.'

'Or she convinced herself.'

'Indeed,' murmured Ruth.

As Fran came out into the warm air of Belsize Park she breathed a sigh of relief. She walked purposefully towards Hampstead tube station, while other people ambled in shorts and summer clothes, enjoying the sunshine. She was deep in thought and worried. Three men dead. Three men killed in the same way and most probably by the same – experienced – hand. No, thought Fran, trained! A trained hand. Ex-army, perhaps. A mercenary. Capable of a stealthy and deadly approach. And, of course, if that was true, Carole Ann hardly fitted the profile. And the knife had never been found. But it was damaged. Someone in Fowchester had that broken knife. Someone connected with Carole Ann or Michael Summerton. But who?

Carole Ann hadn't seemed surprised when O'Neill called and suggested she might be able to help with their enquiries.

'Will I go straight back to prison?' she asked.

O'Neill smiled. ' "Enquiries" means what it says – I enquire and you answer.'

He couldn't help noticing the rose-coloured blouse she wore knotted at the waist over black leggings. Her hair she'd tied in a loose pony tail, she wore no make-up and she looked younger and more vulnerable.

As they left, Enid Braithwaite stood by the kitchen door and caught O'Neill by the sleeve. 'You listen to me, young man, I've been in this game for some years now – looking after ex-cons and bad ones – and I'll tell you this: she's a good one.' She let go of his sleeve to put a gnarled hand on Carole Ann's shoulders. 'Now you stick up for yourself, love, and don't be browbeaten into saying something you'll regret later. I know you didn't leave the house on those nights. I was here, I know what goes on. Understand . . . I know what goes on.'

At the station Carole Ann was booked in and her name added to the holding list. O'Neill had arranged for a police matron to be in attendance and she would provide meals and anything else Carole Ann might require. O'Neill hoped Carole Ann's stay wouldn't be too long, but her keenness to go back to prison might, in fact, prolong things.

He took her to an interview room, selected a detective constable called Stacey Robinson by looks alone, deciding he wanted one with a kind intelligent face and he'd let her set up the tape recorder.

Carole Ann sat, nervous and silent. Occasionally she stared round the windowless room. She refused coffee but asked if she could roll herself a cigarette and have an ashtray.

'I can get you some ready rolled if you like,' suggested O'Neill.

'I prefer to roll my own,' she said, not looking at him.

While DC Robinson went for the ashtray and coffee for O'Neill, he said, 'You're not under arrest, Carole Ann, I want to be reassuring you about that. But I think you may have to spend the night in the cells – and in the morning I'm sure we'll have finished our enquiries.'

She stared up at him with a slightly incredulous look on her face and seemed about to say something, but at that moment the DC arrived with the ashtray and coffee and the moment was lost. O'Neill switched on the recorder that sat on a shelf beside him and said, 'Right then . . . the time is 3 p.m, Wednesday 27 July 1994, at Fowchester Police Station. Those present: Detective Chief Inspector Connor O'Neill and Detective Constable Stacey Robinson. Interview commencing' – he glanced at his watch and waited – '3.01 p.m.'

He smiled reassuringly at Carole Ann, knowing that, nervous and fearful, she would take the easy course and reply in monosyllables. Quite where to start he didn't know. 'You'll be wanting to tell me about your time in prison,' he said. Carole Ann looked down at her tobacco and, taking a cigarette paper, she arranged the tobacco thinly along its length, raised the thin tube to eye level and then licked the edge of the paper and sealed it. 'I learned how to do this,' she said, 'and how to tend a garden.'

'How did you cope with prison life?' asked O'Neill as he signalled to DC Robinson to give her matches.

She lit the cigarette and inhaled deeply. 'I coped quite well after the first few months. It was safe in there.'

'Safe? What do you mean?'

'I mean, I didn't feel in any danger.'

'Among criminals? Didn't you feel safe living in Belsize Park with Michael?'

'I did until . . . until he died. Then I didn't feel safe any more.'

'Why not?'

'I don't know. I suppose I felt I should have died in his place. He was more talented than me. I was just a waitress.'

'So you felt guilty that you were alive?'

'Yes.'

'Are you sure that you didn't feel guilty because you'd killed him?'

She stared at the cigarette in her hand and then slowly raised her eyes to meet O'Neill's gaze. 'I don't know. I'm not sure. I felt guilty . . . but just for being alive. The other prisoners helped me feel less guilty. There are some victims on the outside but everyone is a victim in prison. It wasn't my fault I didn't die.'

'What exactly do you mean when you say "everyone is a victim in prison"?'

'I mean that if you're in prison it's because someone's let you down – cheated, lied, abused you, been cruel. Someone had to make you what you became.'

'Is that what Michael did? Did he harm you in any way?'

'No. We loved each other.'

'Who harmed you, then – making you into a victim?'

Carole Ann frowned. 'What are you trying to get me to say?'

'I'm not trying to trap you. I'm just trying to get at the truth. Let's go back to the night Michael died. You pleaded guilty. So I'm presuming you were thinking you were responsible.'

'I was.'

'In what way?'

'I could have—' She broke off.

'You could have saved him? Is that what you're going to say?'

'I don't know. You're confusing me. It was all clear . . . once. The police told me I must have done it. There was no one else there. My fingerprints were on the knife. He didn't have any enemies—'

'Are you sure about that?'

The blue eyes bored into O'Neill's. 'I'd known Michael from when we were very young. We had no secrets. We both did what we had to do. We had to survive.'

'And what did you do to survive?'

'We lived together, we loved and trusted each other. That's all.'

'What did you do to be surviving, Carole Ann? Do you mean money?'

Carole Ann shrugged and looked uneasy. She picked up the matchbox in front of her and began to play with it. O'Neill watched her steadily. She avoided his eyes and he could see she was becoming increasingly evasive. It was hard to know whether to push this line or move on. He decided to move on.

'Fair enough, Carole Ann,' he said gently. 'We'll be moving on now to the night Alan Lattaway was murdered.'

Carole Ann's hands dropped the matchbox as though it was red hot but she continued to stare at it silently.

O'Neill waited, he knew she'd speak in time; it was just a question of waiting. The minutes ticked slowly by. DC Robinson began to rearrange her feet. O'Neill stared at the top of Carole Ann's head and felt the beginnings of a strong desire to snatch the box away from her. But still he waited.

Eventually Carole Ann lifted her head. Her eyes had filled with tears. 'It must have been my fault,' she said miserably. 'I don't why, but it must—'

'Be explaining what you mean,' said O'Neill.

Carole Ann lowered her head and mumbled. 'Could I do these things and not know?

'Do what things?'

She looked up sharply. 'You know what I mean, Chief Inspector. Could I kill three men and not know. Could I be so mad that I could kill and not remember doing it?'

'It's unlikely, but . . . unhappy people do block out bad memories.'

Carole Ann seemed to stare into the distance. 'I have bad memories. People die in my dreams all the time.'

'What people?'

Shrugging, she said, 'I see Michael die and—'

'And your mother?'

This time there was a noticeable tremor of her hands and a widening of the eyes. 'What do you know about my mother?' she demanded.

O'Neill knew this nerve was the rawest of all. 'Tell me about her.'

'She's dead.'

'I know she's dead. Tell me how she died.'

There was another long pause before Carole Ann murmured, 'It was my fault – it was. She hanged herself because of me. She was in prison because of me—' She broke off, then continued, 'I'm a murderer.'

'Tell me why you'd think that, Carole Ann?'

O'Neill waited as, again, she lowered her eyes and then placed her hand across them. When she spoke again her voice was more angry. 'I'm around, and people die. And your soft voice doesn't fool me. You know I'm guilty so why don't you just stop playing this game?'

'Look at me, Carole Ann,' said O'Neill. 'Look at me and admit you killed those men by the river.'

Carole Ann didn't look up.

'Look at me,' repeated O'Neill.

This time she looked him straight in the eyes. 'I killed them. Shall I say it again and then you can arrest me?' This time she looked defiant, her eyes bright, her voice firm. 'I killed them,' she repeated. 'I killed them. I killed them.'

Chapter Twenty-Two

O'Neill cursed himself for generally cocking up, but all wasn't lost yet. 'Tell me how you did it, Carole Ann. Be explaining exactly how you killed two grown men.'

'I stabbed them,' she announced dully.

'What with?'

'With one of Miss Braithwaite's kitchen knives.'

'Where is it now?'

'I washed it and put it back.'

'Now tell me how you killed them. Starting from why you were on the river bank in the first place.'

'I went to meet Alan there. I'd seen him fishing before; we'd talked. I quite liked him. But then he attacked me, so I stabbed him in the chest.'

'Why did he attack you?'

'I don't know. I think he wanted sex.'

O'Neill let that pass. 'How many times? Show me.'

She raised her right arm high above her head and brought it down twice.

'He didn't raise his arms to try to defend himself?'

'He pushed me away but I came back at him.'

'And were you covered in blood?'

'Yes.'

'What did you do with your bloodstained clothes?'

'I put them in with the rubbish for collection.'

O'Neill stared at her. 'I'm thinking,' he said slowly, 'that the word "rubbish" is the most appropriate word you've used so far. It's all crap and you know it.'

Carole Ann's pretty blue eyes didn't blink.

'I'll give you one more chance, Carole Ann,' said O'Neill. He waited for her to respond. When she didn't, he said abruptly,

'Take her down, Constable. When she's ready to talk, let me know. Interview terminated at 3.45 p.m.' He switched off the machine.

Carole Ann stood up. 'Am I under arrest now?'

O'Neill shook his head. 'You're still helping us with our enquiries and I'd be grateful if you would try and do just that.'

'Have I made you angry?' she asked, looking worried.

'No. I'm disappointed that you couldn't tell me the truth, that's all.'

She paused for a moment in front of O'Neill but he'd already steeled himself not to look at her.

When she'd left the interview room O'Neill sighed; he didn't understand her. Probably never would. In his opinion men were much easier to interview. Even the devious, cunning ones tried to be too clever, too devious – plied lie upon lie until one lie too many trapped them. Carole Ann was different – she lied badly, but was it fatalism or simply that she was genuinely far too clever a liar for O'Neill to fathom? Or could she be lying to protect someone? Was she there, did she watch? Did she perhaps not do the killings herself but watch someone else kill? Was that what she did for kicks? Too passive to kill but keen to be a voyeur. If that was the case she was insane but hiding it well.

O'Neill left the interview room, went back to his office, closed the door, walked over to his filing cabinet, opened the drawer and realized he no longer had a supply of Irish whiskey. He'd vowed only to drink in company and never to swig it from the bottle, which, he thought, was a sure sign of an alcoholic. Perhaps when Fran came back she'd go to a pub with him.

He stood for some time in front of the photos of the scene and the drawings Fran had made. They were poor drawings – he had to admit Fran was no artist – but there was something else that bothered him. He continued to gaze from photo to drawing but after a short time his mind roved back to thoughts of social drinking.

In the police cell Carole Ann sat hunched in one corner on the thin mattress. She'd felt a sense of panic when the door had first clanged shut, now she felt more peaceful, she was safe here. Confinement was something she'd got used to and what did it matter if it was a room somewhere or a cell? She was free in her head. In her head she could remember Michael.

Why she'd lied to O'Neill she didn't know, or at least she did know really but found it hard to admit. She wanted to be back in prison. Wanted to feel safe all the time. If she didn't convince O'Neill she'd stabbed those men he would release her, and without Michael so-called freedom wasn't worth having. Just lately she'd begun to feel paranoid. Even before the arrival of the press she'd felt like that. As if someone, sometimes, was watching her.

In the early evening O'Neill went straight to Enid Braithwaite's house. He hadn't got a search warrant but he felt Enid wouldn't find a few questions and a preliminary knife check too worrisome.

Dave Reynolds was sitting in the dining room in front of a bowl of thin apple pie topped with matching thin custard. He looked up as O'Neill entered and O'Neill thought he saw a hint of pleasure or relief in his expression. As though even police company was better than no company at all.

Enid wedged herself by the kitchen door and said, 'I'll be in my room when you want me. I hope you're looking after Miss Forbes, Chief Inspector?'

'I am indeed,' said O'Neill.

Dave Reynolds spoke only when he heard Enid's door close and the strains of Cliff Richard drifted through.

'Don't fancy apple pie and custard, do you?' he asked O'Neill.

'I haven't got a sweet tooth,' said O'Neill as he sat down and stared at the untouched pie.

'How is she?' asked Reynolds.

'Telling me a pack of lies.'

'What about?'

'She's confessing to both murders. Or at least she's trying to.'

'Why would she do that?'

'I'm guessing she wants to go back to prison. What about you?'

Dave shrugged. 'This is no life. Stuck here. No money, no friends, and food worse than prison. What's the fucking point?'

O'Neill shrugged. 'I can't answer that one – but if you're planning a job, don't do it on my patch, Reynolds. I've got enough to cope with.'

'I'm always planning jobs, Mr O'Neill, but even to commit crime these days you need a bit of money.'

'Tell me about Carole Ann?' said O'Neill, anxious to get back to the point of his visit.

'We don't talk much. She's a quiet person. We've had a few chats about prison – we've got that in common.'

'Did she mention any friends on the outside?'

'Nah, no one. The only real friend she had was Trish in prison. She writes to a penfriend every week. She does talk about that bloke Michael she was supposed to have killed.'

'You don't think she did it?'

'No.'

'Why not?'

'I think she was set up.'

'By whom.'

'I don't know. The police didn't find out – I don't expect they even bloody tried. She sort of confessed, didn't she? Why should they bother? But I think someone had it in for her.'

O'Neill smiled. 'Come on, Reynolds, you must have some idea who would want to set her up.'

'Why should I? The only thing I know about her is she likes men.'

'What's that supposed to mean?'

Reynolds began to roll a cigarette. 'If you were a good-looking woman and hadn't had a man in years and you had no money, what would you do?'

'You don't mean she's on the game?' asked O'Neill in surprise.

'Don't put words into my mouth. But if men are grateful they might want to show their appreciation.'

'Meaning you?' said O'Neill, slowly catching on to Reynolds' drift.

Reynolds stared silently at his perfectly rolled cigarette.

'Here?' asked O'Neill meaningfully. Reynolds still didn't reply.

O'Neill tried again, watching as Reynolds lit his cigarette and inhaled deeply. 'She did know the victims, didn't she?'

Reynolds shrugged. 'All I'll say is she goes walking by the river late at night. Old Braithwaite doesn't know, she bolts up at midnight.'

'How does she get back into the house, then?'

Reynolds smirked. 'I come down about twelve-thirty and unbolt the door. She didn't ask me to; I suggested it. I know when she's going out. She knew those blokes all right, but she wouldn't have killed them.'

172

'I'm tired of hearing that,' said O'Neill. 'I think anyone's capable of murder given the right circumstances, the right provocation. Even you, Reynolds.'

Reynolds smiled. He was pleased to be a suspect! O'Neill sighed. Holy Mother help me! He'd got one suspect trying to be jailed for murders she didn't commit and another vague 'possible' who seemed to be delighted to be included with the others.

'When she went to the river,' he asked Reynolds, 'did you follow her?'

Reynolds raised his eyebrows. 'You want to know if I killed them out of jealousy, don't you? Well, I didn't. There's no payoff for that sort of murder. I'm a criminal for profit and you know that well enough – you've checked out my record. I wouldn't kill anyone for nothing. I'm not a bloody psychopath. DC Preston asked Miss Braithwaite if she was sure I was in and I was, because I unbolted the door.'

'Convenient,' muttered O'Neil. 'And you haven't answered my question. Did you ever follow her down to the river?'

Reynolds glared at him and said angrily, 'I'm not a bloody peeping Tom either.'

O'Neill walked to the door. 'What time did she come in on those two nights?'

Reynolds smiled cockily. 'About one-ish.'

O'Neill stared at Reynolds until he grew uncomfortable, then he said, 'You're not trying to set her up, are you, Reynolds? Because you're doing a damned fine job of it. Rejected you, has she? Once was enough, was it?'

Reynolds scowled angrily but said nothing.

'I'll call again, Reynolds, and be assured I'll be keeping a special eye on you.'

Outside Enid Braithwaite's back room, 'Living Doll' was in full swing. He knocked loudly, and after some time and a scraping of chairs she came to the door and stood with her arms folded beneath her huge chest. 'He's not a bad lad, you know,' she said. 'His trouble is he's got only one topic of conversation and that's crime. Still, all ex-prisoners are like that. No time to get any real hobbies on the outside, I suppose. Now me, I could talk about Cliff Richard till the cows come home—'

'I'm sure you could,' O'Neill interrupted her, 'but I'm wanting to check your knife drawer.'

'Whatever for?'

'Miss Forbes says she borrowed a knife from you.'

Miss Braithwaite gasped and looked outraged by the suggestion.

'Well, she's lying. She never did.'

'I'll just check. Will you come with me?'

'I suppose so. I don't like being disturbed in the evenings. I'm getting on, you know. I'm in my seventies.'

'And you're looking wonderful, Miss Braithwaite,'

She smiled and smoothed down the front of her blue-flowered Crimplene dress.

He followed her through to the kitchen and she opened a drawer to the left of the sink. 'Now these are my knives,' she said, gathering them up in one hand. 'This is my bread knife,' she said, showing him a wooden-handled knife with a serrated straight edge. 'This is my vegetable peeler – I've got two the same, nice and small they are, and I use this one for chopping vegetables. I'm not so fast I can use a really sharp blade.'

O'Neill stared at its ridged blade. 'What about carving the joint?'

'We don't have many joints,' she said, peering at him as though he'd made an improper suggestion. 'But on special occasions I do use my electric carving knife – it's not so hard on my wrists, you see.'

'And that's all?'

'Well, dear. What did you expect? I'm not a hotel chef, you know. Good plain cooking is what I do best.'

O'Neill tried to forget the sight of that apple pie. 'I'd like to search her room now, if that's all right with you.'

'You go ahead, I'm going to sit myself down again. You know where it is.'

In Carole Ann's bedroom he began to search the small chest of drawers, her wardrobe, even under the bed. He found nothing of any interest. Her possessions were so few he felt slightly guilty to be there at all. It was like searching the room of someone who didn't exist. The only photos he found were placed carefully in a small pile in her bedside drawer, some of Michael Summerton alone and some of them together. Smiling, happy, a good looking couple. Had marriage been a possibility, he wondered. Had their lack of formal commitment created problems for Carole Ann?

174

By the side of the photos was a writing pad with the beginnings of a letter

Dear Josephine,
   I do hope your father is still improving.

That was all. This must be the penpal, he thought. And what did you tell a penpal? The answer came back – everything!

Chapter Twenty-Three

Fran arrived back in Fowchester as darkness fell. The travelling and the day in London had exhausted her. The train had seemed excessively warm and airless, as though the hundreds of bodies had left their warmth and fetid air behind and she and a few other late travellers had been left to soak it all up. She longed for a warm bath and clean cool sheets.

Once inside the house, she kicked off her shoes and walked straight upstairs to run the bath. When the knock at the door came she decided to ignore it and stood undressed and waiting for the bath to fill. 'Go away,' she muttered. 'Leave me alone.' She guessed it was the charity person who'd left two plastic bags for her to fill with old clothes, but the only clothes she had were old and she liked them that way.

The knocking didn't stop. When it did, the letter box opened and the unmistakable voice of O'Neill shouted, 'I know you're in there, Fran. I'm needing a good woman to talk to.'

'Need on,' said Fran sourly as she stared at the inviting bath water.

'I'm not going away,' shouted O'Neill. 'And the neighbours are watching.'

Fran snatched her white bathrobe from the hook, hurriedly put it on and stomped down the stairs. O'Neill stood at the door, smiling broadly and holding a bottle of wine. 'I'm a reformed man,' he said. 'I've decided to drink the grape instead of the grain. And I want to discuss the case with you.'

Fran sighed. 'Come in, boss. I was about to get in the bath – I'm shattered.'

'Don't let me stop you. You go ahead; I'll open the wine.'

Fran was about to say wine was the last thing she wanted. But what was the point? O'Neill's selfish streak always seemed to

176

guarantee he got his own way. 'The bottle opener's in the kitchen drawer on the left,' she said as she walked up the stairs.

From the bath she could hear him sorting through the drawer. She couldn't relax.

'Fran!' he shouted after a few moments.

'What?'

'I can't find it.'

Fran wanted to say something cutting about being a detective but she didn't. Instead she said, 'Try the right-hand drawer.'

Her relaxing bath was already ruined so she got out, dried herself quickly and threw on a ghastly red and gold kaftan that her father had given her for her last birthday. It was cool because it billowed like a tent and was at least four sizes too big for her, but at least the colour might make O'Neill think she looked drained and tired enough for him to let her have a early night.

In the kitchen O'Neill had already poured the wine and started making toasted cheese sandwiches.

'Sit down, Fran,' he said, as if he were the host. 'You're looking great. I'm longing to know what you found out.'

Fran smiled. So much for looking knackered! He handed her a glass of wine and the toasted sandwich, and she had only taken one sip and one bite before he said, 'Be telling me all about it.'

Fran rested her elbow on the table. 'I'll have to précis it, Connor. It's been a long day.'

'Take your time,' said O'Neill. 'We've got all night.'

Fran's heart sank but she began, talking fast and hoping he wouldn't interrupt too much.

He didn't, he let her relate her day in as much detail as she could muster. 'Anyway,' she continued, 'even though both accounts differ, it seems they both saw someone enter the house after Carole Ann and Michael came in that night.'

'Male or female?'

'There's the rub, boss. The dotty one seems to think it could have been female but the other witness just saw a shape.'

'Did the intruder have a key?'

'It doesn't seem so. The pair staggered in drunk and failed to close the door properly. So if someone who didn't live there came in after them, the house was obviously being watched for their return.'

'I take it they closed their own room door,' said O'Neill.

Fran shrugged. 'Someone got in with a key or the door was on the snib. Because if the murderer had a key to the room, then they'd have had a front door key cut as well.'

O'Neill nodded thoughtfully. 'So if we're assuming Carole Ann didn't do it, the murderer was a real opportunist and didn't have a key, so presumably they intended to pick the lock or—'

'I think he hung around the bathroom,' interrupted Fran. 'The room was a bedsit with a kitchen alcove but the bathroom was down one flight of stairs. If either left the room for a few moments and closed the door they'd have been locked out. So they put the door on the snib. Which means anyone could have got in.'

'Was the room dark?' asked O'Neill.

'Not especially. There was a small window with curtains and a skylight with a blind but it could have been different then.'

'Let's suppose they had the same. What about the hall?'

'A timed light. Short timer. Black outside the actual room. What are you getting at, boss?'

'I'm beginning to think you're right, Fran. Carole Ann went downstairs at some point and while she was in the bathroom our murderer got in the room and killed Summerton. He wouldn't have stirred. Why should he? He was drunk and asleep. Silently, our murderer pulls back the bedclothes – if he had stirred, he'd have thought it was Carole Ann anyway – then he delivers the fatal blows, covers him up and Michael Summerton's life blood seeps away—'

'But that means—'

'That means, Fran, Carole Ann got back into bed with a dead man.'

'And that explains why she has no memory of sounds or even sensing someone else was there. She just wasn't there at the time. She got back into bed, unaware that Michael was dead. We can't be certain that she did leave the room, though.'

O'Neill nodded. 'There's only one way to find out.'

'How?'

'Hypnosis.'

Fran nodded. 'All this is fine, boss, but where does it get us? Carole Ann's innocence on this one doesn't help us find the murderer of the other two.'

'Oh, but it does. The same person has just killed two men that knew Carole Ann.'

178

'She did know them, then?'

'I'm not sure how well. Dave Reynolds seems to think they may have paid her for the privilege, but then he's a "profit criminal" so his philosophy is nothing for nothing. I haven't questioned her about that yet, not in any detail.'

'You've interviewed her, then?'

'Sure I have. She's in the cells. She tried to confess. Obviously wants to go back to prison.'

'So really we're none the wiser,' suggested Fran.

'No. One killer. A ten-year wait to kill again. Deliberately targeting Carole Ann. What does it sound like?'

'Revenge.'

'Sure. These are revenge killings. Someone in Fowchester has waited ten years to incriminate her again.'

Fran sighed. 'This is too much for me, boss. What in God's name did she do? There's no evidence of her wronging anyone. If you ask me she was the one who was wronged. And anyway, why not just kill her and be done with it?'

O'Neill refilled Fran's wine glass. 'Because, Fran, this murderer regards death as the easy option. Carole Ann has to suffer.'

'We have to clear her first, then?'

'I'm not sure, Fran. I think we should release her. We can't keep her indefinitely.'

'We really need to check where certain people like Ian Bishop were ten years ago, don't we?'

'Sure we do, Fran, but that'll take time,' said O'Neill thoughtfully. 'I'm betting Dave Reynolds was in prison and I'm pretty sure Charles and Nina Gardener were living in Fowchester ten years ago. But there are newcomers—'

Fran finished her wine. 'While you're at it, boss, you could check on Enid Braithwaite. Maybe Carole got on a bus once and sat on one of her Cliff Richard records.'

O'Neill laughed, 'Fran, you're good for the crack, you really are. That's made my day.'

It was midnight when O'Neill decided to go. He could see Fran was exhausted, her face was pale, her eyes red-rimmed.

'I'm going, Fran,' he said. 'You're bushed and I'm going back to the office.'

'What for?' asked Fran sleepily.

'I want to read those reports on Carole Ann again. The answer must be staring me in the face but I've missed it.'

'Do you want me to come with you?' Again O'Neill resisted the urge to hug her. Instead he said, 'You're a real trouper, but you get some sleep and be at the office by nine. I want to interview Carole Ann again. She may well have changed her mind about the relative joys of captivity by then.'

'Is it safe to let her out even if you can convince Ringstead she's innocent?'

'Let me worry about that, Fran. Go on, go to bed.'

Fran stood up stiffly from the kitchen table, her bottom was numb and the kaftan had stuck to the back of her legs. 'Good night, Connor,' she said, then added, 'I have had a thought about motive.'

'Fire away.'

'Drugs.'

O'Neill nodded. 'I wondered about that too. I'll think about that one and I need to think about the press. Once they know how long Carole Ann's been in custody they could be starting another furore.'

'Don't tread on Ringstead's toes, O'Neill.'

O'Neill grinned cheerfully and Fran knew he didn't give a toss about Ringstead, his toes or any other part of his anatomy.

O'Neill read the reports for some time, stared again at the photos of the dead men and the drawings that Fran had made. He was beginning to see a glimmer of light. But he wasn't sure yet, not absolutely. At 3 a.m. he bedded down between two chairs in the rest room, then at seven he showered and shaved and ate a fry-up in the canteen. And for the first time in ages he felt optimistic.

Once Fran arrived he launched straight into his plans. 'I'm thinking, Fran, we should tell the local press first. Tell them we're planning Carole Ann's immediate release and that the Home Office is being asked to review her trial and undoubtedly her innocence will soon be proved.'

'You can't do that, boss,' replied Fran. 'I'm shocked you should even think of releasing her—'

'I've got nothing to hold her on, only her cobbled confession, which wouldn't hold up in court.'

Fran laughed. 'I wouldn't be too sure of that, boss. They convicted her last time.'

O'Neill shrugged. 'Sure, but this time we're going to keep her under surveillance. She'll be safe. We'll direct the press to Belsize Park and that'll keep them going for a while.'

'Ringstead won't like it.'

'Ringstead won't know it was us.'

'How?'

'Just use a disguised voice, Fran. You can do it.'

'Me!'

'It happens all the time. Go on. Use a phone box in the town.'

Fran hesitated.

'Go on, Fran – go. I'll tell Carole Ann the good news and release her as soon as I've arranged surveillance.'

Fran still felt reluctant. If Ringstead ever found out about the leak to the press both their jobs could be on the line. And if the Lothario on the *Fowchester and District Times* recognized her voice she could well be obliged to have more than a drink with him. If he was that good with women she could hardly say she had made a great sacrifice for the sake of their jobs. She smiled. She could always pretend she'd made the ultimate sacrifice . . .

'Don't be standing with a smile on your face, Fran – just do as I'm telling you.'

'You could be sorry,' said Fran as she walked to the door.

A few minutes later the phone rang. It was the desk sergeant. 'Chief Inspector, we've got Mr and Mrs Gardener here to see you.'

'OK, send them up.'

When Nina Gardener walked in, O'Neill could see she'd had a hard time, her eyes were red and swollen with crying and she had a bruise on her right cheek. Charles was stony-faced. This time, though, O'Neill was on home ground.

'I'd like to talk to you both – separately,' said O'Neill.

'I hardly think that's necessary, Chief Inspector, I do know the truth at long last,' Charles blustered. 'And I think she should now confess to you.'

Chapter Twenty-Four

Charles Gardener strode off without a backward glance and Nina watched him go with a look of tired relief. O'Neill pointed to a chair and she sank down gratefully as if her body were as heavy as her spirits. O'Neill sat opposite her and leaned towards her. 'You'll be wanting to tell me all about it, Mrs Gardener.'

She stared at him for a moment as if not comprehending, and then said, 'Call me Nina; Mrs Gardener sounds so proper and I haven't been very proper. I've been awake all night. I've been misguided – I wasn't always a . . . flirt.'

O'Neill thought that a mild interpretation but didn't comment. Instead he said, 'I want to know about your relationship with Alan Lattaway. Were you in love with him?'

O'Neill could see by the expression on her face that she was shocked at that suggestion. 'Oh no, I liked him, felt sorry for him and there was a – how can I describe it – a basic animal attraction between us, that was all.'

'And you saw him on the night he died?'

'Carole Ann's told you, has she? That's why I came, I had to.'

O'Neill gave her the benefit of an unblinking gaze and she looked away embarrassed.

'Would you be explaining that, Mrs Gardener?'

There was a long pause, in which Nina stared at the floor, then finally she said, 'I arranged the alibi with Carole Ann but I've thought better of it. I've told Charles, of course. I don't know if he'll forgive me or not, but I thought when you found out I was the last person to see Alan Lattaway alive you could well think I'd murdered him.'

Now it was her gaze that held O'Neill's. He stayed silent.

'I thought if Carole Ann could give me that alibi then I'd be safe.'

182

'You can be telling me about it now,' he murmured.

She looked at him sharply. 'But you know—'

O'Neill smiled encouragingly. 'Be telling me.'

Nina trembled slightly. 'I thought you knew,' she said. 'I . . . I arranged with Carole Ann to say I visited her that evening – late. I thought we could help each other but . . . then I realized that she might have killed Alan. I shouldn't have got so involved with her in the first place.'

'Why did you get so involved, Mrs Gardener?'

'I liked her, felt sorry for her. I thought I could help.'

'You haven't done much for her so far, have you?'

Nina shook her head miserably. 'I was too optimistic. Charles suggested she could work on our garden but I baulked at the idea. I thought . . . if you must know, I thought she was too attractive.'

'I see,' said O'Neill. 'You could play away but not Charles.'

'That does sound hypocritical, I know, but I didn't want to put temptation in his way.'

O'Neill raised an eyebrow. 'Are you sure you didn't fear Carole Ann might kill him too?'

'Don't be ridiculous,' she snapped. 'Carole Ann—'

'Carole Ann what?'

'Nothing.'

'When I asked you what you both talked about during your prison visits you were evasive. Why?'

'Because those talks are confidential and it wouldn't have been ethical or fair to Carole Ann.'

O'Neill nodded, as if in agreement, but then said, 'Is it ethical to withhold information that might prove her innocence?'

Nina fiddled with the cuff of her white blouse. 'Put that way, of course not, Chief Inspector, but she didn't say anything which might have done that. I have to say, most of our conversations concerned prison life – it was as if she had never lived before. As if she'd blotted out her past.'

O'Neill sighed as he realized the interview was going nowhere. 'Just one more question, Mrs Gardener,' he said, 'before we go back to the river bank.'

Unease crossed her face but she smiled a forced professional smile and said, 'Go ahead, Chief Inspector, I've got nothing to hide.'

'I believe Carole Ann had a penfriend.'

'Yes – a girl from London. I think she wrote very frequently. Carole Ann enjoyed receiving her letters and sometimes mentioned them. Why do you ask?'

O'Neill didn't reply to her question but said instead, 'Did you see anyone on the river bank that night?'

'No.'

'Where did you have sex?'

Nina coloured slightly at the bluntness of his question. 'There, of course, by the river.'

'You didn't think someone might see you?'

'I've told you there was no one there; it was dark, but . . . if you must know, the idea of being seen did rather increase the excitement.'

'So you didn't care if you were seen?'

'I didn't say that. Of course, I would have been mortified.'

'Did you practise safe sex?'

'Really,' said Nina, clenching her hands together with obvious irritation. 'Aren't you being a little overzealous?'

'Not at all. I'm wanting you to answer my questions. Did you use a condom?'

'No. I'm on the pill.'

'Right, Mrs Gardener, take your time and be telling me exactly what happened that night.'

'I refuse to go into details,' she snapped.

O'Neill realized that he was taking a rather perverse delight in seeing her so agitated, but that wasn't his motive. He wanted a picture in his mind. A picture that would conjure up the scene.

'I want to know what you were wearing, where you parked the car. What the weather was like, were there any lights to be seen? Where was Alan when you arrived and what was he doing? Did you . . . make love standing up or lying down?'

'What difference does all this make?' she asked angrily. 'Why on earth should I cooperate?'

O'Neill smiled. 'If you don't, Mrs Gardener,' he said slowly and with emphasis, 'I might be thinking you guilty of murder. Already you've committed adultery, fabricated an alibi, lied to your husband, and you've only come here today because your husband insisted. You're not in the least concerned about your past client and I personally think you're a lying, scheming, selfish woman and it's up to you to prove to me you didn't kill one or both men.'

Nina opened her mouth, either to argue or to complain, then decided that perhaps neither would help, closed her mouth and placed her right hand over her eyes. Eventually she said, 'Very well, 'I'll tell you about it . . . it was a warm humid night. He'd rung me earlier. I didn't promise to go but he said he'd be fishing. I couldn't settle at home so I slipped on a plastic mac in case it rained . . . I was naked underneath and I drove to the picnic area further along the river, parked the car – there were no other cars there – and then walked down to him. It was very dark but I had taken a torch. I remember seeing his big red and white umbrella. I couldn't see him at first. He heard me coming, though I was wearing sandals – the ground was dry and the twigs cracked. As I approached he came out from under the umbrella. He said he was pleased to see me. I switched off the torch and for a while we stood and kissed. Then we lay down on the tarpaulin. Shortly afterwards I went home. It was less warm then and clouds seemed to be gathering. I didn't hear anyone or see anything.'

'What was he doing as you left?'

'He said that he felt like fishing then and he sat on his little canvas stool and picked up his fishing rod.'

'Did you actually see him start to fish?'

She shook her head, removed her hand from her eyes and said, 'May I go now?'

'Sure. You can go, Mrs Gardener.'

Quickly she got to her feet, as though afraid he might change his mind. As she got to the door he said, 'If I were you, Mrs Gardener, I've give up prison visiting as a hobby, I think you're temperamentally unsuited to it.'

She didn't bother to turn, she just said caustically, 'Thank you so much for your advice, Chief Inspector,'

Unwilling to let her have the last word, O'Neill said, 'And be sure to take it.'

O'Neill waited for a while for Fran's return. When she didn't arrive he went down to the cells. The police matron reported that Carole Ann had slept well and eaten breakfast. When he opened the cell door Carole Ann was sitting bolt upright. She half stood up as he entered but then sat down again with her back straight and a determined expression on her face.

'As soon as my sergeant is back you'll be released, Carole Ann.'

She gasped audibly, 'No, please. Let me stay here. Please.'

'Be giving me a good reason for keeping you here?'

She looked suddenly defiant. 'I'm a murderer.'

'Try again.'

She stared at him and he could see the fear in her eyes. 'You know I'm scared,' she said.

'Why are you scared, Carole Ann?'

She looked down at the stone floor for several seconds and then slowly raised her eyes to his. 'Someone out there is after me.'

'I know,' said O'Neill. 'But not to kill you. I think this person just wants you back in prison for good. I think they were peeved you only served ten years. Why, I don't know, but I'm thinking I might know who.'

'I've never hurt anyone – only Michael, I suppose, and I didn't do that consciously.'

'You didn't do it consciously or unconsciously, and I think I can prove it.'

'I don't believe you.'

'You don't have to, but I'd like you to cooperate with us.'

'I just want to stay here.'

O'Neill crouched down in front of her. Carole Ann avoided his eyes. 'Look at me,' said O'Neill. Slowly she looked up. 'I want you to show some spirit. Stop being a victim. That's what you are. You're the fall guy and you've got to start fighting.'

She stared at him blankly and O'Neill resisted the urge to shake her. Instead, taking her gently by the shoulders, he said, 'It's time for the truth, Carole Ann, and a bit of action.'

'It's not always wise to tell the truth,' she said dully.

O'Neill shrugged. 'I'm trying – you can damned well meet me half way. You'll be taken back to Miss Braithwaite and I'm putting you and the house under protective surveillance. The press should be off your back for a while. I want you to walk around with your pretty head held high.'

Carole Ann managed a weak smile. 'No man's called me pretty . . . for a long, long time.'

'That doesn't mean men don't see you as pretty, Carole Ann. Are you going to be showing the world that you're not going to be a victim any more?'

'It's easy for you. You've got power. I've got nothing, only guilt and fear.'

'Jasus, woman. You've got your health, good looks, intelligence—' He broke off abruptly, realizing that platitudes had never helped him. And that fear of fear itself didn't go away with a pep talk. He smiled. 'You're right, life's a bastard but you have to carry on.'

Carole Ann shrugged. 'I'll do what you say. It takes a while to realize that there's no one I can hurt now and that without prison I have to make my own decisions.'

O'Neill nodded. 'Sure, and I suggest you be making that decision now. Just tell me about your walks along the river – that's just one step. The second step is to tell me about your relationship with both men.'

He waited, saw a slightly obstinate look in her eyes, but then she slumped her shoulders as if giving up the unequal struggle.

'You're right, I know you're right. I will tell you.'

'Will you come along to the interview room?'

'No, I'll tell you here.'

'Go ahead, then. Be telling me.'

'I'd only been here a couple of weeks. The days were so long, I couldn't sleep. I started creeping out occasionally after the door was bolted. I just walked down to the park. Sometimes I sat on the swings for a while until the cold drove me back. Then when the weather improved I began to walk along the river and that's when I met Alan. We just talked. I really liked him. We'd sit there under his striped umbrella. He'd share his sandwiches with me. In a way it was a little glimpse of what freedom could be like. Once he lent me some money – I didn't ask, he just did—I never got round to paying him back. It's too late now—' she broke off, her eyes glistening with tears.

'So you didn't have sex with him?'

The abrupt question did the trick. 'No. I did not,' she said firmly. 'Dave Reynolds thinks I did because I slept with him once. After ten years of celibacy. Well, he was in the next room. And for an ex-con he's not a hard man. Deep down I don't like sex much. I just like kind words . . . well, you know . . . Michael was a romantic—'

'Be keeping to the point, Carole Ann,' interrupted O'Neill gently. 'Did you see either man on the night they died?'

Carole Ann shook her head. 'Not on those nights. There was a chance of rain and I knew Alan was meeting someone that night. Then, I didn't know who she was, but I do now. He still loved his wife. I felt sorry for him but I didn't kill him or—'

'I know that,' said O'Neill. 'Tell me, when you were talking to both men did you sit under the umbrella?'

She frowned, puzzled. 'Yes, it was sort of cosy and sometimes it got a bit chilly. But is that important?'

'It could be. And no one saw you?'

'I don't think so. Someone may have seen the light of our torches, I suppose. But I didn't see a soul.'

'Did you go back at night *after* Alan was killed?'

She nodded. 'I went back and stood on the spot where he fished. And I cried. For the first time in years I cried. I stood there, just thinking—'

'And you didn't feel in any danger?'

'No. I must admit I thought Jill's lover had killed him – to get him out of the house. Alan told me he was being pressured. When Patrick King died I was so shocked and scared. They were nice men, both kind.'

'Did Patrick lend you money?'

Carole Ann nodded her head sadly. 'Fifty pounds. As soon as I can, I'll pay back his wife. If I get a job.'

'When you get a job,' said O'Neill firmly. Carole Ann smiled bleakly. Then he asked, 'Why didn't you tell me you and Nina had concocted an alibi?'

She shrugged. 'I don't know. Her alibi might have helped to clear me but I wasn't sure I wanted to be free.'

'And now?'

She stared at him for a moment. 'I'm still not sure. Being free is scary and lonely. In prison you have no decisions to make, the days pass as they do on the outside and sometimes they seem just as long.'

O'Neill knew what she meant. The days, weeks and months after Jenny's death were to him an endless grey tunnel of guilt, misery and sadness. But one day the sun had shone again and he'd laughed occasionally. Sometimes since, he'd even felt moments of happiness untinged by guilt. It could be the same for Carole Ann.

Patting her on the shoulder, he pointed to the open cell door. 'There it is,' he said. 'That's freedom. Don't believe all that crap about freedom of the soul. You need physical freedom as well. Go on, be going through the door now.'

She stared for a long time at the open cell door, then, straighten-

188

ing her shoulders and lifting her head high, she walked slowly towards it. She didn't look back at O'Neill or the cell.

It was an hour later when Fran came back. 'Where in heaven have you been?' asked O'Neill. 'I thought you'd been kidnapped.'

'No,' said Fran wearily. 'The local press mogul wasn't convinced by a corny Brummy accent. I had to meet him and now he thinks he's on a promise.'

'Will he do it?'

'Do what?'

'You know what I mean, Fran.'

'Of course he will, it's the best story he's had in years. He says, too, he'll fix it with Ringstead, some fictitious nonsense to satisfy him.'

'He's the least of our worries, Fran. I've released Carole Ann and I've arranged for someone to watch the Braithwaite house, just in case.'

'You think the murderer will actually try to kill Carole Ann?'

'Why not? She's been released.'

Fran smiled. 'You know who it is, don't you?'

O'Neill didn't answer.

'I'm impressed.'

'Sure you are, Fran. I'm impressed myself.'

Chapter Twenty-Five

The next day the *Fowchester News* headline was stark: Forbes Free.

O'Neill debated with himself about doing the search that day. He'd got men deployed outside the Wanderer pub and outside the Braithwaite house. He didn't want to alert the murderer. But he did want to visit the pub.

He arrived well before opening time to find Roger drinking his Glenmorangie and obviously cheerful.

'Drink, Chief Inspector?' he asked as he raised his large body into a semi-standing position.

O'Neill shook his head. 'I'm here purely on business. I'm wanting to have a look round upstairs. A view of the river, you understand.'

'Right, squire. I'll show you round,' said Roger amiably. Upstairs, pointing to a door at the end of a dimly lit corridor, he said, 'That's Julie's room. That looks out on to the river.'

'Where is Julie today?' asked O'Neill.

Roger scratched the back of his bull neck. 'She's got a day off. She went home last night.'

'Home?'

'Down South somewhere. She's got a father and brother living there – so Connie tells me, Julie doesn't speak to me. Still, barmaids come and barmaids go, don't they? I expect she'll be gone soon. They get fed up with the quiet life. She's no trouble really, goes swimming once or twice a week, doesn't make any noise and she's quite a good cook.'

'So you expect her back this evening?'

'Yeah, she gets back about midnight usually.'

'Did you take up references?'

'Course we did. We don't want to get landed with anyone dishonest, do we? Shall I leave you to have a look round?' He felt in

190

his trouser pocket, then, handing O'Neill a bunch of keys, said, 'This one opens Julie's room. Our rooms are open – help yourself.'

O'Neill nodded. 'There's a small window on the top floor; what room is that?'

'Just a boxroom, load of old rubbish in there.'

O'Neill glanced up towards the narrow staircase.

'Too narrow for me,' said Roger with some satisfaction.

'One more question,' said O'Neill. 'Are there any knives missing from the kitchen?'

Roger looked surprised. 'Not that I know of. Why?'

'I just wondered,' said O'Neill.

'I could ask Julie about the knives; she's got her own set.'

'Where's she keeping them?'

'In the kitchen. She says hers are better quality than ours. Do you think one of them was used for the murders?' asked Roger, his small eyes bright with interest.

O'Neill didn't give him the satisfaction of an answer.

In the boxroom, O'Neill went straight to the window and looked out. The river glimmered serenely in the morning sun, the nettles on both banks stood straight and still. From this vantage point O'Neill couldn't quite pinpoint the murder area. When a figure did come into view it took him a second or two to realize it was a man. If someone watched from this window, he thought, they'd need binoculars.

He looked round the square room and at its bric-à-brac.

There were two tea chests filled with old clothes, three dusty lampshades stuck on top, an old iron, a radio, one or two hideous paintings but no sign of any binoculars.

Julie's room he examined carefully. He passed his hands under the mattress, through the few clothes that hung in her wardrobe, checked her bedside cabinet and her chest of drawers. A black swimming costume was folded up together with neatly folded underwear. She had a few paperback books and magazines in her wardrobe, an unused writing pad and envelopes in her bedside cabinet, and that was all. Apart from one photograph, set in an oval frame: of a young man wearing shorts and sun glasses against a background of trees but with the corner of a building in the background.

He didn't waste time searching Roger and Connie's private rooms. Roger was so unperturbed about his search that he assumed he had nothing to hide. And anyway, time was short.

As he left the pub he spoke to Roger and Connie together. 'My visit today is a secret,' he said. 'I don't want anyone to know, and that includes Julie and the cleaning staff. If I find out you've told anyone I'll make sure, Roger, you lose your licence. D'ye understand?'

'What *is* going on?' demanded Connie. 'No one here had anything to do with the murders. You're only picking on us because we're near the river. Half of Fowchester treks up here in the summer. What about the council estate? I bet it's some one from there.'

O'Neill ignored her but smiled and said, 'I'm wanting to see the kitchen, Connie.'

She turned to Roger, who said, 'Go on, Connie, show the Inspector the kitchen; he only wants to check the knives.'

Connie shrugged. 'It'll be body searches next. You must be desperate, Mr O'Neill.'

In the kitchen she opened the knife drawer and after a quick glance said, 'They're all there.'

'You're sure?'

'Of course I'm sure,' she said, picking up two carving knives, one chopping knife, a bread knife and two small-bladed ones.

'What about Julie's own set?' asked O'Neill. Connie raised her eyebrows and sighed. 'On the work surface over there near the sink.'

O'Neill walked to the sink and on the right side noticed the knife holder, a sloping wooden box with holes, six holes, six knives. He examined each shiny blade. They were all present and correct.

'I hope you're satisfied, Mr O'Neill,' said Connie, still annoyed.

He wasn't, of course. 'Remember, Connie. Tell no one I've been here today.'

Connie managed a resigned smile that seemed to suggest O'Neill was a madman or a small child that need pacifying.

The night was mild, the sky cloudy and the three-quarter moon often hidden behind the clouds. The river glided by, the black surface rippling slightly from time to time. O'Neill and Fran sat in an unmarked police car watching the last of the customers leaving.

'What are you planning to do when she does arrive? asked Fran.

O'Neill smiled. 'I'll think we'll just play the waiting game for a while. I want to take her off guard. She might put up a fight if she hears us coming up the stairs.'

'What about backup?' asked Fran.

'We can do this on our own,' said O'Neill. 'Sure we can.'

Theirs was the only car in the car park now, They slumped low in the front seat so that they couldn't be seen.

'She could be suspicious if she notices the car,' observed Fran.

'We'll pretend we're a courting couple. She'll not take any notice.'

Fran raised her eyebrows at his optimism and stared ahead, expecting to see Julie's Mini at any moment. They waited and waited. By 1 a.m. the pub lights were off, Even Connie and Roger, Fran decided, had become bored with the wait. She noticed O'Neill had closed his eyes, but she could tell by his breathing he wasn't asleep. She stared into the darkness and it was then she heard the car engine. Fran touched O'Neill on the arm just as the Mini drove up and caused the sensor lights to go on. The immediate area of the car was now flooded with light. Julie got out of the car but didn't glance towards theirs. She was carrying a large shoulder bag. She locked the car and turned.

Abruptly O'Neill said, 'Go, go, go.' He was out of the car first and calling out, 'Josephine Price. Police. I'd like a word.'

He doubted that in the glare of the sensor light she could see him properly, but he could see the startled expression on her face. He walked towards her with Fran close behind. The bag hit him full in the face. Staggering slightly, he fell back against Fran but managed to grab her to stop her falling and looked up in time to see Josephine Price running and casting off her clothes and shoes as she ran. Christ! the river. He ran on, seeing her white underwear bright in the darkness and then hearing the splash as she dived into the river. White arms struck out in the blackness. He paused at the river bank, Fran was beside him now, slightly breathless, getting her two-way radio out and calling for backup. He hardly noticed. He was too busy stripping off his clothes.

As the shock of the cold water hit him he couldn't speak aloud, but he gasped, momentarily winded. Then he began swimming, urging his arms and legs to work faster. He hadn't swum in years and by now she was well ahead of him. He was vaguely aware of Fran screaming at him to go faster. As he turned his head he could see she was running along the river bank beside him. The thought

193

that he mustn't let himself down in front of Fran spurred him on. He stared ahead at the expanse of river, his arms and legs now fully coordinated, his strokes strong and steady. It was then he realized he could no longer see Price. He paused for a moment, hearing Fran shouting.

'She's gone under, Connor. She's gone under!'

'Where, for God's sake?' he managed to shout back.

It was then he felt the hand grab his left ankle – she was behind him. He kicked out; she pulled, suddenly she was on his back with an armlock round his neck and he was going under. In the black water he couldn't see anything but he was aware of her strength. He jabbed with his elbows, kicked out with his legs, but still she clung on to his neck. He was aware of going down, aware that he'd always feared death by drowning, aware of his lungs full to bursting. Then suddenly his feet hit the river bottom and the realization that it wasn't that deep gave him renewed strength. He jabbed both feet down to give him an upwards thrust and began prising her fingers from round his neck. She kneed him in the kidneys, but the effort weakened her grasp and he sensed she was losing strength. He twisted violently and managed to grasp her hair. He pushed himself upwards, still holding her hair, and although she flailed with her arms and legs, he knew by this time he was winning.

The first face he saw clearly was Fran's, looking pale and anxious, then Ringstead's, looking somewhat disappointed, and finally the faces of two ambulance men, thankfully clutching huge red blankets.

'Hospital!' said Ringstead tersely. 'That river could be polluted.'

O'Neill heard some wag say, 'Well if it wasn't, it is now,' but he smiled. He was just glad not to have drowned.

It was the next morning that Josephine Price/Julie Johnson was brought to the interview room for questioning. She sat sullenly as O'Neill switched on the tape recorder and stated the date and time and names of those present.

'You've been read your rights,' said O'Neill. 'Would you like a solicitor present?'

She shook her head, then stared at Fran, who sat in the corner of the room. 'I've got nothing to say,' she said directly to Fran, as though O'Neill didn't exist.

O'Neill sat back in his chair, crossed his legs and folded his arms.

'I'm prepared to sit here all day, Miss Price, if necessary. And I can be telling you that we already have evidence against you.'

There was a long pause before she said, 'What evidence? I didn't kill those men.'

'And you didn't try to drown me?'

She gave a harsh little laugh. 'I'll say in court I was just hanging on to you because I was in difficulty.'

'At least you're realizing you'll be in court.'

'You're just trying to set me up. I only wanted to escape from you.'

'And why did you even make an attempt?'

She shrugged and a self-satisfied sneer crossed her face. 'Using a false name, not paying tax and insurance. But that doesn't mean I murdered anyone. What motive could I have, anyway?'

'Revenge,' said O'Neill softly.

'For what?' she snapped. 'I only knew those men by sight. Why would I want to kill them?'

O'Neill stared at her and continued to stare at her. She returned his stare unflinchingly, as though she was merely guilty of trying to evade arrest and of assaulting a police officer. As though murder simply wasn't her style.

'Let's just be talking about revenge,' said O'Neill. Then, adding the final words in a whisper, he said, 'You'll be wanting to tell me all about Carole Ann.'

Chapter Twenty-Six

At the sound of the name Carole Ann, O'Neill saw the muscles tense in Josephine's jaw and neck. 'Your penfriend for many years,' he said.

'Prove it.'

'Oh, I'll be proving it,' said O'Neill.

Josephine Price stared down at the table for some time as if working out exactly what to say, then she looked across towards Fran. 'Even if I was her penfriend,' she said, 'that doesn't prove I killed anyone.'

'That's true,' agreed Fran. 'It also doesn't explain why you didn't make yourself known to her or why you followed her to Fowchester.'

'I didn't want actually to meet her. I just like writing letters. She's not my only penfriend. As for following her to Fowchester, that was coincidence – there was a job and I took it. Jobs are hard to find, you know.'

A knock at the door interrupted the interview. A uniformed PC placed a heavy thick plastic bag on the table in front of O'Neill, gave him a wink and walked out.

'You know what's inside the bag, of course, Miss Price?'

'I might do,' she answered sullenly.

'Sure, you do,' he said. 'It's a pair of binoculars we found in the boot of your car.'

'There's no law against bird-watching. That's what people do in the countryside.'

'And the knife?'

'What knife? I've got a set of knives. Cooks have knives, you know.'

'To be sure, I know that,' said O'Neill. 'But this knife is special. The tip broke off – just a fraction, but you made one abortive thrust and it must have happened then.'

196

He watched her face carefully. This time he'd hit home. The surprised look that crossed her face made it obvious she hadn't known about the knife.

'Lots of knives must be broken,' she murmured. 'What about blood? That's not real evidence.'

O'Neill managed a tight smile. 'I did expect to find some blood-stained clothing, you're right, but of course you overcame that, didn't you? You swam naked. Took the poor bastards by surprise. What did you do, swim up and rise up out of the water like some demented mermaid?'

'Don't call me demented. I'm not demented. I only did what was right. She had it to coming to her – the stupid lying evil bitch—'

'Calm down,' said O'Neill. 'Take your time. Be telling me all about it.'

Price's eyes glistened with anger and then her shoulders sagged as if she'd lost spirit. 'She deserved it, you know.'

'But did those two men you killed deserve to die?'

She smiled a nasty bitter smile. 'They were just convenient, weren't they? If it hadn't been them it would have been that lodger of hers, Dave, or even Miss Braithwaite. I chose the wrong ones to kill.'

'So you killed two totally innocent men in an attempt to get Carole Ann back in prison?'

'Yes. She wrecked our lives. I wanted to wreck hers.'

O'Neill's back and neck muscles tensed in anger. He'd tried to be dispassionate but his dislike of this woman grew by the second. He reminded himself he didn't believe that anyone was born evil. He believed events and other people slowly tainted the life and spirit of a previously normal person. Perhaps, he thought now, he'd been wrong.

'What if I told you Carole Ann wouldn't have minded going back to prison?'

'You forget I know all about her,' said Price with a smirk. 'She might have been next anyway. She was just beginning to think somebody was after her. Getting a bit paranoid, she was. She told me her innermost secrets, you know. One day she would have admitted she lied about my father. Then I would have killed her or got someone to do it for me even if she was in prison.'

'What about Michael Summerton?' asked O'Neill.

'What about him?'

'I'm thinking you were quite young at the time, sixteen or thereabouts. Did you have help?'

'I did not! I killed him. She loved that no-good bastard. My Dad was worth ten of him and her mad mother wrecked our lives. We had to move, you know. We had hate mail and petrol bombs and people screaming at him in the street. Her mother got the sympathy, everyone said he deserved what he got . . . my dad was blind and disfigured by that bitch. He wasn't the same man again and neither was my brother. She should have killed him.'

'Your older brother?' interrupted O'Neill.

'Yes . . . my brother – ' she paused, as if realizing O'Neill's innocent enough question hid far more meaning. 'He's had nothing to do with this,' she said sharply. 'He's a good person. He looks after my dad when I'm working.'

'Your dad needs looking after, then?'

Price stared down at the table and when she looked up her eyes were filled with tears. 'He's senile now. The doctor says the shock of the attack caused it. He's dying slowly.'

'I'm sorry,' said O'Neill.

A tear from her right eye coursed slowly down her cheek. O'Neill watched its slow unchecked passage until it disappeared beneath her chin. One tear that represented the bitter wasted lives of so many. He sighed. 'I think we'll end the interview now, Miss Price. You will be formally charged later today. We shall, of course, oppose bail.'

It was later that day that they went to see Carole Ann. They found her huddled in her armchair watching TV with the sound turned down. She looked pale and apprehensive.

'We have the murderer in custody, Carole Ann,' said O'Neill as he perched on the end of her bed.

'Who? Why did he do it?'

'Not a he. A she. Someone called Julie Johnson – cook and barmaid at the Wanderer.'

A look of puzzlement crossed Carole Ann's face. 'I don't know her. What's she got to do with me?'

'You do know her. Josephine Price – your penfriend.'

Colour flooded her cheeks. 'Oh my God . . . but I never met her. Why . . . why? I thought she was a friend . . . I told her everything.'

'Precisely, Carole Ann. Dates, times, places, people . . . feelings. She knew everything or nearly everything about you. Have you kept her letters?'

Carole Ann nodded dumbly.

'You see, Josephine Price, known as Julie Johnson, was the daughter of the man your mother attacked all those years ago. They were only children at the time, but children with grudges grow up, and as adults it became a full-blown desire for revenge. So far she's admitted to the killings here . . . but not the one in London.'

'What do you mean?' asked Carole Ann.

'I mean she had a hand in Michael Summerton's death. I think she was her brother's accomplice. Witnesses at the time seemed confused about someone entering the house. Male or female, they said, but I think it was both of them.'

Carole Ann's face had grown pale again now. She looked about to cry. 'You're telling me I didn't do it. You're telling me I definitely didn't kill Michael.'

'Sure I'm telling you that,' said O'Neill, smiling. 'Why else would I be wasting my breath?'

'What happened, then?'

'Now, you could be telling me that. Tell me about the evening of the night that Michael died.'

With her head on one side, Carole stared thoughtfully ahead. 'We were at Jack Straw's Castle, the pub in Hampstead. We were alone but everyone was chatting together, we were laughing quite a bit. We stayed on till closing time—'

'Nothing happened that was unusual while you were there?' interrupted O'Neill.

A trace of irritation crossed Carole Ann's face. 'I don't think so . . . oh yes, I remember now, but it couldn't have been important – Michael did have a jealous streak anyway.'

'Tell me about it.'

Carole Ann shrugged. 'It was nothing really, just that Michael said he didn't like the way the young barman looked at me. He said he kept staring at me. Michael went up to the bar and said something. It was too noisy to hear what was said but I think they had a row.'

'Would you recognize him again?'

Carole Ann smiled ruefully. 'My memory's not that good.

Anyway, you don't really notice barmen, do you? I know he was young with dark hair – that's all.'

'So you walked home after closing?'

'Yes, we didn't rush. It was a lovely evening. We sort of sauntered home hand in hand.'

'No one followed you?'

Carole Ann smiled. 'You don't know Hampstead on a warm summer's night, do you, Chief Inspector? There were people in front, people behind, lots of people.'

O'Neill nodded. He didn't know Hampstead at any time of the year. 'When you got to your house, do you remember closing the front door?'

'Not really. We had had quite a bit to drink.'

'And then you went to bed?'

She nodded.

'And then what did you do?'

'I went to sleep and when I woke up Michael . . . was dead.'

O'Neill shook his head. 'Come on, Carole Ann, think – you'd had quite a bit to drink, you've said that. But what were you drinking on a warm night?'

'Lager. I was drinking lager.'

'How much?'

'I can't remember . . . several half pints. Why do you want to know how much?'

'Don't you think that drinking lager in such volume, that some time in the night you would have been wanting to go to the bathroom?'

She opened her mouth to speak but no sound came at first. Then she said hurriedly, 'I do remember. I do. I did get up. I'd forgotten that. When I came to the bedroom I noticed Michael had stopped snoring – he always snored when he was drunk – and he'd stopped . . . oh no . . . oh my God . . . you're telling me he was dead then . . . you're saying I got into bed and he was dead—' She broke off as tears threatened to overwhelm her.

O'Neill leaned across and patted her hand. 'We can be leaving this until another day, Carole Ann.'

'No, I want to know now,' she said, roughly wiping the tears from her face.

'I'm only guessing,' said O'Neill. 'But I think Josephine and her brother were lurking in the house just waiting for the right

200

moment. She was probably a look out; the brother did the deed. His father was ex-army, invalided out due to a bullet wound sustained in Northern Ireland. No doubt he'd taught his son how to use a bayonet or a knife to best advantage – even perhaps as a game.'

'But what about Alan and Patrick? Why did she kill them? I went to prison for something I didn't do – wasn't that enough?'

O'Neill shook his head. 'I think it probably was for the brother but Josephine was more vengeful. She didn't care who she killed to get back at you.'

'But it was my mother who attacked that man, not me. And his name wasn't Price.'

'They changed their name by deed poll. Josephine probably chose the name Julie Johnson at random. No one thought to check, why should they? Roger at the pub hired her – no tax, no insurance, either false references or none at all.'

'Why me, though?' She gazed at him with sad puzzled eyes.

O'Neill shrugged. 'She saw you as the cause of her father's injuries. She didn't believe he sexually assaulted you.'

'I was just a child at the time.'

'Josephine was even younger but she obviously found out what had happened when she grew older. Maybe her brother fuelled her desire for revenge or maybe she was the most vengeful. I think she'll want to take the blame for Michael Summerton, and to prove it was her brother after all this time will probably be impossible.'

Carole Ann nodded and hung her head. 'Chief Inspector . . . I . . . its very difficult for me but I want to explain—' She looked up again, her eyes bright with tears. 'I . . . lied.'

'What did you lie about, Carole Ann?'

Her voice barely a whisper, she said, 'I lied to my mum . . . Colin Blake never touched me that night. I said he did because she liked him. He was divorced, so she said they were planning to marry. I couldn't bear it; she was leaving me alone more and more and I thought he might turn out like Richard Dixon. When he came to the door, I thought. . . . I thought if I said he'd assaulted me she'd stop seeing him. I didn't want a man living with us. I didn't think she'd do anything like that . . . I couldn't have known, could I?'

'You were only a child,' murmured O'Neill. 'Go on.'

'I was angry that she'd left me alone that night. I was really scared but once I'd told her, it was too late. I lied to so many people I convinced myself it was true. But when she went to prison I couldn't visit because how could I look her in the face? So when Michael was found dead I supposed I could have done it and somehow it seemed ... fair. My mum had been sent to prison and died there and that's where I thought I belonged. It was a sort of justice.'

There seemed nothing more to say then. 'We'll be in touch, Carole Ann. We'll be talking again,' said O'Neill.

At the bottom of the stairs Edith Braithwaite and Dave Reynolds stood waiting expectantly.

'We'll be seeking compensation,' said Dave.

O'Neill ignored him, smiled at Edith and said, 'She'll be needing a cup of tea now.'

Outside in the car, O'Neill sat with his hands on the steering wheel and muttered sadly, 'From one little lie – one measly sodding little lie told by a frightened child – all this.'

Fran touched his hand. 'Just one thing puzzles me, Connor – the postmark on the letters.'

'I think when she was home on her days off she wrote back to Carole Ann, probably a few letters at a time and got her brother to post them for her so the postmark would always have been a London one.'

He drove back to the office in silence but as he got out of the car, said, 'I wouldn't be surprised, you know, if Carole Ann didn't carry on writing to Josephine.'

'Neither would I,' said Fran.

As they walked into the police station Fran said, 'Thanks, Connor.'

'And what would you be thanking me for?'

She didn't answer, just smiled at him, but whatever she meant, it gladdened his heart.